A man's chuckle brought his eyes open

On the other d at ease, was so e, but would never forget. Short blond hair, lean face. Too dim to see his eyes, but Finn knew they were an unnaturally light blue.

His hand flashed toward the door, but it was too late; a distinct *click* reached his ears.

"Going somewhere?" The Devil smiled, looking more like a rock star than he did, black boots, polished to a high shine, with black jeans and a gray T-shirt. "No need to rush off. We have things to catch up on, you and I."

Finn glanced quickly toward the driver's window; heavily tinted, and tightly closed. Somehow he knew there would be no help from that area.

"We have nothing to talk about," he said flatly to his unwanted visitor, determined to brazen it out.

The blond man shook his head, chuckling again. "Oh, but we do." The limo began moving, and Finn knew he was in for the ride of his life.

By Terri Garey

DEVIL WITHOUT A CAUSE
SILENT NIGHT, HAUNTED NIGHT
YOU'RE THE ONE THAT I HAUNT
A MATCH MADE IN HELL
DEAD GIRLS ARE EASY

Devil Without a Cause

TERRI GAREY

AVON

An Imprint of HarperCollinsPublishers

AVON BOOKS
An Imprint of HarperCollins*Publishers*
10 East 53rd Street
New York, New York 10022-5299

First Avon Books mass market printing: June 2011

Avon Trademark Reg. U.S. Pat. Off. and in Other Countries, Marca Registrada, Hecho en U.S.A.
HarperCollins® is a registered trademark of HarperCollins Publishers.

Printed in the U.S.A.

10 9 8 7 6 5 4 3 2 1

Acknowledgments

Having always been fascinated by legends and stories surrounding Satan's biblical fall from grace, I hope you'll enjoy reading a new version of this age-old story from a different perspective, that of the arrogant fallen angel whose lust for the flesh led him to defy his Creator. Tales of the Devil exist in almost every culture, with the battle of good vs. evil often reduced to horns vs. wings and pitchforks vs. harps. Somehow I tend to think that it's a lot more complicated than that.

Huge thanks, once again, to Erika Tsang and all the great folks at Avon HarperCollins and the Jane Rotrosen Agency, and to everyone who asked to read more about the wickedly complex character of Sammy Divine.

Special thanks to Jyrki Linnankivi and Finnish rockers The 69 Eyes, who not only provided some of the inspiration for this novel, but are living proof that good guys can wear black.

Devil Without a Cause

Chapter One

"You went to the wedding, didn't you?"

The woman in Samael's bed rolled lazily onto her stomach, propping her head on one slender arm. Her dark hair, gloriously mussed from love-making, spilled over her shoulders, framing a face that would've been perfect if not for the coldness in her eyes, the petulant curl of her ruby red lips.

"I have no idea what you're talking about." Samael—Prince of Darkness, Ruler of the Under-world, the Great Shaitan—stared into the fire, taking another sip of wine.

"Liar," she said softly. "You may lie to the world all you wish, my darling, but you can't lie to me. Bethlehem Baptist Church, just outside of Atlanta,

Georgia, yesterday afternoon. The bride wore white and carried a bouquet of pink tulips." She laughed dismissively. "How utterly unimaginative. Still, the irony of the situation is amusing, don't you think?"

The man before the fire gave no response. Like the woman on the bed, he was naked, but where she lay in comfort amid goose down quilts and velvet pillows, he sat sprawled in a hard wooden chair, carved with symbols and blackened with age. His long legs were stretched toward the fire, the flames catching the blond hairs on his calves and turning them to burnished gold. A silver chalice rested on his flat belly, clasped in a hand adorned with two rings: a plain band on his thumb, a heavy black and silver pentacle on his ring finger.

"Just imagine," the woman went on, tauntingly, "the great and mighty Satan, brought to his knees in the twenty-first century by a mere mortal woman."

"Yes," Samael said, turning his blond head to pierce her with disturbingly pale blue eyes, "just imagine."

She ignored the warning in his gaze. "And the name of the church! Bethlehem Baptist—" Her laughter trilled again, filling the otherwise empty chamber. "Oh, it's too delicious for words."

"Perhaps you should keep the words to yourself, then," he murmured, his voice deceptively gentle. "After all, you wrote the book on true love, didn't you? You and Adam, all alone in your garden paradise."

Her laughter stilled.

"Until you saw me, of course," he went on, "and decided your hairy ape of a man wasn't good enough for you. An angel was far more interesting quarry, wasn't he?"

"You're an angel no longer," she hissed. "Besides, I don't recall you putting up much resistance at the time."

"You were like ripe fruit," he said, meeting her anger with seeming indifference. "Dangling yourself before me, tempting me with the sweetness of your juices and the soft sheen of your bare flesh." His voice hardened. "Little did I know how such softness and sweetness hid the rottenness at your core."

"You wanted me!" she screeched, jerking herself upright. Her breasts heaved, dark hair tumbling around her shoulders and dripping like trails of ink over her pale skin. "You've blamed me for eons, when you were just as much at fault as I! I won't have it, do you hear? I'm sick of the guilt, sick of the blame! *I* was the one who was punished—shoved out into the cold to give birth in pain and suffering to a whole new race, while *you*"—she raised a shaking finger, pointing it at him—"*you* were given a kingdom!"

"Ah, yes," he said calmly, "the kingdom of the damned. Better to rule in Hell than serve in Heaven, and all that. Still"—he looked back toward the fire, taking another sip of wine—"it would've been nice to be given a choice."

"You *had* a choice." She rose from the bed, clad in nothing but her hair and her fury. "And you chose *this*." Proudly, she swept a hand down her body, but he kept his head turned away.

"No, Lilith," he said. "You tricked me." With a snap of the wrist, he flicked his remaining wine into the fire, where it hissed and sizzled amid the embers. "As I have tricked you."

As if on cue, a small creature crept from the shadows, its sickly yellow-green color almost as ugly as its features: bulging eyes, pointed ears, and a tail like that of a lizard.

"Ichor," Samael said lovingly, "come sit with me."

Lilith stared with loathing as the lizard-thing

clambered up the arm of the wooden chair and perched there, raising its chin to be scratched.

"Ichor? You named it after something as revolting as *pus*?"

"Why not?" he asked lightly. "It's what I created him from. Are my creation skills not up to your usual standards?" His lip curled in a parody of a smile.

"Why would you keep such a creature?" she asked, taking a step back. "It's beyond disgusting."

"He's useful, as are his brothers."

Several more creatures crept forth from the shadows, as the one on the chair made small *chirrup*ing noises of contentment, tilting its scaly head for easier access to Samael's fingers.

Lilith leapt back onto the bed, clutching a pillow to her nakedness as even more of the creatures oozed forth from the darkest corners of the room. "Sammy," she said warningly, "keep them away from me."

"I can't, my dear," he said, giving Ichor a final pat. He turned his head to look at her, a fiendish look in his bright blue eyes. "They're drawn to wickedness and depravity, and you present an irresistible temptation." He smiled wryly. "Sound familiar?"

She shook her head, staring with horror at the encroaching army of creatures, all of them now advancing steadily toward the bed. "You can't," she said feverishly. "I'm an immortal, just like you! You can't kill me!"

He laughed. "Who said anything about killing? Though you may long for death before a century or two has passed."

Her look of panic was briefly replaced by one of intense concentration.

"You can't transport yourself anywhere from here," he said smoothly. "This is my realm, not yours. My inner sanctuary. You have no power here."

"No!" she shrieked, tearing her eyes from the creatures to stare into his. What she saw there gave her no comfort, however, for she began to shriek even louder. "I'm glad your little human whore married another, do you hear? It hurts, doesn't it?" She scrambled to her feet on the mattress, back against the headboard, pillow still clutched in her arms. "It hurts when someone you love doesn't love you back!"

"Pain is relative, darling," he said silkily, "as you're about to discover."

"All these months in my bed—you were lying

to me, keeping me busy so I wouldn't go after her again, weren't you?" She was frantic now, trapped, with nowhere to go.

"Oh, Lilith," he said mildly, cocking his blond head. "How could you have forgotten? Lying is what I do best." He made a *tsk*ing noise. "And besides, you're in *my* bed now."

"I knew better than to let you bring me here," she spat, glaring at him.

"'Come into my parlor,' said the spider to the fly,'" he quoted. "How does it feel to be caught in a web of your own making?"

The first of the yellow-green creatures climbed atop the mattress, quickly followed by others on each side. They darted toward Lilith's toes, snapping and biting at them with razor-sharp teeth.

"You should've left her alone, and not forced me to choose between the two of you." He watched, deaf to her shrieking, as despite her kicking and flailing, she was covered in a swarm of lizard-like imps. "You thought you'd won, but you were wrong. I chose *her*, which meant I had to let her go to keep her safe." He gave a short laugh. "Too bad there's no one here to do the same for you." A wave of his hand, and the frenzied woman on the bed was gone, the creatures with her.

In the sudden silence, the one remaining on the arm of Samael's chair gave a questioning little chirrup.

"Yes, Ichor," he said absently, reaching again to stroke its scaly head. "It was far too kind of me to let her keep the pillow."

"Master." A shadow separated itself from the wall. "A thousand pardons."

"What is it, Nyx?"

Black as night, with wings of ebony and a form as shadowy as the darkness where he had been concealed, the Chief Servant of Darkness bowed low before his master. The only color he possessed was in his pupils, slits of red barely visible in the dim light.

"I'm sorry to trouble you, O Mighty One, but you've been summoned."

A bark of laughter escaped Samael's throat. "Another midnight Mass? Another chanting group of robed sycophants wielding bell, book, and candle, perhaps?" He waved a hand negligently toward the shadowy figure. "Don't trouble me with such nonsense, and get me some more wine."

"Immediately, my lord." The gurgle of liquid came as it poured into the chalice. "This is not an ordinary summons, I fear, or I would not have brought it to you."

"Indeed?"

"He says his name is Gabriel, my lord." Nyx's voice was hushed. "He is surrounded by light. Light such as I have never seen."

Despite the crackling fire, the sudden stillness within the chamber was tinged with ice. Ichor's pointed ears drooped, and he quickly climbed down from the chair, retreating to the shadows from whence he came.

"Gabriel is here? Within my walls?" Samael rose from the chair, his naked body gleaming in the firelight, and very carefully put the chalice of wine down on a side table inlaid with squares of ivory and onyx.

"In the outer temple, my lord. He would come no further. He bid me tell you he waits for you there."

"Well," said the original Fallen One, with a sardonic curl of his lip, "let's not keep my dear brother waiting too long."

Only a quick blink betrayed Nyx's surprise. In silence, he helped his master dress, bringing forth the jeans and T-shirts so favored in today's modern age, and waiting as a selection was made. He knelt to assist as Samael stepped into a pair of black jeans and gleaming boots of black leather. A soft gray T-shirt, a black belt with a silver buckle, a wrist cuff of braided leather, and it was done.

Dressed and ready, Samael paused before the full-length mirror that stood beside his bed, and smiled. No mortals observing him now would realize who they were facing. They would see only what he wanted them to see, a virile, good-looking male in the prime of his life. The ability to blend was a talent he'd mastered long ago, and if he wanted someone's attention, he knew full well how to get it. Running a careless hand through his short blond hair and smiling a grim smile, he left his chamber behind and strode down hall-ways made of stone toward the cavernous room known as the outer temple.

It was a long walk, but he was in no hurry, despite what he'd said to Nyx. He could've willed himself there in an instant if he'd cared to, but instead he walked, and as he walked, he remembered.

Wind, cool and invigorating, and the glorious sense of weightlessness that accompanied flight. The pin-pricks of distant stars against the night sky, the brilliant smear of a million galaxies, like glitter tossed carelessly across the heavens. Innocence, laughter, and joy as he and his brother angels darted in and out among the cosmos, their wings outspread, naked and unashamed as they played, secure in the knowledge that they were loved and protected by the One who created them.

He remembered, too, the shame and the fear of that day in the Garden, when he had lost his innocence and angered his Creator. Oh, how he'd wept, how he'd begged to be forgiven—to no avail. He'd been cast down from the lofty heights, stripped of his wings; sometimes, in the night, he felt a faint tingle between his shoulder blades and felt anew the pain of his loss. He'd been blamed for defiling mankind and bringing an end to Paradise, when it was mankind, and their emphasis on the flesh, who'd defiled *him*.

Jaw set, Samael kept walking, not noticing or caring that Nyx followed several feet behind, a silent and shadowy figure at his back. After the Fall, he'd made sure mankind suffered, just as he had suffered. Abandoned by the One, shunned by his angelic brothers, he tempted, as he had been tempted. He lied, as he had been lied to. And when they succumbed to lies and temptation— just as he had—he punished them as he had been punished, by everlasting damnation in the pit of despair.

The hallways rang with his footsteps, but he didn't hear them. Another memory surfaced: a young woman with laughing eyes and a kind heart, streaks of pink in her dark hair. He'd lost her, too—lost her to the Light that had already cost him so much. There'd been other women through the centuries, of course, long dead now, but she still lived. She lived, and she laughed, and she'd clutched her pink tulips during her wedding to the man she'd chosen over him, and try as he might, he couldn't bring himself to hate her for it. For she had been the one who'd known him for what he was, and forgiven him anyway—the only one in all these eons who'd shown him an ounce of genuine compassion, despite the blackness that stained his soul.

Light gleamed at the end of the corridor, as unwelcome as the one who brought it. A few steps more and he was in a chamber, huge and vaulted, full of echoes and dust and silence. A man stood waiting at the far end, his features obscured by the brilliance that seemed to emanate from his very pores.

"What's the matter, Gabriel?" Samael asked coldly. "Afraid of the dark?"

"Samael," said the figure, in a voice filled with sorrow. "My long-lost brother." The light dimmed, fading to reveal a tall man with brown hair, worn long and free, dressed in a white robe and sandals. "My eyes delight in the sight of you, yet my soul will forever grieve over what you've become."

"Spare me your pity," Sammy said, planting his booted feet and crossing his arms over his chest. "The time I could've used it is long past." He raked a scornful gaze over his visitor. "You look like a wandering prophet. This is the twenty-first century, you know; camels and cave markings have been replaced by cars and computers."

Gabriel shook his head, a slight smile lifting one corner of his lips. His garb changed, morphing into plain khaki pants and a blue chambray shirt, long hair clubbed into a ponytail. "Better?" he asked his host.

"No," Sammy growled. Despite his open hostility, a small part of him was pleased to see his old friend and erstwhile brother. He clamped down viciously on the feeling, and trampled it into dust. "What do you want?"

Gabriel was silent for a moment, merely looking into his eyes.

Uncomfortable to find he could not easily meet them, Sammy felt his anger rise.

"Speak and be done with it, damn you," he ground out. "My patience grows short."

"Your patience was ever short," said Gabriel, "as was your humility. Even now you taunt the heavens with your pride and your hubris, establishing yourself within these once hallowed walls"—he gestured toward the vaulted ceiling—"built to proclaim the glory of the One."

Samael made a noise of disgust. "Solomon built this temple to proclaim his own glory." He smiled grimly. "His spells and incantations are what keep this temple hidden in plain sight, invisible to the eyes of mortals. He used that same magic to force my demons to build it, so why shouldn't I use it now that he's dead?" He shook his head, smiling wryly. "The mighty King Solomon, keeper of all the world's mysteries, save one—that of death itself. All the treasures he collected in the name of the One now belong to me, including this dusty monument to greed and glory."

Gabriel frowned, looking troubled. "You take such joy in profaning what was intended as house of worship."

"Is that why you're here? An avenging angel, come to smite me with your flaming sword of righteousness?" Sammy spread his arms wide, as if baring himself to a blow. "Go ahead. Oblivion would be a welcome change after all these years in Hell."

"I will not fight with you, brother."

"We are brothers no longer," Sammy snapped, dropping his arms. "Now get to the point, or get out."

A heavy sigh came from the angel at the far end of the room. "I wanted to help you, you know."

Sammy said nothing.

"I would've spoken on your behalf, but the One forbade it, saying whatever befell you was meant to happen."

"Meant to happen?" Sammy scoffed. "So I was created merely to be punished, is that it?"

"His ways are not our ways," Gabriel answered quietly, "and it is not for us to question them."

"Not for you, perhaps," came the grim reply. "I question them every day."

There was a silence, in which Gabriel turned away. He moved to an old stone altar, touching the tip of his finger to the dust that coated it, revealing white marble, veined with gold.

"Must your minion be present while we talk?" he asked quietly, changing the subject. "The dark one, skulking in the doorway. He disturbs me."

"I don't care if he disturbs you or not," Sammy said smoothly. "Nyx is my faithful servant, and my ever-present shadow. His loyalty, unlike that of others I've known, is unquestioned."

Gabriel stiffened, setting his shoulders and resting both palms flat on the altar. "Formed from the darkness that was always within your soul, I suppose," he answered quietly. "And yet still you question the One's judgment—do you think He did not know the darkness was there?"

"Why have you come?" Sammy growled, scarce able to control his growing rage.

Gabriel turned, facing him head-on. "I want to make you an offer," was his unexpected reply. "One you would do well not to refuse."

Rage was replaced by surprise, followed by mocking laughter. "An offer?" he asked, when he was able. "What could you have that I would possibly want?" Against his will, an image flashed into his mind: wavy brown hair, flowing in the wind, the laughing smile his long-ago brother had flashed over a shoulder as they raced together through the skies.

Gabriel said nothing for a moment, then looked pointedly toward the impassive black-winged shadow still standing by the door. "This is a private matter, between you and me."

"Do not listen to him, Master." Nyx stepped forward, voice low and urgent. His eyes glowed red, and were fixed on Gabriel. "His words are poison, steeped in honey. He dares to come here and make demands—let me kill him for you."

Two powerful beings—one black as night, one clothed in light—exchanged baleful stares.

"You are welcome to try, demon," Gabriel bit off tightly, "but I wouldn't advise it."

Nyx took another step forward, the tips of his wings beginning to quiver like the fur of a black cat poised to pounce.

Sammy allowed himself a small smile, knowing his servant would not attack until given leave to do so. "My, my. Nyx is usually so quiet and unobtrusive. He doesn't seem to like you."

"The feeling is mutual. He is an abomination."

"Where are your feelings of brotherly love, Gabriel? Nyx cannot help who he is, any more than you can."

"Your mockery is wasted on me, Samael"—Gabe's blue eyes fastened once again on his—"for I know the secrets of your heart."

A sneer of disgust twisted Sammy's upper lip. "You know nothing." He turned on his heel, and began to walk away.

"I know about Nicki Styx, and what you did for her."

He paused, back stiff.

"I know why, as well."

For the space of a few heartbeats, Sammy fought the urge to raise his hand and release his faithful servant, who eagerly awaited his signal.

Mastering his temper, he merely turned his head and clipped, "Leave us."

"But—"

"Leave us," he repeated, in a voice that brooked no argument.

With a final red-eyed glare at Gabriel that made clear his feelings on the matter, the Chief Servant of Darkness stalked silently from the chamber, his disapproval lingering like the shadows he himself resembled.

Samael allowed the silence that followed his departure to go on, to build. He said nothing, nor did he look at his old friend. Instead he strolled toward a marble bench, festooned with cobwebs, his footsteps echoing coldly in the vaulted chamber. A quick flick of a finger, and the bench was clean, the dust and detritus of centuries gone as though it had never been. "Where are my manners?" he asked smoothly, and a table appeared, topped with a pitcher and two goblets. "Sit. Heaven is so far away . . . you must be parched." As he poured, more items appeared: a tray, laden with fruit and a loaf of bread, still steaming from the oven. "Not exactly ambrosia," he said wryly, "but a nice, full-bodied cabernet is as close as we come in this world."

Only then did he turn, holding out the goblet to Gabriel, who made no move to take it.

"Suit yourself." Sammy shrugged, and took a sip of his own.

"Earthly pleasures like food and wine will not fill the emptiness within your soul," Gabriel said. "Haven't you learned that yet?"

Sammy's eyes narrowed over the rim of his goblet. "You dare much, *brother*," he said, imbuing the word with as much sarcasm as he could, "for one who dines each day on pompous platitudes and the lies fed to children."

"Blaspheme all you like," the other man said calmly. "I've come to help you."

A noise of disgust answered him.

"Hear me out." Gabriel's eyes, warm brown shot with golden flecks, were trained on his. "I offer you a chance for redemption. A chance to show the One that you regret your disobedience, that you still want forgiveness."

Sammy laughed, but it was an ugly sound. "And therein lies the problem, old friend." He turned away, slapping his goblet down on the table so that a tiny portion of liquid spilled over the rim. "I don't regret anything, except believing in forgiveness to begin with."

"You lie."

"Yes, I do!" His sudden shout filled the chamber, echoing against the cold stone walls. Whirling to face Gabriel again, he added, "I lie, as I was lied to! I tempt, as I was tempted! And when the temptation proves too much"—here his voice lowered—"and it *always* proves too much—it fills me with pleasure and satisfaction." His lip curled. "The only thing that gives me greater pleasure is sex. Lots and lots of sex."

Gabriel's lips thinned, but he said nothing.

"I feel sorry for you," Sammy spat, hoping to find a weak link in Gabriel's armor. "You've never known the touch of a woman, have you? The silky feel of her hair, the softness of an inner thigh, the curve of a breast within your hand. Have you read the Song of Solomon, Gabriel? Do you ever wonder what you're missing?"

To his surprise, the angel nodded. "I do. But I don't act upon it, for it is forbidden the sons of the One to sleep with the daughters of men."

"He didn't forbid *me*!" Sammy shouted in reply. "Why is that, I wonder? Why didn't He tell me that what I did was wrong *before* I did it?" A sweep of his arm, and the contents of the table crashed to the floor. The question he'd asked himself for eons came bubbling to the surface, along with his rage. "If He's so all-powerful, so all-knowing, then why didn't He stop me, Gabriel?"

The silence within the chamber was absolute, save for the hollow sound of the now-empty goblet as it rolled into a corner.

"I don't know," Gabriel murmured, in a voice filled with compassion.

Having no need of compassion, Sammy raked a hand through his spiky blond hair.

"It's not too late, Samael." Gabe took a step closer.

"Samael is dead," he answered harshly. "And what is left is the stuff of nightmares."

"That's not true"—Gabe took a step closer—"and you know it. Even now you feel tendrils of who you once were stirring, moving murkily beneath the darkness that cloaks you."

"How poetic," he sneered.

"How frightened you are." Gabe shook his head, a bemused smile on his face. "The Prince of Darkness, the Great Deceiver, who deceives even himself."

The urge to kill, to rend, to maim rose like a black fog in his mind, testing, probing against the edges of his sanity. He let it feed for a moment before forcing it away, blessedly taking much of his anger with it. "Go away, Gabriel," he answered wearily, "before I show you what truly lies beneath the darkness."

"For the sake of what we once shared, in a long ago time when we were both innocent and unaware, I beg you, old friend, hear me out."

"Stop it," Sammy said, scrubbing a hand over his face. He still wanted to smash his fist into Gabriel's perfect face, rip the hair from his heavenly head, and cast him down deeper than the deepest pit ever created. Instead he found himself growling, "Say whatever it is you came to say, and then get out of my temple."

Gabriel smiled, and something painful twisted inside Sammy's chest, like a knife to the heart he no longer had. Before he gave in to the urge to put a fist through those gleaming, perfect teeth, he turned away, staring at a dusty marbled column as he listened.

"You showed mercy to the woman you love, and in doing so, you opened a crack in the blackened shell of misery and bitterness that surrounds your heart."

Yes, Nicki had found a way inside his heart without even trying, and nestled there still, damn her.

"Been spying on me, Gabriel? I never took you for a voyeur—how very naughty of you."

Gabriel ignored the sarcasm. "Let me show you how to widen that crack, to break free of the path you've taken."

"Oh, by all means," he replied, with exquisite politeness. "Please. Show me."

"Join me in doing what you were created to do, brother. I have a lost soul in need of a guardian angel, and I offer you the job."

For the first time in several thousand centuries, Sammy found himself at a total loss for words.

"A mortal woman, in need of intervention and guidance. You could help her—indeed, you could save her."

Laughter, low in his throat. Swiveling his head, he found his voice. "Why, in the name of all that's unholy, would I want to do that? Less souls for your side, more for mine, remember?" He shook his head, amazed by the suggestion. "Save her yourself."

"I seek to save a different soul today," Gabriel answered quietly. "Yours."

Time, which there had been too much of, seemed to stand still.

"The gates of Heaven have been closed against me for eons. Are you saying they are now open?" How he despised the flicker of hope that made him ask the question.

His old friend shook his head. "No, sadly they are not—not yet. But if you do this, if you show me that you haven't forgotten who you once were—who you *are*—then you give me a reason to beseech the One on your behalf."

Sammy rolled his eyes. "Oh yes, beseech away, Gabriel. I'm sure it will do a tremendous amount of good."

"You forget my position. I stand at the One's right hand. He will hear me, I know it."

"So you want me to turn my back on everything I've done, everything I've created, for the *chance* I might be forgiven? You want me to sheathe my claws, retract my horns, give away my *kingdom*"— he swept an angry hand expansively over the echoing chamber—"for the mere *chance* of regaining what I once had?"

"Ah, yes," Gabriel said calmly, eerily echoing the words Sammy said to Lilith earlier, "the kingdom of the damned." He looked around as well, taking in the dust, the cobwebs, and the utter emptiness that surrounded them. "I can certainly see why you wouldn't want to give it up."

Too astounded to be angry, Sammy merely stared, disbelieving, as Gabriel shrugged.

"Consider it a challenge, if you must. Do it as a favor to an old friend, do it to prove you still can—do it out of boredom, for Heaven's sake— just *do* it."

Unbelievably, despite the transparency of Ga-

briel's arguments, he found himself tempted—
once again—to do something he wasn't supposed
to. He was the fucking Prince of Darkness, for
fuck's sake, and he could do anything he damn
well pleased. "Do you know, Gabriel," he said quietly, "that's the first thing you've said to me that
makes sense."

Nothing was beyond him, including helping a
few pathetic mortals find happiness.

Or not.

Turning away from the flash of eagerness in
Gabe's eyes, he nodded thoughtfully, mind already working. "I'll do it, but I'll do it *my* way.
None of your mealymouthed prayers or good
deeds or sackcloth and ashes." He shot his old
friend a warning look. "You'll stay out of it, do
you hear?"

Gabriel nodded, smiling. "I'll stay out of it."

Eyeing him narrowly, Sammy replied, "Why do
I suddenly feel as though I'm not the only liar in
the room?"

Gabriel stiffened, but Sammy was in no mood
for further debate. "Tell me her name and where
to find her. Then leave it to me."

There was a slight hesitation. "Her name is
Faith McFarland, and she lives in Atlanta, Georgia. She—"

Cutting him off with a raised palm, he swiveled his head. "I'm quite familiar with Atlanta," he said shortly. "Is this supposed to be some kind of joke?"

"Coincidence only," said Gabriel, "though I'm told that Southern girls can be somewhat"—he hesitated—"interesting. It's no surprise that—"

"That's enough," he said curtly. Gabe was about to mention Nicki, and Sammy couldn't have that. Nicki was his, and not up for discussion. "I can find out everything else I need to know about Faith McFarland on my own."

"Arrogant ass," Gabriel murmured. He turned away, crossing his arms over his chest. "And I'm not referring to a donkey either."

Sammy suppressed the urge to smile. "We're done here." Striding toward the arched doorway where he'd entered, he added, "If I need you, I'll let you know, but in the meantime, get the hell out of my temple."

"I warn you, Samael," Gabriel said loudly, his voice echoing in Solomon's grand chamber. "Do not betray my trust. This is your last chance at redemption."

Not bothering to reply, Sammy walked away, knowing his former brother-in-arms would not—and could not—follow. The outer temple was one thing, but the hallways of his stronghold were deep and dark, and just as he was banned from the skies, his private domain was anathema to an archangel. The very walls themselves would repel the light and goodness of one such as Gabriel.

For a moment he heard nothing but the angry rush of blood in his ears, and the sound of his own footsteps behind him, echoing coldly through hallways of stone.

A few seconds later there was a faint rustle of wings as Nyx returned to his usual position, a silent shadow at his back.

"Master?"

He didn't deign to turn around. "Yes?"

"Surely you don't mean to do as he asks."

Dark laughter snaked its way into the corridor. "Oh, Nyx." Samael tossed his answer carelessly over a gray-clad shoulder. "I gave Gabriel my word, after all, and you know how much that means to me."

The nightshade's eyes flared a brighter shade of red as his unholy chuckle joined that of his master.

Chapter Two

Brain stem glioma.

In the quiet of the chapel, Faith McFarland put her head in her hands and cried. She'd been crying on and off all night, unable to take her eyes off Nathan's pale, sleeping face. Her son—her beautiful little boy—had a tumor at the base of his brain. What was she going to do? How would she cope? How could she *fix* it?

"God," she moaned. "Oh God, please help me."

Just two months ago Nathan had been a happy, healthy preschooler, obsessed with cars and SpongeBob SquarePants. Then came the headaches, the vomiting, the lack of appetite and energy. What she'd hoped was just an intestinal bug had become a nightmare of epic proportions—blood work,

CAT scans, and MRIs, all culminating in the horrible news she'd gotten yesterday afternoon.

"I'm sorry," Dr. Wynecke had told her, "but the MRI confirms a small lesion at the base of Nathan's skull. We'll need to get a tissue sample to determine if it's malignant."

Her first thought had been that she'd misheard him—the words he'd used made no sense. But there had been no mistaking the look of concern and sympathy in his eyes, and no mistaking what he'd said next.

Cancer. Immediate surgery. Biopsy, possible chemotherapy, radiation therapy.

Which was why she was sitting here now, in an empty chapel at Columbia Hospital, while her only child was lying on an operating table, his life in someone else's hands.

"Please," she whispered, raising her eyes to the wooden cross on the wall before her. "Please don't let him die."

"Do you think He hears you?" came a voice.

Startled, she looked around, but there was no one.

"Do you think He cares?"

She stood, grasping the empty pew in front of her.

"He doesn't, you know. The life of one poor, sick

child means nothing to Him in the big scheme of things."

It was a man's voice, smooth and matter-of-fact. Frightened, Faith moved to leave the chapel, but stopped short at the distinct *click* coming from the chapel door. "Hello?" she asked loudly, wiping tears from her face with one hand. "Who's there?"

No one answered. The ensuing silence was laden with tension, causing the hair on the back of her neck to prickle. Moving quickly to the door, she tried the handle, but it was locked. Glancing nervously over her shoulder, she pounded on the door with her palm. "Hello? Is anyone out there? Can anyone hear me? I'm locked in."

"No one hears you," the voice said, "except me."

Faith spun around, beginning to panic. One way in, one way out, and the way was blocked. "Help," she shouted at the top of her lungs, pounding at the door.

Columbia was a busy hospital. There'd been plenty of people around when she'd made her way here after they'd taken Nathan to surgery, unable to stand the sight of his empty hospital bed.

No one came, and try as she might, she could hear nothing on the other side of the door.

Willing herself to calm, she scanned the quiet

chapel. No cameras, no speakers, just a small room, plain wooden pews filled with a scattering of Bibles, a prie-dieu for kneeling, and a simple cross on the wall. Blinking back tears, she hammered again on the door with her fists. "Help, someone! I'm locked in the chapel! Let me out."

"'Malignant' is such an ugly word, isn't it?" The man's voice came from nowhere, and from everywhere. "A big, ugly word that just doesn't fit with the image of such a small head, capped with brown curls, just like his mother's."

Faith lifted a trembling hand to her mouth and pressed it there, hard, to keep back the sobs that rose in her throat.

"So helpless," the voice went on, "so innocent. Nathan trusted you to keep him safe—yet you're helpless as well, aren't you?"

"Stop it!" she screamed, frightened out of her wits. *Who was it? Who could possibly be so cruel?* "Leave me alone!" Crying harder now, she tugged on the door handle with both hands, desperate to leave the voice and the chapel behind.

"I can help you, Faith McFarland," said the voice. "I'm the only one who can help you."

Faith slumped against the door, leaning her forehead against the wood. Nathan would be out of surgery soon; she needed to be there for him. "Let me out," she begged tearfully, with no idea whom she was pleading with. "Please."

"I will in a moment, but first we need to have a little chat."

She didn't understand where the voice was coming from. Unmuffled, no electronic echo or hiss, as clear as if someone were standing beside her—but there was no one there.

"I'm sorry to tell you this, but when your little boy gets out of surgery, you're going to get some very bad news."

Faith's legs were suddenly boneless. She sank to the floor, unable to hold herself up.

"It doesn't have to be the end of the world, however," said the voice calmly, impervious to her grief. "I can still help you."

"Who are you?" she shrieked, at her wit's end. "What do you want?" *No escape, no one to fight.* "Let me out!"

The light within the chapel began to grow dim. As she crouched there, on the floor, the room darkened until she could no longer make out the cross on the wall, or the prie-dieu in front of it. The world shrank to a small circle roughly ten feet in circumference, illuminated only by a single track light in the wall above her head.

"I don't want much," said the voice, now coming from the darkness itself. A man's hand, adorned with a thick silver ring, came into view, grasping the end of a pew. "Just your soul."

Her blood ran cold, but she had no time to process, as the man stepped fully into the light. He was blond, he was handsome, and he was smiling. *Smiling, the sadistic bastard.*

She scrambled up from the floor, never taking her eyes from his face. Hoping the surrounding darkness would work to her advantage as it had to his, she eased toward a corner, keeping as many pews between them as she could. Once she reached the shadows, she ducked, and having nowhere to go, rolled beneath a neighboring pew. Maybe she could hide until someone came . . .

"Is your son's life worth so little that you would cower away from the one person who could help you save it?" the man asked, but she didn't answer.

Laying her cheek against the carpet, Faith fought to control her breathing, to slow the racing of her heart, to *think*.

"Ah, well. I can wait. Time is something I have plenty of." Wood creaked as he settled himself in one of the rear pews. "All the time in the world, in fact. Too bad Nathan can't say the same."

More tears welled, slipping over the bridge of her nose to fall soundlessly to the carpet.

"He'll be waking soon, wondering where his mommy is, I would imagine. Too bad he doesn't have a daddy, by the way—boys need a father, after all, or so I'm told."

Faith said nothing, refusing to think of her scumbag ex-boyfriend, who'd pressured her to get an abortion when she'd told him she was pregnant, and then dumped her when she refused. She'd let him go, knowing that anyone who could shirk his responsibilities that easily would make a terrible father. She and Nathan had done just fine without a man in their lives.

Just fine. Until now.

"Doesn't matter now, I suppose," the man went on. "Poor little tyke isn't going to make it to his fifth birthday—"

Her breath hitched at the cruelty of the statement.

"—unless you come out of there and talk to me. I can make it all go away, you know."

She didn't believe him. Of course she didn't believe him. He was just some lunatic who'd followed her into the chapel and somehow managed to lock them both inside. Sooner or later someone would come and let them out. And when they did, she was going to press charges, big-time.

"Remember how he used to call your cat Memmy instead of Emily? So adorable, though I'll never understand why people feel the need to humanize their pets by giving them proper names."

Her mouth went dry.

"What about the time he got hold of the baby powder and smeared it all over the living room? It looked like a sack of flour had exploded in there—such a mess." The man chuckled softly. "Took you two days to wash and vacuum it out of everything, but you couldn't bring yourself to punish him because he looked so guilty when he was caught." He sighed. "Ah, memories. Hold on to them, Faith, for they'll soon be all you have left of Nathan."

"Why are you doing this?" she choked, unable to remain silent any longer. How did he know about her cat, about the baby powder? Those memories were her own, and nobody else's.

"Come out," he said firmly. "Stop hiding from me. Stop hiding from the truth."

And so finally, because she felt she had little choice, she crawled out, feeling the cheap carpet burn her elbows. Then she stood up, keeping the length of the chapel between them.

"Ah," the man said. "That's better. Now I can see your face, and you can see mine."

She didn't believe that statement, unless he could see in the dark. She, on the other hand, could see him quite clearly.

The single remaining track light angled down on him like a spotlight, leaving him fully exposed. Coldly handsome, blond-haired and blue-eyed, dressed in black jeans and a gray T-shirt. He was leaning back in his seat, both arms resting on the back of the pew, a thick bracelet of braided black leather on one wrist.

There was another silence, in which she could literally hear her own heartbeat, thumping madly in her ears. He made no sudden moves, merely watching her watch him, and she got the feeling that he *could* see in the dark, because he was looking straight at her.

"Who are you?" Faith whispered, terrified. Strangely fascinated by his male beauty, and cold to the marrow of her bones, she knew the dizzying fear a mouse must feel when pinned by a snake.

He cocked his head, giving her a wry smile. "Can't you guess?"

She said nothing, unable to formulate the words to express what she was thinking.

"Is it the lack of horns? No pitchfork or forked tail?" He sighed. "I only break them out on Halloween these days, or the occasional midnight Mass. Best to blend in."

She was afraid to blink.

"Don't worry, Faith," he murmured, looking directly into her eyes. "I rarely get a chance to say this, but in your case, I truly *am* the lesser of two evils."

Faith spread her hands against the wall, letting her fingers send her brain the message: *This is real, this is happening.*

"Let me go," she said shakily. "I need to go."

"Right now, as we speak," the man replied, ignoring her plea, "your doctor has just removed some sample tissue from the base of your little boy's brain. A quick examination under a microscope is going to reveal cancer cells, which will multiply, growing larger until the resultant pressure on Nathan's brain stem costs him his vision, his hearing, his balance—and ultimately, his life."

The choked noises she heard were coming from her own throat. Giving in to them, she leaned her head back against the wall and set them loose in raw, wracking sobs.

She no longer cared who he was, or why he was there. She only cared about Nathan—her sweet, smiling Nathan—who lay still and silent on a table somewhere, unaware of what was happening to him.

"There are options, I suppose," the man went on, relentlessly. "Surgery, chemotherapy, radiation. All guaranteed to seriously affect Nathan's quality of life before he ultimately dies. Vomiting, diarrhea, hair loss . . ."

With a shriek of rage and grief, Faith threw herself forward, hating him more than she'd ever thought it possible to hate anyone. Darting around the edge of a pew, she flew down the center aisle, wanting only to shut him up, to stop the words that spewed from his mouth like poison.

He watched her come, unmoving, with a dispassionate expression that made her want to rake her nails across his face until he felt some of the agony she was feeling.

She'd almost reached him when, in the blink of an eye, he was gone.

Staggering to a stop, Faith grabbed the back of the nearest pew, unable to believe what she was seeing. *It was a nightmare, it had to be a nightmare . . .*

"You're wasting time," he said coldly, from somewhere behind her. "Do you want me to save your child's life or not?"

Closing her eyes, Faith drew upon what little

strength she had left. Her flare of rage had died as quickly as it came, leaving her feeling like a spent match. A deep breath, then another, as she fought to bring her sobs under control. "How"— she swallowed hard, willing her voice to work properly—"how can you do that?"

"I can do anything," he answered, not quite so coldly this time. "For the right price."

She felt her way along the edge of the pew until she could sit, facing the voice that came from the darkness. Swiping her hands over her face, she then clasped them in her lap to still their shaking. "What do you want?"

"Only what belongs to me," he said smoothly, "and I want you to help me get it."

Daring greatly, she swallowed hard, and willing her voice not to tremble, asked, "If you can do anything, then why do you need my help?"

His teeth gleamed in the darkness as he smiled. "I didn't say I *needed* your help, Faith. I said I *wanted* it."

He came forward, into the light, resting his hands on the back of the pew in front of her.

"And in case you haven't figured it out yet, I have a devil of a temper when I don't get what I want."

She stared at him numbly. "You can't be real."

Her eyes searched his face, as though memorizing his features. "You can't be . . ."

"Oh, but I am." He reached out a hand—a perfectly proportioned, normal man's hand, no leathery scales or razor-sharp claws—and said, quite simply, "Take my hand, and come with me if you want Nathan to live."

And because she'd do anything to make sure Nathan lived, she did what he said, and that's when the nightmare truly began.

The instant he touched her, everything changed. One moment they were in the chapel, and the next they were in the operating room, where a small, draped figure lay facedown on a table, surrounded by people and equipment. It was Nathan; Dr. Wynecke was probing a blood-stained opening at the base of her son's skull, the instruments in his hands sharp and shiny.

Faith cried out, shocked, but Dr. Wynecke's concentration remained unbroken, and the nurses and the anesthesiologist ignored her as though she were invisible. The blond man squeezed her hand, and as much as she hated it—and him—the contact steadied her.

Pressing her other hand to her mouth, she struggled for composure, then froze at the sight of a shadowy figure lurking motionless in the corner.

A seven-foot-tall, black-winged creature, watching Nathan's surgery with eyes that glowed red.

"Don't be afraid," the blond man said soothingly, in her ear. "He's not here for you."

Faith tried to pull away, but he wouldn't let her, tightening his grip. "Let me go!" she shrieked, panicky. She had to get between Nathan and that, that . . . *thing*. "Dr. Wynecke! Nurse!" she shouted, abandoning all pretense of quiet. They needed to stop the surgery, do it another day— "Behind you! Watch out!"

The surgical team might as well have been enclosed in a soundproof bubble for all the attention they paid her.

"Meet black-winged Nyx," the Devil said calmly, "who waits in the shadows, eager to pierce the veil between life and death."

Horrified, she shook her head, unable to believe what was happening could *possibly* be real.

"Nyx is my chief soul eater, and he's hungry. He awaits my permission to unfurl his wings and settle himself on top of your child like a psychic vulture, a vulture no one will see or hear or even begin to detect"—Satan ignored her moan of terror—"and then he will rend and rip at the invisible threads that bind the boy's soul to his body." He shook his beautiful blond head ruefully, as though sorry to be the one to give her such bad news. "The veil has already been thinned by the use of anesthesia . . . The boy's soul floats above him now, vulnerable, and ripe for the taking."

Faith clawed and slapped at him with her free hand. "Let go of me," she shrieked. She'd throw herself on top of Nathan in the middle of surgery if need be, anything to put herself between her child and that . . . that *monster*, but her efforts to escape were pointless. Satan spun her like a toy and held her against him, back to chest, forcing her to watch the scene in the operating room.

"I can stop Nyx anytime I like," he murmured in her ear, "but you must give me a reason."

She whimpered, helpless and frantic, but no one heard her. No one, that was, except the black-winged creature, who raised its head and looked directly at her. There was no expression on its face, because there *was* no face, really. Just a black hole with glowing embers for eyes, the vague outline of pointed ears, a nose, a pointed chin.

Her knees nearly gave out.

The Evil One gave her a shake. "Focus," he said sharply. "Your son's life in return for one small favor. You choose."

"Yes!" she cried. She'd do anything to get that

thing away from Nathan. "Send it away, please! Whatever it is you want me to do, I'll do it!" she sobbed, boneless with terror.

He gave a dark chuckle. "Good."

And then they were back in the chapel, just like that.

Faith wrenched away, unable to stand his hands on her another second, and grabbed the back of a nearby pew. Mind reeling, dizzy, she wondered if she'd gone insane, or was just about to. "Send it away," she repeated frantically, shaken and sick. "You have to send it away!"

"It's gone," he confirmed. "For now."

Bile rose in her throat, hot, burning, but she forced it back, nearly choking on it.

"Calm yourself," the Devil said. "Nathan is no longer in danger of dying today. I'll even let him go home from the hospital this time."

The casual way he said "this time" made her heart stutter. The pew beneath her hands was the only thing grounding her, so she gripped it as hard as she could and took a deep breath, refusing to give in to madness.

"We'll make a bargain, you and I." She could hear the smile in his voice, and hated him for it. "I'll cure Nathan in return for one small favor. Your little boy will start feeling better the moment he wakes up, and you'll be able to take him home. He'll have a miraculous recovery. Whether he stays there, happy and healthy and completely cured, will be up to you."

She forced herself to look at him, steeling herself against the cold male beauty of his features—a mask, she now knew, to hide the horrors beneath. "What kind of favor?"

"A small one," he said soothingly.

"What favor?" she repeated stonily, not buying it for one second.

"Nothing you can't handle, I assure you." His smirk made her skin crawl. "I'll give you one month to enjoy the improvement in Nathan's health, and then I'll come back and ask for your help in return. It's just that simple."

One month. It bought her some time, but then what?

"You must understand, Faith," he said gently, as though he actually cared, "if you do nothing, Nathan will die. If you agree to do as I ask, he'll get a second chance at *life*. What does it matter what the favor is? If you're the woman I think you are, you'll easily accomplish what I ask."

The soothing tone of his voice was merely a façade, like his handsome face and stylish clothes.

He was evil incarnate, and never in her life had she felt so helpless.

Just in front of her, in the back of a pew, was a worn Bible. It had probably been a source of comfort to many others who'd come to this chapel over the years, but it was no comfort to her today. Where was God when she'd cried out for salvation, and gotten damnation instead?

Faith steeled her resolve, realizing that once again—as she had when she'd found herself pregnant and alone—the only person she had to rely on in this situation was herself. Nathan needed her, so she did her best to compose herself, wiping the tears from her face with both hands. "Please," she whispered. "I'll do whatever you ask. Just let my son live."

Chapter Three

"Great show tonight, Finn. You *rocked* the place, man!"

Finn Payne took the bottle of water he was handed as he stepped offstage, offering no comment except a breathless nod. His body and brain were still buzzing, still riding the crest of the wave; chaos, sound and fury, strobe lights and screaming fans, the siren-sweet call of the dark music that was his life. It was like a drug, all-consuming, tireless in its demand to be heard.

As he strode down the backstage hallway, mind and body racing, his eyes barely registered the people around him; security guys mostly, roadies and technophiles, the human machinery that kept his career in high gear. The music was still in his head, lower now, a raging river instead of a flood.

"In here, Finn." Someone touched his elbow. He'd reached the door to the green room, held open by a security guy who kept his eyes trained on the corridor as he ushered him inside.

Once in, Finn caught a glimpse of himself in the mirror. Dark hair spiked with sweat, soaked white T-shirt, designer jeans that fit like a second set of skin. He was breathing hard, riding high.

Finn Payne, once a member of the rock band Apocalypse, now in the middle of a thriving solo career. Top of the world, top of his game.

The door closed behind him, and he was alone. The silence would've been deafening, save for the music in his head, slowing to undertones no one ever heard but him.

Two decades of decadence were leaving their mark; there were creases at the corners of his green eyes, and shadows beneath them.

Turning away, Finn tipped his head to guzzle the last of his bottled water. The notes within him still pulsed, throbbing in rhythm with his heart.

"Let me know when you're ready to release the hordes," John, the security guy, stuck his head in the door. "Every chick in Atlanta is banging on the backstage door tonight."

Finn shook his head. "I'm heading to the hotel for a shower and some sleep. Where's the limo?"

"You're leaving?" John was shocked. "But you've got some real babes out there!" There was never any shortage of women on the road—many of them all too happy to share a wild night of rock-star craziness, a lazy afternoon of room service in some nameless hotel. "These Southern girls are wild, man."

Finn shook his head, grabbing his bag of personal stuff off the floor. "Tell the crew the party's on me." He waved a hand toward the fully stocked bar. The dark mistress who was his muse was the only one who mattered, and she was already leaving him—the buzz from the show was starting to wear off more quickly these days. All those nameless, faceless girls . . . He wasn't up for another night of nameless, faceless sex. "I have a few days off before the end of the tour. I need to recharge."

You're getting old. A whisper, inside his head, both seductive and insulting.

Finn's muse was still there, and she never minced words.

Prove yourself worthy, she whispered. *Go back for an encore.* Feel *the music . . . make them hear it. Drown yourself in their applause.*

Finn shifted his bag onto his shoulder and left the room, repeating his request for the limo. Within minutes, he was being ushered down yet another hallway, then into an underground parking lot. More screaming from some girls who were lying in wait, flash bulbs and a hurried entrance to the limousine, and then the blessed slam of the door.

Falling back against the cushions, Finn closed his eyes and released a sigh. It was a stretch limo, designed to carry at least eight without crowding.

A man's chuckle brought his eyes open and his head up.

On the other side of the backseat, sprawled at ease, was someone he'd met only once, but would never forget. Short blond hair, lean face. Too dim to see his eyes, but Finn knew they were an unnaturally light blue.

His hand flashed toward the door, but it was too late; a distinct *click* reached his ears.

"Going somewhere?" The Devil smiled, looking more like a rock star than he did, black boots, polished to a high shine, with black jeans and a gray T-shirt. "No need to rush off. We have things to catch up on, you and I."

Finn glanced quickly toward the driver's window; heavily tinted, and tightly closed. Somehow he knew there would be no help from that area.

"We have nothing to talk about," he said flatly to his unwanted visitor, determined to brazen it out.

The blond man shook his head, chuckling again. "Oh, but we do." The limo began moving, and Finn knew he was in for the ride of his life.

"There was a time when you couldn't wait to see me," Satan said idly, watching him. "Remember how hard you worked to figure out how to call me forth from the depths of Hell? It was touching, really, how you pored over those dusty old books—you used to wear glasses as a teenager, didn't you?"

"My time isn't up yet," Finn said, knowing the terms of the bargain as well as he knew his own name. *He was barely thirty-six.* "The bargain isn't over until I'm dead." He held up a fist, displaying a silver ring etched with a starburst of arrows.

"Ah, yes, the Ring of Chaos." Satan's pale blue eyes danced with amusement. "The source of both madness and genius, coveted through the ages for the creative talent it inspires in its owner. Vincent van Gogh only got to wear it a few years before it drove him insane. How many times have you wished you could take it off, I wonder?"

Finn said nothing, lowering his fist to his knee.

"Tell the truth, Finn . . . wearing the ring is a bit more challenging than you expected, isn't it? Everything you wanted—fame, fortune, the world at your feet—in return for knowing that you can only have it for so long. In the end, you'll go raving into darkness, a moldering pile of bones, a lost soul, forever writhing in torment." The Great Deceiver flashed a smile, teeth gleaming white against his tan. "Will you make it to forty, I wonder?"

"Add a few black roses, and it sounds like a great design for a T-shirt," Finn replied shortly, refusing to be intimidated. "I'll get my merchandising people right on it."

The Devil laughed. "You could always give up the ring, you know, if it becomes too much for you."

Finn eyed him warily.

"Of course, if you do that then you'll have reneged on our bargain, and your soul becomes mine to claim as I will." A tilt of his blond head. "It's been twenty years, Finn. How long will you wear it?"

"As long as I want," he growled. "A deal is a deal."

"Is it?"

Finn leaned forward, elbows on his knees, going eye-to-eye with the Devil for the second time in his life. "As long as I wear this ring, my soul is my own," he stated boldly. "So get the hell out of my face."

"You're wrong," Satan whispered, blue eyes lit from within. "As long as you wear that ring, your soul belongs to Chaos, that dark, beguiling creature you call your muse. She will bring you the music and the words that bring you the fame and fortune you crave, and in the end, she will bring you to me."

Finn's blood ran cold.

"A fickle mistress, that one."

Before his eyes, the blond man faded, leaving only the echo of his words to disturb the quiet. "Written any new songs lately?"

Chapter Four

Friday nights at the Ritz-Carlton meant private parties, and plenty of people who didn't necessarily want to go home when their parties were over. Not being one of them, Faith hid a yawn behind her hand, and tried to look alert behind the front desk. It was just past midnight, and the lobby was full of people, most of them spillovers from the bar. She wanted to be home with Nathan, feeling him curled up in the bed next to her, smelling his little-boy smell and getting poked by his little-boy elbows and knees. She'd taken more late shifts than usual this past month so she could make all his doctor appointments, and juggling shifts was wearing her out.

Wishing she could take off her shoes, Faith glanced around the busy lobby, hoping to remain invisible. Today she'd taken Nathan to see his pediatrician, who'd been very pleased at the results of Nate's last blood test. She'd been pleased, too, but she knew the real reason she'd gotten Nathan back, and her joy was tempered by constant worry, because her month was almost up.

What would the Devil ask for in return?

"Look alive, Miss McFarland," said Herve, the night manager. The creep liked to sneak up on her, and spent too much time eyeing her ass when he thought she wasn't looking. "You seem a bit tired. Been burning the candle at both ends?"

"Of course not, Mr. Morales," Faith answered, straightening. She had to stay on her toes—she couldn't afford to lose her job, particularly not the health insurance. "Is there something I can do for you?"

"Not at the moment," he said crisply, "but one never knows." Then he turned and walked away, his stiff-backed posture as obnoxious as the rest of him.

"Sneaky weasel," she mumbled beneath her breath.

"Why, Faith—" A man's voice made her jump. "It's lovely to see you, too."

A frightened squeak died in her throat as she looked across the marble counter and met the ice blue eyes of her worst nightmare.

"You're looking well," Satan said smoothly, resting well-manicured hands on the counter. His blond hair was carelessly tousled, the perfect contrast to a stylish black sport coat worn carelessly over jeans and a pinstriped shirt. Business casual, *GQ* style. "I'd like a room, please, an executive suite, if you have one available."

Faith willed herself not to faint. She'd almost convinced herself that he'd been a hallucination—a horrible, stress-induced hallucination—but here he was, in the flesh.

Again.

"Come now," he urged, in a lower tone. "I'm not going to bite you. Behave normally, and do as I say."

"I—" Words stuck in her throat. "It hasn't been a month yet," she managed to whisper, tears pricking her lids.

"Monday," he answered, with great satisfaction. "It will be a month on Monday. Nathan has a follow-up MRI that day, doesn't he?" The Devil cocked his head, smiling. "Wouldn't it be lovely if his doctors found his tumor had completely disappeared?" Those ice blue eyes hardened. "Of course, they could just as easily discover that the biopsy results were wrong, and that the cancer has spread."

She stared at him, searching his face for some remnant of humanity, some forgotten quality of mercy, but there was no mercy in him.

"You remember our bargain, don't you? I gave Nathan a one-month reprieve—" He quirked an eyebrow for confirmation. "He *is* feeling better, isn't he?" She nodded soundlessly, and he continued. "Now you must decide if he's to stay that way."

She fought the urge to throw up, and wondered wildly, in the back of her mind, what the Devil might think of ramen noodles all over his sport coat. Licking her lips, she swallowed her gorge and steeled her resolve. "What is it you want me to do?"

"I believe I said I'd like a room," he repeated mildly. "Club level, of course." He pulled out his wallet, handing her a credit card as if he were a real person instead of Lucifer himself. The name on the card read Samuel B. Divine.

"While you're checking me in, I'll fill you in on what you need to do to fulfill your end of the bargain." He glanced idly around the lobby, and even in the midst of her fear, Faith saw that he was drawing plenty of glances in return—mostly feminine, of course. A woman in a red-sequined party dress looked ready to devour him with her eyes, and two women in an alcove were staring, whispering and giggling like schoolgirls.

He noticed, of course, but didn't seem to care. "Ah," he said to Faith, "I used to love Atlanta on a Friday night, but with the Underground gone, good old Hotlanta is just not what it used to be."

She knew what he was referring to, of course, having grown up in the area. Underground Atlanta, the old subterranean entertainment district, had long ago been converted to a shopping mall. Just shops and a food court now, not the party destination it once was.

"Back in the twenties," he went on, as if they were having a pleasant little chat, "it was all about jazz and freedom from Prohibition. If you wanted to hear some great blues and raise a little hell down South without heading to New Orleans, Atlanta was the place to do it. 'Blues, booze, and broads,' as they used to call it. Good times."

Forcing herself to breathe, to behave normally, Faith focused on the computer and the check-in process. Not speaking, just listening. He was like a snake, using camouflage and a forked tongue to get victims used to his presence.

"And the seventies . . ." He gave a low laugh. "Do you know, I actually amused myself for a time by running a nightclub in the Underground called Dante's, where it was all about drugs, free love, and music." He put his elbows on the counter, leaning in toward her. "Do you like music, Faith?"

She nodded warily, doing her best to slow her heart rate and steel herself for what was to come.

"I'm glad," he said, eyeing her calmly. "Now, are you ready to be a big, brave girl, and hear what I have to say?"

No, I'm not ready, I'll never be ready . . .

"I'm ready." She slipped his receipt and credit card across the counter, including a pen for his signature.

"A musician by the name of Finn Payne is about to check into this hotel," the Devil said, signing with a flourish. "He's wearing a ring that belongs to me. It's very distinctive: black and silver with a starburst of arrows. I want it back. Get me the ring before Monday, and Nathan's next MRI will be clear. His tumor will be gone forever."

"Finn Payne," she repeated, disbelieving. "As in *the* Finn Payne?"

Rock star, guitar god. Apocalypse had been her favorite band as a teenager. Even now, though she was closer to thirty than thirteen, she owned every single one of their CDs.

"Oh good," Satan said, smiling. "You *are* a music lover, after all. I was afraid you were just telling me what I wanted to hear."

She shook her head, stunned at the magnitude of what he was suggesting. She'd never stolen anything in her life, and now she was expected to steal from a rock star?

Focus, she told herself sharply.

"That's it? I bring you the ring, and we're done?"

"Well"—he glanced around the lobby again, looking amused—"there *are* certain conditions attached."

"What conditions?" Small hairs rose on the back of her neck.

"First, *you* must handle this personally—you can't assign the job to someone else."

So much for a faint hope of bribing someone on the hotel housekeeping staff.

"And in order to *get* the ring"—he gave her a smirk that made her stomach roil—"you must use the gifts God gave you."

She blinked, wondering if she'd mistaken his meaning.

"After all . . ." His voice turned soft, caressing. "What do you think all that lovely female skin and hair is there for? You're very pretty, and could be even more so if you tried. Good breeder, too, obviously. A wholesome, fertile beauty like you is absolutely irresistible to the average human male. He'll be no different."

Bastard. She didn't say it out loud, but surely he couldn't miss seeing it in her eyes. He'd reduced her to a *thing*—something to be used—not a person.

"Don't worry, Faith. Most women find him quite good-looking, in a darkly brooding sort of way. You might even find yourself enjoying the assignment."

She said nothing, feeling a numbness creep over her. He was so cold, so icily perfect, as though the unholy fire burning within him was one that froze instead of scorched.

She hadn't slept with anyone since Jason.

Jason, who'd lied to and abandoned her.

"Must I spell it out for you, my dear?" He tapped a manicured finger on the counter. "Seduce the man, and steal the ring. *Do not ask him for it.* Believe me, he'll never give it to you—the ring is far too important to him. The moment he knows you want it, he'll be gone, and you'll have missed your opportunity." An amused smile lifted one corner of his mouth. "Use your womanly wiles to beguile him into thinking you're harmless, as women have done since the beginning of time— and then steal it. Unless, of course"—he smiled in a way that made her blood run cold—"you're too proud to whore yourself for the life of your child."

She stared at him with loathing, but was unable to meet his eyes very long, for they were devoid of soul.

"Now, now," he warned, sotto voce. "I do believe your manager would be very unhappy about the way you're looking at me right now. Isn't that him, over by the elevator?"

She shot a glance over her shoulder, and saw he was right—Herve was currently harassing one of the bellmen as he loaded luggage onto a cart.

Turning away, she stared down at the counter for a moment, schooling her features to calm.

"Oh good," he said approvingly. "You're going to behave." He smiled a perfectly pleasant smile, as if they were having a perfectly pleasant conversation. "You still have a choice, of course." He leaned in, resting his elbows on the counter. "You can say no. Your son will be dead within the year,

but hey"—he shrugged jacket-clad shoulders—
"the rest of us will live to party another day."

Nathan's face flashed into her mind, the way
he'd looked on his last birthday, smiling and
laughing with his friends in the ball pit at Chuck
E. Cheese. The way he looked before he got sick,
and lost all his energy.

"I'll do it." She lowered her head, defeated.

"You're sure?" He cocked his head, obviously
toying with her. "Can't claim later that I didn't
give you a choice in the matter." He chuckled. "I
make it a point of pride to always offer a choice."

"I said I'd do it," she repeated tersely, looking
nervously around. The woman in the red dress
was still watching, sipping her wine and staring
avidly at the blond sex god who was checking
into the hotel, clearly hoping to meet him.

"In that case . . ." Satan reached into his jacket
pocket and pulled out a slim black notebook.
"Once you have the ring in your possession, you
must summon me to come get it." He held the book
out to her, looking her directly in the eye. "Do you
understand? You must summon me properly as
described in this book, with all ceremony due me
as the High Lord Prince of Darkness, or we do not
have a deal."

Faith swallowed again, her mouth gone dry. "Why?" she managed to ask, eyeing the book as though it were a snake. "You can obviously come and go as you please . . . why would you need to be summoned?"

He gave a low chuckle, and repeated nearly word for word something he'd said to her in the hospital chapel. "I didn't say I *needed* to be summoned, Faith. I said I *wanted* to be." The look he gave her was chilling. "It's a matter of respect, of commitment . . . call it the icing on the devil's food cake."

She wanted to look away, but didn't dare.

"And know this." He never took his eyes from hers. "Once I am summoned, I will never truly leave you. Having summoned me, having committed theft on my behalf, your soul will be mine when you die, whenever that may be." His smile made her blood run cold. "In return, I give you the life of your child. You and he will have decades ahead; you'll get to see him grow up, graduate college, get married—maybe even enjoy a few grandchildren. I'll do nothing to interfere with your natural life cycle, but in the end, making a deal with the Devil means your soul belongs to me." He gave a low chuckle, tilting his head to regard her in the friendliest of fashions. "We'll be bound together, you and I."

Horrified, she blinked back tears, tears she knew were useless. "Is there . . . is there any other way?" she whispered. "Couldn't you just"—a plea for mercy slipped out—"just let us go?"

Her plea for mercy went unanswered, and so, hand shaking, Faith reached out and took the book, giving in to the fact that there was nothing she wouldn't do for the life of her child—nothing at all.

"Welcome to the Ritz-Carlton, Mr. Payne. Please come this way." Faith kept her concierge staff smile firmly in place as she led the man and his two-man entourage toward the private elevators.

The past hour had been both the shortest and the longest of her life—she'd been so distracted that she'd almost forgotten her name tag, remembering to remove it only at the last minute during her mad rush to greet Finn's limo. She'd made as many last-minute, emergency arrangements as she could, including calling her buddy Alberto in valet parking, who had given her a heads-up when a black stretch limo, followed by a black SUV, pulled up to the Ritz's private entrance at 1:12 a.m.

"The bellmen will bring up your luggage while I show you to the penthouse," she said, swiping the key in the elevator.

"Thanks," Finn murmured, in the smooth, smoky voice she'd heard many times before—on CDs, of course. A quick glance at his face made her heart skip a beat; he looked just like he did in the magazines. Green eyes, creased at the corners; short dark hair. Signature goatee, neatly trimmed. Unlike some of the other rockers who occasionally stayed at the Ritz, drunk or hungover after a night of partying, Finn Payne was alert, aware, and disturbingly vital.

The elevator door opened. "After you," he said politely.

Hoping it wasn't obvious how badly her hands were shaking, she stepped inside with the three men and used her key to access Club Level One, sixteenth floor.

She got a brief glimpse of Herve, talking to one of the parking attendants, as the elevator door closed. *She could lose her job over this.* "My name is Amy," she said cheerfully, lying through her teeth, "and I hope you'll consider me at your service during your stay."

He was looking at her, and she hoped he liked what he saw. *For Nathan's sake, he needed to like what he saw.* To her great good luck, she'd dressed for work tonight in her favorite pink top, a silky button-down that she'd unbuttoned one deeper than she was normally comfortable with. Her black pencil skirt was tighter than the one she usually wore, which was at the cleaner's. She'd taken her hair down from its ponytail and reapplied her makeup, borrowing some from one of the maids, smoky eyes and pale pink lipstick to bring out the auburn in her hair.

"Is there anything special I can do for you while you're here?" she asked, forcing herself not to break eye contact with Finn.

The two security guys shot each other an amused glance, but Finn was the one who answered. "Just room service and quiet, thanks."

She blinked, still dazed by the irony of how her girlhood fantasy had been turned into a nightmare. Finn Payne, rock star, was standing right *here*, right next to her, and instead of love at first sight, followed by happily-ever-after, this evening was nothing but a tawdry means to an end.

She was staring, and he knew it, giving her a small smile before glancing away. He seemed distracted, tired maybe, but she couldn't let that stop her. She had to get his attention, and keep it for the rest of the evening, because she couldn't afford to fail.

"Whatever you need during your stay, Mr. Payne," she said softly, refusing to give up. "Anything at all."

He looked at her again with those dazzling green eyes, and she gave him a small smile, definitely flirting and definitely hoping he noticed.

He was gorgeous—a rock god. *She was in trouble.*

The elevator came to a stop, and the door opened. Faith led the way down a short hallway to two double doors. As she walked, she made sure to hold her shoulders back and put a little extra swing in her step, knowing all three men would be watching. It felt strange for a moment, being a woman instead of the desperately worried mom of a seriously ill toddler, and she was afraid she might've overdone it.

"Thank you very much, miss," one of the security guys said, and the smile on his face told her she'd done it just right. "We'll take it from here." He reached out a hand to take the key cards.

"May I—" Faith handed them over, shifting her gaze back to Finn. "May I pour you a drink?" She had to do something before she lost her nerve.

There was a pause, then Finn gestured toward

the door. "That would be nice," he said. He had a slight smile on his face, which, along with the cute little goatee, gave him the diabolically handsome look that had made him a superstar.

Oh shit, was her last thought before she stepped into the suite.

Chapter Five

She was nervous, and he was glad of it, because if she wasn't nervous it would've told him that she'd done this a million times before, and oddly enough, he didn't want to believe that. She was pretty, sweet-looking, with a vulnerable curve to her mouth that made him wonder what it would be like to kiss it.

He hadn't wondered anything like that in a long time.

Finn let his gaze settle on the back of her head as she stepped into the foyer of the penthouse. Wavy red-brown hair, just past her shoulders. Nice figure.

"Thanks, guys," Finn said to the security team, "you can head back to the party. I'll be okay here."

"We're checking out the suite first," said John, in a voice that told Finn there was no point in arguing. "Wait here."

Finn nodded as they fanned out for a quick check, then turned to the girl. She looked uncertain, as if she were about to bolt, and he found himself hoping she wouldn't. Earlier in the evening he'd wanted nothing more than to be alone, but the limo ride had cured him of that. He doubted he was going to get much sleep tonight; why waste the evening sitting alone and feeling sorry for himself?

"A scotch and soda would be nice," he said. "Would you like to stay and have one with me?"

She flashed him a smile before heading toward the bar, revealing a dimple in one cheek. "I'd love to."

The suite was big, decorated in yellows and vivid reds, framed by a wall of windows overlooking the Atlanta nightscape. Too big for just one person—it would be cavernous when she left, and what a waste that would be.

"All clear," came John's voice, a moment later. "All clear in here," said Larry, from a different direction. John strode back in the room and went straight to the windows, drawing the curtains shut. "You're staying in tonight, right?" he said to

Finn, over his shoulder. "You'll call if you want to go anywhere?"

Finn glanced toward the girl at the bar. She wasn't screaming his name or offering to have his baby, and the very thought made the idea of spending an evening with her enjoyably different.

He was still here, still alive. The Devil hadn't claimed him on the limo ride over, even when he'd defied him.

"I'm staying in," he said. "And leave the curtains open."

"I mean it, Finn," John insisted, ignoring his request, and twitching the curtains closed. "You sneak off again without us like you did in Dallas, and Derek will have my ass in a sling. Told me he'd fire me next time."

Derek Johnson was Finn's concert promoter, and a damn good one. He did most of the hiring and firing, arranged the venues and the press junkets, and was generally the oil that kept the machinery of his career moving forward.

"I'm staying in," Finn repeated firmly, "and nobody can fire you but me."

"Larry's going back to the party," John said, "but I'm right down the hall. Call if you need anything."

"I'm not going to need anything," Finn said,

letting his exasperation show in the look he gave John. The guys finally took the hint and left, leaving Finn's key card on the table by the front door.

He turned, looking at the girl. She busied herself at the bar, brown curls partly shading her face. Slender, fragile, not at all his usual type, and for a moment, he wondered if he was doing the right thing. She looked so wholesome, so cute, so far removed from the sometimes sleazy world he inhabited.

Then she turned, scotch in hand, and smiled at him, and his doubts vanished.

"Do you sneak away from your security team very often?" she asked, with a grin.

"Not often enough," he said, grinning in return. "It really pisses off the guys. I get dirty looks for days."

She laughed at that. "You're their boss!"

"True," he agreed, "but they have guns."

"It must be hard"—she came toward him, holding out the scotch—"always being seen as a celebrity instead of just yourself."

"It can be," he answered, choosing not to elaborate. "Sometimes I just want to get away, to be alone, you know?"

Her smile faltered, so he made sure to add, "And other times I don't." He took the glass, meeting her eyes and holding them. "Like tonight, for instance."

She took a deep breath, regarding him frankly. Brown eyes, a light dusting of freckles across the bridge of her nose.

"I understand the need to get away," she said softly. "To break out of the mold you're expected to fit."

"I can see you do," he answered, approving of her honesty. They both knew she was supposed to be working, yet working seemed to be the last thing on her mind.

She looked away, laughing a little. "If you really want to drive them crazy, we could sneak up the service stairs to the roof," she suggested teasingly. "Nobody ever goes up there."

For a moment, he was actually tempted, but they'd all been working hard on this tour, and like him, John and Larry deserved a break. If his security team came back and found him missing, all hell would break loose.

"Not tonight," he answered, with a grin, "but I'll keep it in mind if they piss me off."

She laughed, and he liked the sound of it.

"I'm sorry, but I'm not sure I caught your name."

"Amy," she answered, smiling. "Amy Smith."

"Nice to meet you, Amy." He made a sweeping gesture toward the living room. "Maybe you'd like to give me a guided tour of the suite?"

A flash of what looked like panic appeared in her eyes, but a heartbeat later he was sure he'd imagined it. This girl was no innocent—she wouldn't be alone with him in a hotel room otherwise.

"I'd love to," she said brightly. "Gorgeous, isn't it? Everything state of the art and recently renovated." She moved into the living room, going straight to the curtains and opening them back up. "This is my favorite of the penthouse suites. It's not the biggest, but it's the nicest, and the view is great, isn't it?"

"It is," he agreed, but he wasn't talking about lights outside the window. She had a great ass, round and feminine.

Inwardly he shrugged. Earlier he'd told himself no nameless, faceless sex tonight—but she had a name, and it was Amy. A nice, wholesome girl who worked at the Ritz-Carlton; what was the harm in that?

She was going to die. She was going to burn in Hell for all eternity, because despite her best efforts, she couldn't get past the fact that she was alone, in a hotel room, with Finn Payne, a rock legend whose music she'd listened to since she was seventeen years old. Such a bad boy, that Finn Payne; such a radical group, Apocalypse. And here he was now, ten years later, looking at her with those vibrant green eyes, alive and aware.

So far she'd been able to manage some banter about his security team, but what now?

Swallowing her panic, she handed him the scotch. It was then she saw the ring, gleaming on his hand. A black and silver signet, depicting a starburst of arrows in every direction.

"I'm sorry, but I'm not sure I caught your name," he said, taking the glass.

"Amy," she answered, smiling. "Amy Smith."

"Nice to meet you, Amy." He made a sweeping gesture toward the living room. "Maybe you'd like to give me a guided tour of the suite?"

It was on the tip of her tongue to turn craven and say she couldn't, that she had to get back to work. Here she was, in her sexiest top and her tightest skirt, with management aware of her every move . . . but then she thought of Nathan, and that was all it took. She tipped her head to the side and smiled. "I'd love to."

Get a grip, she told herself fiercely, heading toward the window. That little extra swing in her step had gotten her in the door, so she used it again, hoping he was watching. A glance over her shoulder told her he was.

She babbled something about the view, and when she turned around, he was smiling at her over his glass. The look in his eye, combined with that smile, made her knees go weak.

Steady, she told herself.

"Pour yourself something," he said. "Stay and visit with me awhile."

"That would be wonderful," she said, not having to fake the heat in her cheeks. *Finn Payne liked what he saw.* She would've thanked God for it, if she'd still believed in God.

A hint of recklessness led her to choose scotch as her drink of choice, too, though she rarely drank anything stronger than wine.

She caught him looking at her again as she moved toward the couch with her drink, and made sure to cross her legs provocatively as she sat down.

"You're very pretty," Finn said, taking a seat in the chair opposite her.

"Thank you." Her mother had always told her that a simple "thank you" was the best way to acknowledge a compliment. Desperately she searched her memory for any other scrap of motherly advice that might help her in a situation like this, and came up empty—her mom wasn't big on seducing strange men, or stealing. "You're even better-looking in person than I expected."

He sighed a little, leaning back in his seat.

Inwardly she cringed, woefully aware of how out of practice she was on her flirting skills. Men liked to be complimented, didn't they? "I'm a big fan of your music—your *Gothika* CD is one of my all-time favorites."

"That CD came out over ten years ago." He cocked his head, looking at her. "How old are you?"

"Twenty-seven," she said, and immediately wished she'd lied and told him twenty-three. He was probably used to younger women; women with no responsibilities, and no children. "How old are you?" she asked, though she already knew.

"Thirty-six," he said quietly, shaking his glass so the ice rattled. He'd begun to look thoughtful, and she couldn't have that, so she smiled at him, and he smiled back. He took a sip from his drink, and so did she. The scotch burned its way into her belly, and helped crystallize her resolve.

She had to seduce him, and steal the Ring of Chaos.

"I love your latest song, 'Fallen,'" she said, taking another sip of her scotch. "So moody and atmospheric." She shifted her legs, sliding to the edge of the couch. Her skirt slid up with it, but she pretended not to notice, leaning in to give him her sexiest smile.

"I'll be honest with you," she said to Finn, being anything but. "When I saw your name on the reservations list, I knew I had to do just about anything to meet you; I switched shifts with someone so I could be here when you arrived." She gave him her most seductive smile. "I was hoping we'd get to spend some time together, like this, while you were at the hotel." Toying with her glass as if she didn't have a care in the world, Faith ran a finger along the rim.

Finn said nothing, merely looking at her.

She met his gaze evenly, though inside she was quaking. "Are you sure there's nothing else I can do for you while I'm here, Mr. Payne?" she asked him softly.

Chapter Six

He was disappointed. He'd known her less than five minutes and already held some preconceived notion in his mind about her being different, when she wasn't.

He sighed. Here he was, thirty-six years old and unable to have a normal conversation with a woman because all she saw when she looked at him was Finn Payne, the rock world's fucking Prince of Darkness.

She doesn't want to get to know the real you—you're nothing without your guitar. She wants the music, the legend, the fantasy.

He pushed the thought away, determined to prove his spiteful, spoiled muse wrong. He was more than just his music. This girl would know it by the time the evening was through.

"Why don't you call in sick and get the evening off?" he suggested plainly. "We'll order some room service, have a drink and a late dinner." Glancing at his watch, he amended casually, "Or breakfast, whichever you prefer."

So what if she was a groupie? He liked her looks—fair skin, high cheekbones, nice figure. "I'm starving; never eat before a show." He cocked his head, giving her his most charming smile. "And I hate eating alone."

Her face turned almost as pink as her blouse. "I'd love to have dinner with you."

"We can still get room service, can't we?"

"Absolutely. The chef is a friend of mine."

"Great. Call him up."

You're getting old, said the voice of Chaos. *There was a time you'd never choose food over sex.* The voice was fading now, a sour remnant of itself. Hopefully it would be gone soon.

"The steaks are really good here," she said. "The bacon-wrapped fillet melts in your mouth."

"Sounds good," he said. "Order whatever you like."

She smoothed her skirt to a more ladylike length and smiled a more genuine, tentative version of the smile she'd sent him earlier. She'd taken his sidestep pretty well, and he was glad of it. He didn't want or need any drama this evening, and if they ended up in bed together he wanted it to be a natural progression, not a sprint toward a goal.

The smile she sent him showed her dimple, and somewhere inside his chest, a knot loosened, a knot he hadn't even known was there.

There was something about this girl he liked. He was going to rock her world tonight, and he didn't need a guitar to do it.

She'd nearly blown it.

She'd come on too strong, and from the look on his face a few moments ago, she'd nearly lost him.

If he wanted food and company before sex, she'd be happy to give him food and company before sex. It was the least she could do.

"Chocolate cake for dessert," she said into the phone, after ordering two bacon-wrapped fillets.

"None for me." He was smiling at her. She'd been afraid to look too deeply into his eyes up to this point, because she was sure he'd see what a liar she was. But this time she did, and somewhere in those green depths she saw the real Finn Payne: a nice guy who was world-weary, jaded, and *tired*.

Tired in a way that made her want to push his hair back from his forehead and tell him everything was going to be all right. Tired in a way that made her feel guilty, as though she didn't feel guilty enough already.

He smiled at her again, and something unfurled, low in her belly. With a shock, she realized it for what it was: genuine arousal, genuine desire—neither of which she'd felt in a very long time.

"There," she said to him cheerfully as she hung up. "Dinner will be here before you know it."

"Thank you," he said, taking another sip of his drink before putting it down on an end table. "Do you mind if I take a quick shower while we wait? I came straight from the stage."

The image of him onstage was seared into her brain from a concert when she was twenty. The image of him naked in the shower, however, made her mouth go dry. "Not at all," she said brightly, "I'll, ah . . . I'll just call my supervisor while you're in there."

"Great." Finn gave her a grin and stood up. "I'll be out in a few minutes." His green eyes crinkled at the corners when he smiled. "Turn on some music. Make yourself comfortable."

"Thanks."

She watched him walk away. The man knew how to wear a pair of jeans. They fit him like a second skin, and how could *anybody* make a plain white T-shirt look so sexy?

Dammit. He lived up to every single picture she'd ever seen of him, and he was *nice*. He was a celebrity, and she was just a single mother who worked in a hotel, lying her ass off for the chance to steal from him.

Before she lost her nerve, she picked up the phone again and dialed, not the front desk, but her home number. Her good friend and next-door neighbor, Dina, answered.

"Dina," she whispered, glancing anxiously toward the bedroom, "is everything okay? How's Nathan?"

"He's sleeping," Dina replied, "and why are you whispering?"

She'd known Dina for five years, ever since she'd moved into her little duplex apartment. They shared a front porch and a common wall, as well as all their secrets. She'd been there for Dina while she'd gone through a messy divorce, and Dina had been there for her when Nathan was born.

"I'm going to be later than I thought," she whispered. "Can you stay the night? I'm not sure what time I'll be home."

" 'Course I will," Dina said comfortably, having slept over many times. "What's going on?"

"Long story—I'll tell you later. Thank you so much for watching him for me tonight."

Dina made a rude noise. "You don't need to thank me, girl. You know I love that boy almost as much as you do. I'm just glad to have him out of that hospital and home where he belongs."

A lump rose in her throat, and she had to swallow hard to keep back the tears that threatened. *What was she doing?* How was she *ever* going to pull this off?

"Dina?"

"Mm-hm?"

She could hear the jagged burst of TV in the background, and knew her friend was flipping through the channels. "Do you think I'm pretty?"

"Oh Lord," Dina groaned. "What the hell are you up to, girl?"

Faith bit the skin around her fingernail, looking anxiously toward the bedroom where Finn had disappeared. "Nothing," she said, too quickly.

Dina sighed. "Never mind," she said. "Don't tell me. Go on, have a little fun. You deserve it after what you've been through with Nathan. He's fine, don't you worry."

She said nothing, and Dina sighed again. "Yes, you're pretty, and you'd be even prettier if you put a little meat on them bones."

Dina was a full-figured young black woman, and proud of it. "You looked hot when you left for work; that pink top looked good on you. White boys love that sexy librarian look."

"Thanks, Dina," she whispered gratefully, in need of any reassurance she could get. "Call me if Nathan wakes up and needs me, okay?"

"He ain't gonna need you," her friend said complacently. "Auntie Dina is here. You have a good time, and I'll see you in the morning."

Faith hung up, feeling just a teeny bit better until she turned around and faced the reality of the big, empty suite, and heard the faint sound of a running shower from the bedroom down the hall.

Oh shit, she thought again.

Finn Payne was in the other room, naked. Every woman's fantasy come to life, hers for one night only, despite the nightmare that had brought her to this point. In order to steal the ring, she first had to overcome her own nervousness. He was a man, and she was a woman, and that's all there was to it.

Faith took a deep breath and let it out slowly.

Yes, she was about to have a private dinner with one of the world's sexiest rock stars in a luxury suite at the Ritz-Carlton, and despite Finn's immediate preference for food over sex, she had no doubt how the evening needed to end.

Given that she hadn't had sex since before Nathan was born, she only hoped she could remember how.

A knock came at the door while Finn was still in the shower. "Room service."

Faith, who'd kicked off her shoes and unbuttoned another button of her blouse, put her eye to the keyhole. "Leave it in the hall, please," she said through the door, glad she didn't recognize the waiter. He wouldn't know her voice.

"Yes, ma'am." Instantly he did as she asked—this was the Ritz, after all—and left his wheeled cart where it stood. She waited, giving him plenty of time to reach the elevators.

Checking the peephole a final time before opening the door, she ducked her head outside and looked around before snagging the cart, feeling like a criminal. She'd lied to her coworkers and left the desk shorthanded, so she wasn't eager to be seen.

She wasn't eager to get locked out, either, so she used a hip to keep the suite door open, backing in with the cart.

"Let me help," came Finn's voice, behind her, and the weight of the door was relieved. He held it open, standing close to the wall to let her pass.

When she did, she got a whiff of soap and dampness, and with a jolt that set the cart rattling, she realized he'd barely dried off from his shower.

He was wearing nothing but a towel.

"I'll put this over by the table," she said brightly, dragging the cart farther into the suite. He turned to shut the door, giving Faith a great view of his lean back and narrow hips. He had a pair of black wings, ornately feathered, tattooed on his shoulder blades.

"Your tattoo is beautiful," she said truthfully. She didn't care much for ink as a rule, but Finn's wings had obviously been done by a true artist.

"Thanks." He turned from the door to help her with the cart, giving her a wry smile. "Every fallen angel needs his wings." The way he said it made her stomach do flip-flops, and the way he looked—well, the way he looked made her mouth dry and her heart pound. His chest was firm and well-muscled, a faint line of dark hair trailing down until it disappeared into the towel.

"You're blushing," he said with a grin. "I'm making you nervous."

"No shit," she shot back, unthinking.

Finn threw his head back and laughed. "She blushes *and* swears," he said. "So ladylike, yet so naughty. You're an interesting woman, Amy."

"I don't swear that much, really," she said ruefully, knowing she wasn't at *all* interesting, and wishing he hadn't called her Amy.

He was standing on the other side of the cart, the handle of which she still held in a death grip.

"Never seen a man in a towel before?" he asked softly.

"Um . . . not lately," she answered honestly.

Finn laughed again. His towel was riding low, bunched in his fist. "Glad to hear it. I'll just go"— he gestured toward the bedroom—"get dressed, then."

She nodded, grateful for the chance to gather her wits.

"Or I could eat like this. You could get naked and join me." The teasing glint in his eye was still there, but there was a definite hint of possibility there, too, and Faith knew it.

"I'll set the table while you dress." She chickened out.

"Hm," he murmured, eyeing her with a grin as

he walked away. "Not quite as brave as you think you are, I see."

She had no answer for that, because her brain was otherwise occupied. Oh. My. God. *He was hot.* Hormones she had forgotten existed surged to life, bringing a dampness between her thighs, and suddenly Faith remembered what it was like to be a *woman* again. To want a man who obviously wanted her (if the bulge in his towel was to be believed), and to be free to do whatever they— as two consenting adults—wanted to do.

Except she wasn't just consenting—she was instigating—because she had an ulterior motive, which made her a big fat freaking liar.

Finn walked through the bedroom door and out of sight, but before he did—in large part because she couldn't help herself—she admired the view. Then, a blink or two later, she calmly began to set the table. This wasn't about her, it was about Nathan, and it wouldn't do to forget that.

If that made her a liar, then so be it.

Might as well do her best to enjoy it.

Chapter Seven

Finn emerged from the bedroom to find she'd set the table. She stood by the window, staring out as though mesmerized, and he wondered what she saw.

To him it was just another faceless big city, but to her it was obviously home.

"Do you like living here?" he asked, and she jumped.

He wanted her to relax, for purely selfish reasons that he had no trouble acknowledging. He hadn't been on a date—a real date—in so long he couldn't even remember what one was like. She'd gotten so flustered when he'd come out in the towel; women who blushed were pretty rare in his world. At any rate, he didn't want to be *on* anymore tonight. No performing, no posturing, no bullshit. He just wanted to be himself, to be Finn, and see how she responded to that.

"I love Atlanta," she said, turning back to the view. "Except for the traffic. It's beautiful when the dogwood and azalea are in bloom, and the winters aren't too bad. I've lived here all my life." She gave a self-conscious laugh. "Sounds pretty boring, doesn't it?"

He shook his head. "I was an Air Force brat—I always thought it would be cool to stay in one place."

There was a silence, in which he could feel her looking at him.

"I thought you grew up in L.A.," she offered, as if everyone knew where he'd grown up, just because of who he was.

He shot her a wry grin. "That's the official story, I guess." He turned from the window, moving toward the table. "I grew up all over." He pulled out a chair and held it for her, smiling. "I hope you don't believe *everything* you read about me."

"You mean you *don't* own a private island in the Bermuda Triangle where you throw wild parties with celebrities and starlets and models?"

She cocked her head, obviously only half teasing.

He gave a short laugh. "Of course not," he replied, as if the very idea was ludicrous. He waited until she'd settled in the chair to add, "It's in the British Virgin Islands."

There, he'd made her laugh. She smelled good, something light and uplifting that made him want to breathe in deep.

Instead he settled himself in the chair opposite her, looking forward to the meal. "I'm hungry," he said, "how about you?"

"Starved," she answered.

And so for the next half hour, they talked and they ate; him doing most of the eating and her doing most of the talking, mainly because he kept asking her questions. She toyed with her green beans while he decimated his fillet, and pretty soon he knew quite a bit about Amy Smith.

Twenty-seven, degree in business from Georgia State. Grew up in Atlanta with parents she thought were great, lots of friends, liked to go out but took work very seriously.

"Sounds like a nice life," he said.

She laughed at that, spearing a bean or two. "It's had its ups and downs, but yes"—she nodded thoughtfully—"my life definitely has its bright spots."

"Anyone special?"

Her eyes flew to his face.

"Boyfriend, maybe?" Finn shrugged, playing it casual. "As long as he doesn't show up pounding on the door, I'm okay with it." As he said it, he was surprised to realize he *didn't* mean it, and wondered why—he barely knew this girl.

"No boyfriend," she said, putting down her fork to pick up her glass. "I have a four-year-old son."

She barely looked old enough to be anyone's mother, but news of a child didn't faze him; after tonight he'd never see her again.

"Divorced?"

She shook her head. "Never married. He didn't want what I wanted, so we went our separate ways."

Finn nodded as though he understood, but he didn't. What kind of man walked away from his own child, his own flesh and blood, knowing no other man could ever quite fill those shoes?

"What about you?" she asked.

"No kids," he said, shaking his head. "But I wouldn't mind having them one day." *Except he never would, because he'd probably be a lousy father. Always working, always touring . . .*

The overhead light played on her hair, gleaming shades of red and mahogany that reminded him of the wood he used in his workshop. It was his sanctuary between tours, where music and chaos were replaced with the sound and fury of saws, drills, and hammers.

He hadn't lied about the British Virgin Islands—he did have a house there, and it was as close to home as anyplace else he'd been in the last twenty years. It was private, and it was quiet, and he could usually rest there, for a while, until the muse of Chaos roused herself and consumed his mind and body with the need for another song, another CD, another tour.

Another triumph.

"You didn't eat much," he observed quietly.

She looked up. "I don't usually eat red meat," she admitted, "but I thought you might like it."

"Surely you're not still nervous," he teased. "Ever since I put my clothes on I've been a perfect gentleman."

"You have." She smiled, shooting him a glance beneath her lashes. "But you don't have to be, you know."

Despite the open invitation, she was blushing again; no hiding it with skin that fair.

"Good," he replied, "because I've been dying to play footsies with you under the table."

He liked the way she laughed.

"You're quite the tease, aren't you? The last guy I dated had no sense of humor—" Then she stopped laughing, as though she'd said too much. "I mean, not that this is a *date*, exactly . . ." She trailed off.

He raised his eyebrows. "Isn't it?"

She looked uncomfortable. "You're being sweet," she said. "We both know I shamelessly pushed my way in here."

"I'm glad you did," he answered smoothly. He reached across the table for her hand and took it. His hand dwarfed hers. "Let's be honest with each other, shall we?"

Her brown eyes widened.

"For all your bravado, you don't seem like the kind of girl who talks her way into celebrity hotel rooms on a regular basis, so you need to understand something. We can have a great time together tonight, but afterward . . . afterward you'll probably never hear from me again."

He leaned in, smoothing his thumb over her knuckles. "You need to be okay with that. One night, that's all we've got."

"One night," she repeated, biting her lip.

"And in the morning, no hard feelings and no regrets?"

"No regrets," she murmured.

"Do me a favor," he said, his eyes drawn to those sweet pink lips. "Let's pretend I'm not Finn Payne; I'm just some guy who saw you in a crowded elevator and invited you to dinner, and you're not Amy . . ." He hesitated.

"Smith," she provided, a heartbeat later.

"You're not Amy Smith; you're just a beautiful woman about to have a night of wild delight with a total stranger. Sort of like role playing, except we get to play ourselves." He stared into her chocolate brown eyes, wondering if she could possibly be as gorgeous naked as he was beginning to imagine.

She swallowed, squeezing his hand. The tip of her tongue came out to moisten her bottom lip, and his groin tightened.

"Wild delight," she murmured huskily, "sounds good."

"Doesn't it?"

There was something different about her; boldness mixed with vulnerability, shamelessness mixed with shame.

Face of an angel, body made for sin, whispered an amused voice, faintly, in the back of his mind.

Go away, he ordered it, tightening his hand over the girl's. *I don't need or want any chaos tonight.*

Chapter Eight

She could feel the ring beneath her thumb as he gripped her hand. He stood up, drawing her with him. "Come with me."

She did as he asked, choosing to focus on *him*, not her problems. It wasn't hard—she was very conscious of how very male his fingers felt, the sculpted strength of his wrist and forearm, the firm bulge of his biceps. He led her to the couch overlooking the Atlanta skyline and settled her where she had the best view, but she barely noticed, her attention taken by something infinitely more interesting, directly in her line of sight.

Finn gave her a knowing smile, not troubling to hide his erection. Then he moved away, toward the bar. "Wait right there," he said. "Enjoy the view."

She swallowed hard, enjoying the view very much.

Finn poured them both another splash of scotch and came back to the couch, taking a seat next to her. His knee was touching her thigh. "To no regrets," he said, clinking his glass with hers. They both drank, and the burn of the scotch as it worked its way down steadied her.

So much so that when he lowered his glass, she leaned in and kissed him. Gently, slowly, as though they had all the time in the world. Moving her lips over his, breathing his breath and letting him breathe hers, the merest brush of their tongues, mingled with the tang of scotch and the first stirrings of desire.

One night; that's all they had.

She hardly heard the clink of his glass as he put it on the table, vaguely felt him take hers and do the same. All her senses were focused on the taste and the feel of his lips, and sensations she'd forgotten existed.

He shifted, slipping an arm around her shoulders and pulling her closer. The kiss changed, deepening. She was against his chest, and he smelled wonderful; she could barely keep herself from groaning aloud at the scent, the feel of him. Her hand was on his arm, her palm against his bicep, skimming upward over the muscled curve of his shoulder.

He leaned back into the couch, taking her with him. The hard length between his legs left no doubt of his arousal, and Faith felt an answering throb between her own. One broad hand slid up her ribs to cup her breast, and she made an involuntary noise low in her throat, shocked at how good his palm felt against her nipple, even through her clothes.

Suddenly, regrets or no regrets, she couldn't wait to get naked.

There was a slow tug at her waistband, and she helped him pull her blouse free, never moving too far from his lips. Finn's fingers—the ones that could make a guitar sing like an angel—deftly undid the buttons, and then smoothed the fabric from her shoulder. His hand was warm on her skin, sliding down her arm, freeing it from her sleeve; firm on her hip, squeezing her thigh and bottom as though learning the terrain. She brushed his cock with her hand, unable to help herself, and felt it throb in response.

His lips left hers, and then she was drowning in the feel of them on her neck, his breath in the hollow beneath her ear.

"Oh . . ."

She was moaning aloud, and didn't care.

His fingers were at her waist again, this time unzipping her skirt.

"Too many clothes," he murmured, and she couldn't agree more. She pulled back, intending to help, but he forestalled her by cupping one of her breasts in his hand, squeezing and stroking through the fabric of her bra. She caught her breath, gazing down at him, seeing the evidence of her fingers in the wild state of his hair, his lips, smudged with lipstick from her kisses. Without thinking, she reached out to thumb it away, but as soon as she touched him there, he opened his mouth and caught her thumb in his teeth, giving it a gentle nip.

His eyes were a vivid shade of green, hungry and intent, and his hand was still on her breast. It was throbbing, she was throbbing, and if he didn't make love to her soon she was going to incinerate.

Whatever inhibitions she'd had were long gone.

One night with the man of her dreams. She had almost five years of pent-up passion to release, and she was going to use every bit of it giving Finn Payne, rock star, a night of mind-blowing ecstasy.

* * *

Hot, she was so hot. Her breast filled Finn's hand perfectly, driving even more blood between his legs. His jeans had become uncomfortable, but he was in no mood to rush. She felt good on top of him, and he enjoyed looking up at her: strawberry-bruised lips and tousled auburn hair, silky blouse off one shoulder, white bra trimmed with lace.

Her kiss had caught him off guard—the softness of it, the gentleness. No one had kissed him like that in a long time, as though how he tasted and how he felt were more important than who he *was*. He'd wanted to savor it, to make it last, and then the heat between them had flared, making him hungry for more.

"You're beautiful," he whispered.

She turned shy at the compliment, brown eyes slanted at the corners, and he wondered if she had any idea how impossibly sexy she looked. He pulled her down to kiss her again, harder this time, and suddenly lost his desire to take things slow. His hand slipped beneath the lace of her bra, freeing one breast, and with a speed that made her gasp, he lowered his head to lave her nipple with his tongue.

She moaned, and he held her tighter while he

licked and sucked, then let her go slowly with a gentle scrape of the teeth that made her gasp aloud. Her fingers were in his hair, on the back of his neck. She dropped her head, and her breath on his ear made his balls tighten.

"Up," he murmured, his cheek against the soft skin of her breast. "To the bed."

She surprised him once again by giving his head a gentle kiss before moving to do as he'd asked. It was a gesture of tenderness between lovers—even though they technically weren't lovers just yet—and it touched him.

He was used to keeping his lovers at arm's length. Women wanted him because of who he was, and he wanted women for the release they gave him. Tenderness was not usually part of the equation.

This girl, however, seemed different, though he wasn't sure why. It was more than the way she looked; it was something about *her*.

She got up, brushing her hand again over the bulge in his jeans. Already aching, his erection made it difficult to stand.

"Careful," he warned, as he gained his feet, "these jeans are pretty tight."

She looked down, a pleased smile curving her

lips. "So they are," she murmured. "Let me fix that for you."

He caught his breath as her hands went to his waist, deftly undoing the top button of his jeans. He gazed down at her as she worked, thoroughly enjoying the view of one rosy breast, still uncovered, the nipple dark pink and damp from his tongue.

She unzipped his fly partway, then stopped, slipping a hand inside to stroke his groin and belly. Bringing her face up to his for another scorching kiss, she grasped his T-shirt in both hands and raised it over his head.

Shirtless now, he returned the favor, slipping her blouse, already half off and hanging free, from her shoulder. The only thing between them now was her bra, and he had that unhooked in seconds. Then it was gone, and they were both bare from the waist up. He pulled her against him, skin to skin, kissing her again.

"Mmmm," she murmured as her breasts came into contact with his chest, and he agreed completely.

A tug at her waist and a little wiggle, and her skirt dropped to the floor, pooling at her feet. He could see their reflection in the tall glass windows: him, in unzipped jeans; her, in a wispy pair of panties. While he'd never considered white to be particularly sexy, the way she looked in hers definitely changed his mind.

Then he felt her fingers on his jeans again, and closed his eyes as she freed his aching cock.

"No underwear," she whispered, her lips at the base of his neck. "You *are* a bad boy, aren't you?"

He smiled against her hair, liking how she teased him, then caught his breath as she took him in her hand, stroking and squeezing. Such soft hands, warm and insistent . . . His cock throbbed and swelled, her touch turning him hard as iron.

Surprised at how much he suddenly wanted to be inside her, he caught her wrist and said hoarsely, "Let's go in the other room."

She let him go, but not before another slow stroke of her hand had wrung a groan of pleasure from his lips.

Once in the bedroom, he caught her at the foot of the bed and kissed her again, cupping her bottom in his hands. She was soft where he was hard, and seemed to fit him perfectly. Her breath was coming faster now, and she gasped when he pressed their hips together, letting her feel his urgency.

Her hands were like velvet on his skin, slipping below the waistline of his jeans to stroke and touch. He pulled back, ready to take them off, but she was still kissing him, and he couldn't seem to stop doing the same. She urged him a step or two backward, toward the bed.

Her hands moved to his shoulders, and pressed down gently until he fell back on the mattress, landing on his elbows. His jeans were partially unzipped, and he was fully exposed, hard as a rock.

They were both breathing hard. For a moment she just stood there, taking in the view, as did he.

She was just as beautiful beneath her clothes as he'd hoped, slender, with womanly curves in all the right places. Her breasts were full but not overblown, the nipples a dark pink.

As he watched, she slowly removed her panties, keeping her eyes on his face while she did it. He couldn't tell if the color in her cheeks was shyness or arousal, but it didn't matter. The small triangle of curls at the base of her thighs was the same color as the hair on her head, and just as pretty.

He smiled appreciatively, and she leaned in, running her fingers through the dusting of hair on his chest, trailing them all the way down to his groin. His breath hitched at the brush of her fingers along his cock, and he raised his hips to help her as she tugged down his jeans and drew them off. Her hands traveled smoothly back up his calves, soft against the coarse hair of his legs and thighs. She touched him again, and he groaned as she cupped his balls, tight with need. Closing his eyes at the sensation, he felt her other hand moving over his belly and chest, finding the erect nub of his left nipple. He threw back his head and let her do whatever she wanted—she held him there, by both pleasure centers, squeezing and rubbing, as the evening's chaos centered itself into one burning, coiling ache that could only be eased by what she had to offer.

It was slow torture, but he kept his hands to himself, sensing that what she was doing was just as good for her as it was to him. The bed dipped as she came down beside him on one knee, bringing her face to his. "Lie down," she whispered, breath warm in his ear, and he did, stretching out a hand to cup and caress her breast as he did.

So soft, so smooth.

But then she flinched, bringing his eyes open.

"Ow," she murmured, though he couldn't imagine what could've hurt her. "Your ring—could you take it off?"

"I'll be more careful," he replied.

She hesitated, but he was well past the point of

any hesitation, and pulled her down for a kiss designed to make them both forget anything except what they were about to do. Her hair brushed his cheek, and her lips moved against his, quickly matching his hunger. Hands around her waist, he rolled, trapping her beneath him. Unable to help himself, he rocked his hips gently against her, once, twice . . . pressing his hardness against her softness in an unmistakable rhythm.

She broke the kiss, gasping, but he merely transferred his mouth to her breasts, which were inches away, and completely irresistible. His tongue played with her nipples as he sucked, licked, and nipped them both in turn. Her gasps turned to moans, her fingers threading their way through his hair. "Wait," she groaned after several moments of torture, "please."

Though he hated to stop, he forced himself to raise his head from those pink, rosy tips. Running his lips from her collarbone to her ear, he murmured huskily, "Please don't tell me you've changed your mind—I've tried to be a gentleman, but now I need more than footsies under the table."

"No," she said, rubbing one slender leg along his bare thigh, "I haven't changed my mind." Her breath was hot in his ear, and everywhere she touched him, his skin tingled. "I just want to make this last."

And make it last she did, using her mouth to bring him to the brink of madness, and the honeyed warmth between her thighs to pull him in, sheathe him in ecstasy, over and over again. By the time they both fell asleep in the wee hours of the morning, boneless and exhausted, Finn already knew he wasn't going to be content with just one night with Amy Smith.

Chapter Nine

He looked boyish when he slept, younger than thirty-six. His hair was wild from her fingers, and Faith was sure hers was no better. The curtains were open, Atlanta's nightscape casting a soft glow over the darkened room. She'd been lying there, watching the glitter of skyscrapers over his bare shoulder, for well over an hour. It would be dawn soon, and she couldn't wait much longer.

Finn had been the perfect lover; gentle, fiercely passionate. She'd given him everything she had, and he'd given it all back. Her girlhood fantasies had been far exceeded by the reality; his body, lean and fit, his fingertips, hard with guitar calluses, tracing every inch of her skin.

She wanted to touch him, one more time, but

didn't dare. *Why did she have to meet him* now, *like this?* If she'd met him a few months ago, before Nathan got sick, she could've just been herself; he seemed to like her.

And in the morning, no hard feelings and no regrets, he'd said.

There would be no hard feelings on her part. Ever. But what should have been a magical interlude was forever tainted, because no matter what she did, as soon as he discovered the ring gone, he'd remember her only as the girl who stole something from him. Something valuable, and important. It was probably a priceless antique or something—no one made a deal with the Devil over costume jewelry.

Lying there in the dark, listening to Finn breathe, Faith never had any doubt that what she did for Nathan was the right thing to do, but for a moment—just for a moment—it was nice to imagine a different scenario. One where she and Finn and Nathan could all three be together, without the shadow of darkness hovering over their heads. He said he liked kids, maybe he could be happy with a normal life . . .

Dream on, girl, she told herself.

Yes, Finn Payne was every woman's dream.

And now it was time for the dream to be over.

Slowly, so she didn't wake him, Faith slipped from the bed and gathered her clothes, finding most of them in the living room. She dressed quietly, then put her shoes by the door and crept barefoot back into the bedroom, where Finn still slept.

His breathing was slow and deep. She eased into the bathroom, touching the fingers of her left hand to the soap dispenser. Then she came back into the bedroom and waited, gathering her nerve. She already knew what she'd do if he woke up; squeeze his hand, claim a good-bye kiss, and urge him back to sleep, hopefully slipping the ring off in the process.

And if she got caught . . . well, she didn't know what she'd do if she got caught.

Reminding herself that failure was not an option, Faith took one last look at the glitter of Atlanta's skyline, then one last look at the gorgeous man in the bed. When they were both imprinted on her mind's eye, she went to him and gently smoothed the warm, soapy tip of a finger across his knuckle.

He didn't stir, so she did it again. Then she used her other hand to slowly take hold of the ring. It was chunky, very solid, and slid from Finn's finger far more easily than she'd imagined it would.

She had it, clenched within her palm so hard it hurt.

Backing soundlessly from the bed, Faith turned and fled, not realizing she'd been holding her breath until she reached the front door. Taking only a moment to slip on her shoes, she carefully unlocked the dead bolt, cringing at the slight *snick.* Hearing nothing from the bedroom, she gave a silent sigh of relief, and opened the door.

That, of course, was when all hell broke loose.

The blare of a siren jerked Finn from a sound sleep, and for a moment he had no idea what was going on. Another anonymous hotel room in an anonymous city, one with glittering skyscrapers just outside the window. His head cleared quickly, however, and he rose from the bed; the hotel's fire alarm was going off. He was naked, and his jeans were on the floor; as he pulled them on he remembered the girl—where was she?

"Hello?" he called out. Snagging his T-shirt, he pulled it on as he checked the bathroom, which was empty. Grabbing his boots, he headed toward the living room, and found it empty, too. "Hello?" he called again, disappointed to find her gone—he hadn't gotten her phone number.

The fire alarm was still blaring, and his cell

phone began to ring. He ducked back into the bedroom to answer it, not overly concerned just yet about the possibility of fire—he'd been in a lot of hotel rooms through the years, and through many false alarms. His phone was on the bedside table; it was John, his security guy.

"You okay, Finn? Larry's checking with the front desk to see if this is for real, but you should grab your stuff, just in case." John was slightly out of breath, and Finn knew it was because he was already on his way. His team took their job very seriously, and their room was always next door or just down the hall.

"Let's give it a minute," Finn answered wearily. His mood had taken a downturn, the siren annoying as hell, and he didn't relish the idea of charging out the door.

"Excuse me, miss?" John called out. "Is this a drill?"

"Who's that?" Finn asked sharply.

"It's the girl from the hotel," John said into the phone. "Right by the stairs."

The sirens stopped.

Finn greeted the silence with relief, glad he hadn't missed the girl. "Grab her, would you?" he asked John casually. "I wanted to ask her something."

"Sure thing," John said, and hung up.

Finn strode to the front door of the suite, which opened as he reached it. There was Amy, her face pale and set, ushered in by John, who'd let himself in with his key.

"We meet again," Finn said, giving her an intimate smile.

She didn't smile back.

"There's no need to rush off," he said, stepping closer. Her auburn hair was slightly rumpled—he remembered how soft it was, like silk beneath his hands. "How about an early breakfast?"

"I have to get home," she answered stiffly, with none of the warmth she'd shown him earlier.

Finn frowned, wondering what was up. He drew her aside to murmur, "I know what I said about having just one night together, but I had a great time, and I'd love to see you again."

She stared at the floor, blankly.

"I'm going to be in town a couple of days," he urged. "Let's get together again before I go. Give me your cell number."

She shook her head. "No, I'm sorry—I can't do that."

Finn blinked, caught off guard. He saw the look of amusement Larry shot John, and didn't appreciate it, but he'd deal with them later.

"Is something wrong?" he murmured. He thought they'd had a great time together, shared some chemistry.

She pulled away, turning to go as if she couldn't get out of there fast enough. "I'm sorry," she said again, over her shoulder, "it was fun, but I have a boyfriend."

And then she was gone, leaving him with two grown men who—if they didn't stop smirking— were about to be unemployed.

He glared at Larry, whose smirk died, and then turned to John, who shrugged and turned away as if seeing his rock-star boss dissed at the door was an everyday occurrence. "Hey, man"—Larry shook his head, making light of an awkward moment—"you win some, you lose some."

Right, Finn thought, darkly. *Except I always win.*

Not bothering to speak, he went into the bedroom and shut the door very quietly, leaving them to stay or go as they chose. The room seemed bigger, and emptier, than it had earlier. He stretched out on the bed, fully clothed, and stared moodily up at the ceiling, which looked exactly like thousands of other ceilings he'd stared at over the years.

Too many ceilings.

Too many girls.

How could he possibly have imagined this one might be different?

He rolled over, staring at the glittering skyline, and caught the faint scent of her on the pillow. He'd bought so easily into her good-girl routine. Should've known when she proved to be so hot in bed that she was no innocent.

The sheets were bunched in his fist, and Finn forced his hand to relax. *She was no one, and nothing.* It was then, as his palm lay flat, that he noticed his bare finger—the Ring of Chaos was gone.

Ice-cold fear gripped him, but not for long. He leapt from the bed and searched through the sheets, throwing the pillows aside in his haste. Finding nothing, he stripped the bed and shook the bedding out thoroughly, piece by piece, then got down on his hands and knees and checked under the bed.

"John!" he shouted. "Larry!"

He'd never taken the ring off, ever. The one time he'd tried—years ago, in a fit of drunken anger— it had refused to budge, sticking to his finger as though part of him.

"What is it?" John came bursting into the room, Larry hot on his heels. "What's going on?"

"My ring," Finn said, flat on his belly now,

sweeping his arm beneath the bed. "It's missing. I can't find it."

There was a silence. He looked up to see his security team sharing a puzzled glance. "It's a black and silver ring," he snapped, "round, with a starburst of arrows."

"You've got lots of rings, man," Larry said, with a shrug.

"This one I never take it off," he insisted. "My father gave it to me." That was a lie, of course, one he'd used before. His father had never given him anything but an unhappy childhood, then left before he could ask him why.

"Oh."

"So help me find it!" Finn hated to admit to himself how close he was to panic. "Check the living room, the couch, the minibar." Since he rarely raised his voice except onstage, John and Larry got the message, and jumped to do just that.

Together they began to slowly and methodically search every inch of the suite, including the carpet. Finn took charge of the bedroom, checking both side tables, the dresser, the entertainment armoire, all the drawers and cabinets, then went into the bathroom and did the same.

Ten minutes later, the entire suite had been

thoroughly searched, and none of them had found the ring. Finn sank down on the arm of the couch, mind reeling.

"You're sure you didn't take it off?" Larry asked, for the third time.

Finn sent him a dark look in reply, not trusting himself to speak. What if he didn't find it? What if it was all over, here, now, tonight . . .

"Okay, so you never take it off," John said, repeating what Finn had told them earlier, "but what if it slipped off? It could be in the limo, or back at the auditorium."

"I had it on when I went to bed," Finn said tightly, thinking furiously. Had the Devil figured out a way to double-cross him after all these years? That unpleasant visit in the back of the limo earlier could *not* have been a coincidence.

He sighed, scrubbing a hand through his hair.

"What about the girl?" John said. "Maybe she took it as a souvenir or something."

Finn shook his head, impatient. "No," he said shortly, but then thought about it—she'd mentioned the ring, asked him to take it off. He remembered, because he'd been surprised at her claim that it hurt her; the ring had no sharp edges.

Unlike the girl, who'd gone from hot to cold in an instant.

He got up from the couch, heading toward the door.

"Where you going?" Larry asked.

"To find the girl."

"Think she stole it?"

"Maybe," Finn said, shooting him a look, "but we won't know until we ask her, now will we?" His hand looked strangely bare on the doorknob. "Let's go talk to someone at the front desk, find out how to reach her."

Reaching Amy Smith, however, proved easier said than done.

"I'm so sorry, Mr. Payne," the prim little man behind the desk said. He wore a name tag that read "Herve Morales." "We have no one working here by the name of Amy Smith, and even if we did, we don't give out personal information regarding our employees."

"We just want to talk to her," John growled, backing Finn up. "What's the problem?"

The little man regarded John coldly. "As I said, we have no one working here by the name of Amy Smith," he repeated.

John sighed, reaching into his pocket. "Okay, man, how much?"

Herve looked insulted, his nose rising a shade higher.

"Look," Finn said, impatient with the delay. "One of your female staff members saw me to my room last night—young, pretty, reddish-brown hair."

"Was there a problem with your service, sir?" Herve asked, arching a brow.

"No," he said shortly. "I just need to talk to her."

"Enough of this bullshit." Larry stepped up, flanking Finn. "Do you know who this is? This is Finn-Fucking-Payne, man! If he wants your girl's number, you give him your girl's number!"

Herve Morales, however, was not to be intimidated. "This is the Ritz-Carlton, sir, not a dating service."

Finn held up a hand, signaling Larry to tone down the tough-guy routine. It was John and Larry's usual method; good cop, bad cop.

He'd met people like Herve Morales before, and recognized a petty dictator when he saw one. As eager as he was to track down Amy and find his ring, he wasn't out to get her fired just yet.

Single mom to a four-year-old boy.

He had no proof she'd stolen the ring, and even more importantly, he didn't like bullies.

"There was no problem with the service, and I'm not looking for a date," he told the man smoothly. "She dropped something in the hallway outside my suite, and I was just hoping to give it to her."

The little creep behind the desk knew he was lying. "I'm not entirely certain which of our employees escorted you to your room last night, Mr. Payne, but I'll be happy to find out. In the meantime, if you have something you'd like returned to one of our staff members, please feel free to leave it with me." Herve gave him an oily smile. "I'll be sure she gets it."

I'll bet you will, you little weasel.

Over the weasel's shoulder, one of the other desk clerks was doing his best to unobtrusively get their attention. As soon as Finn made eye contact, the guy gave a subtle tip of his head toward the end of the counter. He left the counter and headed toward the elevators, glancing over his shoulder to see if they followed.

"Never mind," Finn said to the weasel. "Sorry we bothered you. It wasn't important."

Larry and John followed him through the lobby and around a corner, where the second desk clerk had just disappeared. The man was waiting for them there, out of sight of the front desk.

"You want to know about the girl who showed you to your room last night?" he asked Finn, not mincing any words. "A hundred bucks."

"A hundred bucks?" John's jaw dropped, even though the man wasn't talking to him.

"Done," Finn said promptly. "Pay the man, John." Finn rarely carried cash, but John would be reimbursed, and he knew it.

Sighing heavily, John did as he was told, digging out his wallet and handing over a wad of twenties.

"Her name is Faith McFarland," the desk clerk said, pocketing the money in one swift motion. "She usually works the day shift, but a few days ago, she asked if we could swap shifts. I figured it had something to do with that kid of hers, so I said sure."

Faith McFarland, not Amy Smith.

Lying bitch.

Just to be sure, he asked, "Auburn hair, late twenties, pretty?"

The guy confirmed his description with a nod, looking nervously over Finn's shoulder, obviously aware his manager could appear at any second.

"How do I get in touch with her?" Finn tamped down his anger to focus on more practical concerns.

"You want her phone number? That'll cost you another hundred."

"For a chick's phone number?" Larry was now officially outraged. "You've gotta be kidding!"

"Done," said Finn, shooting Larry a warning glare.

Sourly but silently, John handed over another hundred bucks.

The desk clerk, whose name tag read "Farouk Jones," pulled out his cell phone and started scrolling through numbers. "Here it is," he finally said, and showed it to Finn.

Finn got out his own phone and added the number to his contact list.

"Her car is still in the parking lot," Farouk offered, clearly eager to be of further service. "I saw it just now when I came in—she hasn't checked out on the schedule yet, either. My guess is she's still somewhere in the hotel."

That bit of information definitely got Finn's attention, giving him a flicker of hope. "Thank you," he told the man. "You've been very helpful."

"Pleasure doing business with you," Farouk

said, beaming. "Please let me know if there's anything else I can do for you during your stay at the Ritz-Carlton."

Finn turned and walked away, wanting only privacy. John and Larry trailed him at a distance, following him back into the lobby, which was deserted this early in the morning. Finn found a secluded corner and punched SEND.

She answered on the third ring, voice tense. "Hello?" There was some kind of rumbling noise in the background, low and steady, and he wondered where she was—a laundry room, maybe?

"Hello," he said tightly. "It's Finn Payne."

For a long moment he heard nothing but the hum of machinery, and feared she was going to hang up. Then she asked, "How'd you get this number?"

"It wasn't hard, particularly once I found out your real name. Faith McFarland suits you much better than Amy Smith, by the way." He was surprised how much that particular lie bothered him. When he made love to someone, he at least wanted to know her name, dammit. "Getting your number wasn't hard at all—I just wish I'd gotten it sooner." She couldn't fail to miss the sarcasm.

"What do you want?"

"Where are you? Are you still in the hotel?"

"That's none of your business," she answered coolly, "and I'm very busy at the moment."

"I'm missing a ring," he said, getting right to the point. "Did you take it?"

"No." Her denial came a second too late. "I didn't take your ring . . . you must've lost it or something."

"I didn't lose it," he said flatly. "I was wearing it when I went to bed—when *we* went to bed—and when I woke up it was gone."

"Are you accusing me of *stealing* something from you?"

You did steal something from me, he thought. *A really nice memory.* "I'm not accusing you of anything," he said. "I'm just asking."

"No," she repeated emphatically. "I didn't take your ring."

He didn't believe her. There was more to this story than met the eye—why the lie about her name and the sudden switch from hot to cold after the night they'd shared? It was as though she really was two different people: one, sweet and tender; the other, an ice queen. Which one was she, and why?

"I need it back," he stated grimly, not bothering to call her a liar. "Give it back, and there will be no hard feelings, no questions asked, no problems."

"I didn't take your ring," she insisted, but her voice shook, just a little. "Lose this number, and don't call me again, ever." Then she hung up on him.

Finn stared at the phone, thinking hard. He should probably call the police—right now, this instant. He *had* to get the ring back.

That noise in the background; where had she been? If she hadn't left the hotel . . .

A quick glance toward the lobby windows revealed the faintest hint of gray. Dawn was just beginning to break in the city of Atlanta, and suddenly he had a sinking suspicion of where she might be.

"No, no, no," he mumbled beneath his breath, pocketing his phone and heading for the elevators as fast as he could.

"Where you goin', man?" Larry and John fell in beside him.

Curiously reluctant to put his suspicions into words, Finn said merely, "The roof."

"The roof?" John's eyebrows shot up. "What the hell would she be doing up on the roof?"

Calling up an old friend, he thought, praying he was wrong.

Chapter Ten

She shouldn't have answered the phone.

She almost hadn't, particularly since the number had been unfamiliar, except she had to be available in case anything ever happened with Nathan—that's what you did when you were the mom of a sick child. Now, despite worries of Nate, she turned the phone off, turning her attention back to what she'd been doing.

The wind was picking up, making the candles flicker. Good thing she'd found this secluded spot in between three huge air-conditioning units, or they'd never stay lit. The hum from the AC units was soothing, its noise drowning out all other sounds, and helping her to concentrate as she stepped back inside the circle she'd drawn in flour on the concrete roof.

Everything was ready: the candles, the pentagram, the inner circle, the bread, the salt, the incense. Sammy Divine had oh-so-thoughtfully provided everything she needed in a leather bag he'd left at the desk. According to the instructions in the book, she was supposed to take the items to a high place, arrange them precisely, and use them in the hour between dark and dawn. She'd set everything up hours ago, before she'd met Finn in the parking garage. Thinking of Finn wasn't helping, however, so she picked up the small metal dish that held burning cones of pine and cedar, and waved the fragrant smoke into all five corners of the pentagram, never leaving the inner circle.

She'd broken the circle to reach the phone, and the book had said to never break the circle.

There was no help for it, she'd just have to start again, and hope for the best.

"I sanctify this space," she said aloud. "I purify it with the elements of air and earth." Her hand was shaking, but she refused to acknowledge her fear, putting the incense down and kneeling to rip apart a loaf of round, unleavened bread. *What if she'd ruined everything?* She barely knew what she was doing as it was—never in her wildest dreams had she ever pictured herself on a rooftop at dawn, calling up the High Prince of Darkness.

Putting the bread on the ground, she picked up a bottle of sea salt and sprinkled it over both halves, then sprinkled it liberally over the surrounding area until the bottle was empty.

Then, with a shaking hand, she pulled out the little black book and began to read aloud, grateful the ceremony was short.

"This place is protected, prepared, and sanctified for the presence of the One Most High, the Lord of Night, Son of Perdition." How she hated most of the titles she was forced to speak. "Samael the Serpent, Samael the Black, Belial the Accuser." Closing her eyes against the first rays of sunlight, gleaming through the skyscrapers. *Had she waited too long?* "I invoke thee, O Wicked One, O Dragon of Darkness, Lucifer, Father of Lies."

The wind freshened, blowing cool against her overheated cheeks, but she kept her eyes closed. She was going to Hell when she died; that was what she was assuring herself of with every second that passed. An eternity in agony, burning in a lake of fire, in exchange for the life of one small, brown-haired boy. Keeping her eyes closed, she searched the darkness beneath her lids for any hope of doing otherwise, for any chance—no matter how slim—to have everything she wanted without giving up her soul, and found nothing but darkness.

The hum of the air-conditioning units kept her grounded. "I invoke thee, Ruler of the Abyss, by this seal of sun and stars, by the power of moon and sky, to come forth."

Nothing seemed to happen, and after a moment she risked a peek to see that the rooftop was much lighter now, morning having nearly arrived.

Had she done something wrong? She'd done as the book instructed; where the hell was he? The ring was burning a hole in her pocket, and she wanted it gone.

Taking a deep breath, Faith struggled not to give in to despair. She'd merely forgotten something, that's all, some step to the ritual. What else had the book said? Oh yes . . . the final step, the one she'd hoped to avoid.

She turned it to the last page, and winced as she read the instructions inscribed there. *Open yourself to the Darkness*, the book said, *embrace it within the very depths of your soul, and acknowledge Satan's power. Only then will his glory surround you.*

Stupid book. Stupid life, stupid roof, stupid fucking ritual. Closing her eyes once more, Faith prepared to surrender herself to the evil that had seeped its way into her world.

"You've got to be kidding me," came a man's voice, and her eyes snapped open in horror. There was Finn, glowering at her just outside the top-most tip of the pentacle.

"Are you trying to get yourself killed?" he asked, fixing her with a grim stare. "This hour of the morning is completely wrong for a conjuring spell."

She was pale as milk, the expression on her face a mixture of shock and fear. Clutching the book to her chest, she snapped, "What the hell are you doing here? Go away!"

"Like hell I will," he replied, furious to have found her this way, doing something no one should ever be foolish enough to do. He kicked over the nearest candle and scrubbed his foot through the chalk outline of the pentagram. "You have no idea what you're dealing with."

"Stop that," she cried, in a voice filled with panic.

He ignored her, striding to the next two candles and kicking them over, too. "Just what the hell do you think you're doing out here, you little idiot?" He felt free to call her that, since he'd practically

written the book on idiocy when it came to calling forth demons. "You think this is some kind of
game?"

The fourth candle went over, too, leaving a spill
of wax on the dirty concrete.

"I'm a Wiccan," she babbled frantically, daring
to lie, "and you're ruining my Solstice celebration."

"Bullshit," he said crudely. "Give me back my
ring."

He kicked over the fifth and final candle without a pause, barely hearing her cry of frustration
over the hum of the air conditioners.

She'd picked a secluded spot, all right, and if
she hadn't made that offhand remark the night
before about escaping to the roof, he'd never have
found her. The sweet, sexy woman he'd met last
night was just a front for evil incarnate, and he'd
been sucked in like a fool.

"You've ruined everything!" she cried, eyes
wild. Tears were streaming down her cheeks, but
they meant nothing to him.

"What did he offer you?" Finn shouted. "Tell
me." He pinned her with a furious gaze, kicking
aside more flour to further break up the five-star
pattern on the concrete. "Eternal life? Money?
What was it?"

She stared at him, stricken.

"I know how it works; I know how he operates." *Yes, he knew all too well.* "He promises you your heart's desire in return for your soul, and you agree to it, secretly thinking you'll have plenty of time to figure a way out of the bargain." He stalked from point to point on the pentagram, scuffing the flour to the wind, circling Faith, who still stood in the middle. "But the bargain can't be broken. Once you make a deal with the Devil, it stays made."

She shook her head, tears staining her cheeks. "You don't understand."

"No!" he shouted, angrier than he'd been in years. "*You* don't understand! The ring belongs to me and I'm not giving it up! And you"—he pointed at her—"you are a fool if you think stealing it for him is going to be to your benefit in any way."

Saying nothing, she sank to her knees, as though her legs could no longer hold her up.

"Believe it or not," he said with a mirthless smile, "I'm doing you a favor. I know what you're up to, Faith, but whatever deal he's offered you, it's not worth it."

Faith dropped her head, resting her palms on the ground. Her hair hung forward, hiding her face. "I'm so sorry," she said, though he could barely hear her.

"Get up," he answered sharply, stepping in to

take her by an arm. The sooner they got off this rooftop the better.

She twisted away in a flash of movement, tossing two handfuls of flour and salt directly in his face. Blinded, eyes burning, he reeled back, and Faith took off. He got an eye open just in time to see her disappear around one of the air-conditioning units, moving low and fast. Blinking and swearing, he did his best to follow.

She was quick, ducking and weaving her way between the units. It didn't take him long to realize that she definitely had the advantage . . . in the predawn darkness, she knew exactly where she was going, while he quickly became turned around inside a maze of noisy, humming boxes. He couldn't hear her, he couldn't see her, and his eyes burned like hell. "Faith!" he shouted. "Don't run away; we can talk about this!"

Eight feet away, too far for him to reach it in time, Finn saw a door open and close. Rushing to get there as fast as he could, he found it locked from the other side. Pounding on the door in frustration, he shouted through it. "Faith!" More furious pounding. "Faith!"

But he heard nothing but silence and the hum of air conditioners, and far away, too faint for anyone to hear but him, a chuckle of laughter from the muse of Chaos.

Finn immediately called John on his cell phone, but it was no good—the key to the inner dead bolt was missing and maintenance had to be called to unlock it. Larry was sent to the parking lot to look for Faith, but not knowing what she drove or on what level she was parked, Finn wasn't hopeful he'd catch her.

She was smart, and she'd be positioned for an easy getaway.

"What happened, man?" John shouted through the door to Finn while they waited for the key. "How'd you get locked out?"

Finn was in no mood to shout explanations. What was he supposed to say, that he'd interrupted the girl in the middle of a Satanic ritual that—if she'd succeeded—might possibly have sent his soul screaming straight to Hell? "It's a long story. Just get the door unlocked, will you?" He hadn't seen her with the ring, but he was more convinced than ever that she had it. The dodgy scenario—lies, theft, the summoning ceremony—it was all too familiar.

John and Larry knew nothing of his past visits to the dark side, and with a familiar stab of frustration and shame, he realized he had no desire to enlighten them.

They'd never believe him anyway.

While he waited, the sun came up. Soon he could see all of Atlanta laid out before him, bright lights fading into big city. The Ritz wasn't very tall compared to some of the other skyscrapers; it seemed small and insignificant, surrounded by gleaming spires of glass pointing their way to a Heaven he'd never see. With a sigh, unable to help himself, he made his way back to the spot where he'd found Faith. The evidence of what she'd been up to was clearly revealed by the weak light of dawn; the crudely drawn pentagram—scuffed and broken, the candles, the bread.

"She needs more practice," came a man's voice from behind him. "Perhaps you should give her lessons."

Finn turned to see Satan step out casually from between two air-conditioning units.

"Don't look so surprised," he said mildly. "Surely you were expecting me?"

"Doesn't sunlight turn you to ash or something?" Finn snapped, meeting sarcasm with sarcasm. "What happened to your legendary preference for the dead of night?"

Those ice blue eyes sent a chill down his spine.

"Daylight works just as well for me," the Devil said. "Light, darkness . . . it's all the same." He wandered away from the AC unit to stroll easily about the roof, going to one of the overturned candles, toeing it with his boot. "I believe our bargain has come to an end."

"No, it hasn't," Finn disagreed calmly, though his heart was pounding. "I haven't given up the ring—it was taken from me."

Satan waved a hand. "A technicality."

"Not a technicality," he answered firmly. "Part of the deal."

The blond man sighed, turning his head to look out over the city. "You humans are so literal," he said idly. "But I suppose you're right."

Hardly daring to breathe, Finn waited, sensing there was more to be said.

"I suppose I could let you live out what's left of your soon-to-be-miserable life. It will be suicide eventually, you know," he added casually, as an aside, "though the official statement will be that it was an accident; another burnt-out rocker who accidentally killed himself in an excess of drugs and alcohol."

"I don't do drugs," Finn answered tersely.

"You will," the Devil answered, with grim satisfaction.

Finn said nothing, waiting to hear more of what fate had in store for him.

Satan smiled, meeting his eyes. "Face it, my friend . . . the muse of Chaos has chosen another. The girl would never have gotten the ring off your hand otherwise, and you know it. The ring chooses its wearer, as it chose you, twenty years ago."

Twenty years ago he'd been a stupid, lonely kid who would've given anything to live the fantasy life he'd created in his head—that of a rich, successful guy doing what he loved to do, which was making music. Music had been all that mattered, and he'd sold his soul for it. When offered the Ring of Chaos, he hadn't hesitated, even though his gain was someone else's loss.

Someone named Mike Gilliam, who'd blown his brains out in the back of a dirty little club in Indianapolis after his career hit the skids, after a skinny little roadie named Finn had stolen the ring for himself.

"She doesn't know the ring's power." The idea of a girl like Faith—so beautiful, so full of promise—in league with Satan left a bad taste in his mouth. "You must've tricked her somehow, the way you tricked me."

"More technicalities." Satan sighed. "How tiresome. Bottom line, take it she did, and you, dear

Finn, are about to become a washed-up has-been. Your career in music is over, because the ring *is* the music—the inspiration it gives your mind, the talent it gives your fingers. It's all that's carried you this far." He made a *tsk*ing noise. "How far do you think you'll get without it?"

"You are one sick bastard." Finn had nothing to lose by getting angry; as much as he wished differently, there was no walking away from this. If he'd known, back when he was sixteen, that all the money and all the fame in the world couldn't buy happiness, things might've turned out differently for him. As it was, money and fame were all he had, and the only life he knew.

"Rich, famous and unfulfilled" was still far better than "once rich, once famous and now dead." He was no Kurt Cobain or Jim Morrison, and had never bought into the "better to burn out than fade away" bullshit.

"You really get a kick out of watching people suffer, don't you?"

The Devil laughed, an unholy fire flickering in his ice blue eyes. "I like you, Finn, did you know that? You've never lacked courage, even as a pimply kid. You figured out how to get what you wanted back then, and maybe you will again. Tell you what . . ." He cocked his head, smiling. "I'll give you two days to get the ring back, unless, of course, Faith succeeds in calling me up first." He shrugged. "I'm helpless against certain rituals and incantations, as you well know."

Finn didn't respond, but neither did he look away.

Satan chuckled, shaking his head. "She certainly bungled it this time, so maybe you'll have a shot at getting it from her before I do. You can't take it from her, though—you've already stolen it once, and that would be far too easy. You have until Monday morning to *persuade* her to return the Ring of Chaos, or it's all over—your career will come to a standstill." He arched an eyebrow. "Do we have a deal?"

And Finn, as he'd done once before in his life, nodded his head and answered, "We have a deal."

Finally the door opened, and Finn stepped inside the stairwell, where he found John and Herve Morales, the asshole who'd refused to give him any information about Faith earlier. Morales's sour expression quickly changed to one of shock, and it was only then that Finn realized he had flour in his hair and on his clothes.

"Don't ask," he growled, brushing past the men to head down the stairs. He needed a shower, and he needed to plan his next move, preferably both at the same time. Luckily he still had some time—despite what Satan had said, summoning ceremonies were not a task to be undertaken in the daylight. He'd thought carefully while on the roof, and his initial desire to see Faith burn in Hell for what she was doing had faded to something more introspective—something he didn't like, but couldn't ignore.

"What happened with the girl?" John was the only one with him as they emerged from the stairwell onto their own floor.

"She took off running," Finn answered shortly. "Call my house manager in the islands, tell him to contact that private detective who did security work for us last summer. We need to track her down, quick."

"We should call the police, or just let that prick behind the desk handle it," John growled.

"Not yet."

John gave him a look, but Finn said nothing, merely waiting while John used his key to open the door to his room, then heading directly for the shower. He didn't want to explain why he didn't want the authorities involved, wasn't even sure he could. The Ring of Chaos now linked his fate to the girl's. By stealing it, she'd put them both in danger, making the same mistake he'd made him-self twenty years ago. He wasn't sure why—or even *if*—he cared . . . the only thing he knew for sure was that he needed to find her.

Let her look him in the eye and tell him she knew what she was doing, and why.

Besides, he had to get the ring back, and the less the world knew about it, the better.

Chapter Eleven

The water in the pool was black, as black as the hearts of the water nymphs who lurked beneath its surface. They were quick, those nymphs, always eager to snatch anything or anyone who wandered too close, but they knew better than to disturb the mirrorlike surface with their ripples when the Prince of Darkness stopped by for a visit.

Sammy breathed in deeply, taking in the quiet. There was utter silence in the cavern, natural sunlight streaming from openings high above his head. Animals and birds shunned the area, knowing that the darkness that lurked underground sometimes welled up into the earth itself, turning twigs into claws, creating death traps from which they couldn't escape. This was an ancient place, a place avoided by everyone, including the dead.

"It's been a long time, Samael." An old woman stepped from the mouth of a cave, well hidden by stones.

"So it has, Ariadne," he returned, unsurprised by her appearance. "You're looking well."

She glared at him, obviously uninterested in pleasantries. "What have you done with Selene?" she demanded. "Where is she?"

"Selene is being punished," he said simply, strolling around the edge of the pool to stand beside the old woman.

"For how long?"

"For as long as I see fit."

Sammy turned, looking down on the pool from his new vantage point. In it, he could see himself as well as the old woman, who, in her reflection, was now a beautiful young woman, with long golden hair. "You didn't think I'd let her get away with challenging me, did you?"

The young woman's mouth twisted. "She cannot help who she is," she said to Sammy's reflection. She met his eyes in the water and said spitefully, "You made her that way."

Sammy shook his head. "Oh no, my dear, don't blame that on me. I brought her to you long ago, after her mortal death, for help and guidance. You were supposed to keep her occupied and out of harm's way, and instead you taught her to weave her poison within the webs of fate."

"Bah," said the woman in the water, "you didn't want her out of harm's way, and you know it."

Sammy laughed, untroubled by the accusation.

"What do you want from me this time, Samael?" she asked his reflection. "And whatever it is, why should I give it to you?"

"That's what I like about you, Ariadne; you always get right to the point."

"Pray do the same."

Sammy's expression hardened, and the woman took note, for she said nothing further, waiting in silence until he was ready to enlighten her as to the reason for his visit.

"I have someone I wish to bind to me," he finally said, "forever."

"There is no such thing as forever," she returned, "you know that. There are only patterns, and circles, endlessly repeating themselves, over and over and over."

"Spare me the semantics," he replied. "Can you do it?"

"Of course I can do it," Ariadne said, "but there is no need." She waved her hand over the surface of the pool, and their reflections began to ripple, changing into something entirely different—a white house, with a wraparound porch, shaded by trees. On the front porch sat a young, dark-haired woman in a rocking chair, reading. "You are already engraved upon her heart," the old woman said, "even though it belongs to another. The binding is unnecessary."

"Damn you," he said angrily, unable to take his eyes from the scene in the pool, "who are you to tell me what's unnecessary?" He knew she was right, of course, but his loneliness had driven him to it, driven him to come here, to the one place where the dead did not follow. As he watched, the girl in the rocking chair moved a hand to her flat stomach, patting it absently as she read. The gesture betrayed what he already suspected, yet cut like a knife. "I can't make her do anything she doesn't already want to do, but you . . ."

Ariadne waved her hand again, and the girl and the house faded. "I can bind her to you, but I cannot make her love you," she said simply. "Even the Great Shaitan is not immune to the laws of the web of Fate."

Samael stared bitterly into the pool, seeing now only his own reflection, and the blackness that surrounded him, as always.

Ariadne turned away, heading back into her cave, and he let her go, knowing himself a fool for wishing for things he could never have.

Nicki Styx was beyond his reach, and part of him, Darkness help him, was grateful for it.

He stayed by the pool a long time, soaking in the quiet. There were no further visions, and he didn't expect them—the pool revealed what it wanted to reveal, when it wanted to reveal it, and he had long ago ceded control of its moods to Ariadne. She was the Weaver, farseeing and complex, and the black pool her familiar. He did not begrudge it, for he had plenty of his own.

After a time, in no hurry to return to the eyes that watched him constantly in Sheol, he climbed the narrow path that led from the cavern into the bright light of day, thinking he might wander down to the sea and watch the waves beat against the cliffs. Ariadne's isle was isolated, a hard little rock in a chain of larger rocks, remote from the rest of the world. He'd brought his favorite pair of Ray-Bans just for the occasion, and slipped them on just as he reached the top.

"What do you think you're doing, Samael?"

Sammy whirled, shocked to hear another voice. He'd been coming to this island for millennia, and never seen another soul save that of the Weaver's.

His old friend Gabriel stood at the head of the path, emanating light, radiating disapproval.

"What the hell are you doing here?" Samael snapped, not at all pleased to see him.

"I'm here to speak with you," Gabe said, taking a step forward. "Without your army of darkness behind you, hiding in the shadows."

Sammy drew in a breath, reining his temper. "How did you find me?" he demanded.

"You're not the only one who knows of this place—we found it together, remember?"

He remembered. They'd circled it, eons ago, he and Gabriel, on a beautiful day just like this one, sea winds holding them aloft, the sun warm on their wings. The skies surrounding them had been cloudless, but a gray fog had clung to the island, shrouding it, marking it as different. It had appeared so barren, yet so alive; its sinister aspect had drawn him like a lodestone. Gabriel hadn't wanted to explore, but Samael had been unable to resist. He'd come back one day, alone, and it had been then that he'd met the old woman who lived in the cavern, and learned for the first time that he and his brothers were not the only immortal creatures in the universe.

"What do you want, Gabriel?" he asked shortly.

"I want to know what you're doing to Faith

McFarland," Gabe answered grimly. "You were supposed to help her, to look out for her—instead, you've turned her into a thief."

Sammy felt his temper rising—he answered to no one. "And a whore," he agreed, flatly. "I made her into a whore, too. Don't forget that part."

Gabriel's eyes flashed, for even angels were capable of anger, particularly when it was on someone else's behalf. He was dressed as he'd been in the temple, khaki pants and chambray shirt.

"You were supposed to stay out of it, mind your own business, remember?" Sammy ignored Gabriel's anger, and brushed past him to the head of the path, following it downward to the sea. "She's unharmed, and the boy is in remission. More importantly, we agreed to do things *my* way."

"You could heal the boy in an instant," Gabriel stated, stopping him in his tracks.

"True," he agreed, eyeing Gabriel over his shoulder. "Is that what guardian angels are supposed to do? Remove every trial from life and grant every wish as though they were someone's fairy godmother?"

Gabriel made an exasperated noise, and Sammy knew he'd made his point. He turned and started again down the path. A moment later he heard the clatter of stone as his former comrade followed.

They made their way in silence, single-file down a narrow track through the rocks. Soon the scent of the sea surrounded them, clean and sharp, and their ears became filled with the rumble of crashing waves, growing louder until they reached the end of the path, which opened onto an empty beach.

There Sammy stopped, feeling the wind whip through his hair, watching and listening to the thundering waves.

The wind and the waves did only as they pleased.

Nature had no need of a conscience, and neither did he.

It was several minutes before Gabriel, who watched the waves in silence beside him, finally spoke.

"What are you up to, brother?"

His anger had passed, or Sammy might've struck him for using the word. As it was, he merely shrugged, still watching the waves, and stated, "I'm helping her. Her son is home from the hospital, isn't he?"

"You're using the child to get something you want. That was never part of the bargain."

"Speak to me not of bargains," Sammy said, not realizing how he'd fallen into a much older speech pattern, "for you know nothing of them. Everything you have has been given to you with an open hand." He demonstrated, opening a hand to the cool touch of the wind, though his eyes stayed on the waves. "Beloved of the One, the universe your playground," he added, without heat. "You know nothing of struggle, of pain, or of loss."

"That's not true," Gabriel said firmly, but Sammy chose not to hear him, listening only to the crash and boom of the sea, pounding stubbornly against the rocks that surrounded the island.

"I told you I would do this thing my way," Samael repeated, keeping his eyes on the ocean. "Go back where you belong, Gabriel, and don't come here again."

Gabriel's laughter took him by surprise. "I'm not one of your servants, Samael." He shook his head, apparently amazed by his old friend's arrogance. "You do not command me. You reign within your hidden temple, and you play at evil among the shades of dead while you torment the living, but mostly you just hide—you hide from the One and you hide from yourself." The angel took a step back, unfurling his wings. The sea winds caught them, buffeting the edge of his feathers, bearing him aloft, where he drifted. "We are brothers still, born of the same womb, that of the infinite universe. You hate me now for what I am, as I hate what you have become, but our fates will always be entwined." The winds bore him higher, out of reach. "For that reason, and that reason alone, I give sway here today. Do what you will with Faith McFarland, at least for now, but do not disappoint me, my brother."

Then he dissolved in a burst of light that made Sammy shield his eyes, despite the Ray-Bans.

"Showoff," Sammy muttered beneath his breath, then turned back to the waves, letting them soothe the jealousy that had speared his veins at the sight of Gabe's feathers, fluttering in the wind. The wind taunted him by bringing one of them to rest in the sand near his feet, where without hesitation, he crushed it beneath his heel.

Chapter Twelve

What, in the name of Hell, was she supposed to do?

It had been almost two hours since she'd left Finn locked on the roof of the hotel, and Faith's nerves were shredded. She'd driven home in a state of near panic, anxious to get somewhere safe, knowing there was no such place. Now she paced the floor of her living room by the harsh light of morning, impatient, wired.

She needed to get rid of the ring, *now*.

Finn knew her name and her phone number—he'd be sure to go to the police. They'd find the ring in the backyard where she'd buried it, and put her in jail. She'd have no chance to re-create the conjuring spell, no chance to fulfill her end of the bargain. Nathan had a doctor's appointment in two days. She'd be a criminal . . . they could take her little boy from her, put him in foster care . . .

Faith put her head in her hands, and forced herself to stop pacing. Taking a deep breath, she moved to the window, eyeing the street through the blinds. A bird trilled from the tree in her front yard, and Mrs. Dawson, her neighbor, was outside watering her roses.

She was a thief, who'd used her body to get what she wanted.

She needed to focus on dealing with the Devil, yet the face that kept forming in her mind was not one of cold blue eyes and lean cruelty, but Finn's, green-eyed and soft, the way it looked this morning before she'd lied and told him she had a boyfriend. Before she'd thrown flour and salt in his face and locked him on the roof.

Whatever deal he's offered you, it's not worth it, he'd said. How did he know so much about what she'd been doing on the roof?

Bring me the ring by Monday, Satan had said, *and Nathan's tumor will be gone forever.*

Closing her eyes against the morning's glare, Faith drew a deep breath, unable to stop reliving every nightmarish moment of the morning just past. The fire alarm, the sickening feeling in the pit of her stomach when she'd thought herself caught, the even more sickening feeling when she had been. That moment when she'd seen Finn standing there, so angry . . .

She'd lied to him, tricked him, and treated him badly when he'd been nothing but good to her—it was wrong, and she was ashamed.

A lump rose in her throat, but she refused to give in to tears again—not yet.

Faith rubbed her eyes and sighed. She'd always known that getting caught had been a possibility, she'd known she'd feel guilty no matter what happened, but she'd never expected the time she'd spent with Finn to be so . . . earth-shattering.

She had to put those memories away for now, lock them up and bring them out later, when things calmed down. As to the theft, her only defense at this point: deny, deny, deny. Maybe Finn had filed a complaint with hotel management; if she was caught with the ring she'd lose her job . . .

"Mommy?"

Nathan was in the doorway, looking sleepy and cute and totally, one-hundred-percent adorable. She swept him up, banishing all bad thoughts to the corner of her mind where she'd trained them to hide. "Good morning, Superboy," she told him, kissing the curls on top of his head. A big patch of hair on the back of his head had been shaved for surgery, but was already growing in. "Were you good for Auntie Dina last night?"

"Mm-hm," Nathan confirmed sleepily, squeezing her neck. "We played cars."

Faith smiled, knowing how crazy Nathan was about cars. Dina would've probably preferred just *one* car—one with a good-looking guy behind the wheel—but she was a good sport when it came to playing with Nathan.

"For hours," Dina added with a yawn, shuffling in wearing a pink robe and pajamas. "We played cars for hours. Any coffee?"

"I'll make it." Faith gave Nathan a final hug, then put him down. "Thanks so much for staying last night, Dina."

Her friend waved a hand in dismissal, still yawning. "No problem. We watched a VH1 marathon of Michael Jackson videos, didn't we, baby?"

"I can moonwalk, Mommy! Watch me!" Nathan immediately became animated, executing a clumsy backward maneuver that made Faith laugh. He laughed, too, and her heart swelled to bursting at the sound.

That's what they needed around here . . . more laughter.

Unable to resist another kiss, she cupped his

little face in her hands and planted one on him. "I'll get you some juice."

"Okay." He returned her kiss, then darted away while she moved into the kitchen to get the juice and make coffee. "Can I watch TV?" He climbed on the couch, scooping up his favorite stuffed dog as he got settled.

"Go ahead. It's Saturday, cartoons are on. I'll make us some breakfast."

"What about you?" Dina asked. She took the TV remote from Nathan and turned the channel to cartoons. "How was your evening?" She came into the kitchen, giving Faith a sleepy once-over. "You got lucky, didn't you?" she whispered, shooting Nathan a glance to make sure he wasn't listening. "Who is he?"

"Nobody special," Faith lied, willing her hands not to shake as she poured Nathan's juice. She didn't want to talk about Finn right now.

Dina, of course, didn't buy it. "You all right? What happened?"

"It was a long night," Faith answered, with a sigh. She was so tired—the last twenty-four hours had been a maelstrom of anxiety, ecstasy, guilt, and panic. She had no idea what was going to happen next—all she could do was wait until dark when she could once again try to call up the

Devil, and hope he got there before Finn—or the police—did.

"There was a lot of craziness, most of which you wouldn't believe if I told you." She wanted to tell Dina everything, but believed—for her friend's sake—the less she knew the better.

"*Good*, wouldn't believe you, or *bad*, wouldn't believe you?" Dina asked, obviously anxious to hear more.

Faith held the coffeepot under the faucet, letting it fill. "Both," she answered, unable to help thinking about the good part of the evening, being held in Finn's arms, so close she could feel his heartbeat as he moved against her, inside her, lips searing her skin . . .

"Ooeee," said Dina, stepping in to take the coffeepot, now about to overflow, from Faith's hands. "You got it bad. I can see it all over your face. Now who is he?"

"Oh, Dina," she groaned. "I'm in such trouble."

Dina put down the pot and held out her arms. "C'mere, baby," she said, as though Faith were Nathan's age.

Faith went into them without hesitation, wishing she *was* Nathan's age, when life had seemed so simple—Cheerios or Cap'n Crunch? Barbie, or My Little Pony?

"Tell me," Dina urged, but Faith was afraid to. How could she tell her closest friend and next-door neighbor that she'd made a deal with the Devil, and that the police could show up at any moment? How could she tell Dina that she was a thief, and that she'd slept with a total stranger last night with only one goal in mind, which was to steal from him?

And what about when she said, *Oh, by the way, he's a rock star*; her friend would think she'd finally cracked—lost it over the strain of Nathan's illness, gone off the deep end.

Burying her nose against Dina's neck, she wondered again if maybe she *had* cracked; her heart certainly felt full of jagged edges.

"Faith McFarland, twenty-seven, lives at 1421 Magnolia Trace, Marietta, Georgia."

Finn wrote the address down on a pad. "Marietta? Not Atlanta?"

"Marietta is just north of Atlanta," said the voice on the other end of the phone. "Easy commute." Bert Kudlow was the brother-in-law of his housekeeper, and had proven his worth last summer when he'd upgraded the security system for Finn's island house. He did background checks and private investigations on the side. "Never been married, drives a dark blue 1995 Volvo. Some credit card debt, but her rating is good; pays her bills on time."

Finn couldn't care less about her credit rating or what kind of car she drove—he just needed to get to her before she did something stupid, like conjure up Satan. "How far from the Atlanta Ritz-Carlton?" he asked.

"About forty minutes," Bert said. "At this time of morning you should be okay traffic-wise; everyone's coming into the city while you'll be going out."

"Thanks, Bert. Stick close to your computer in case I need you again."

"Sure thing."

Hanging up, Finn tore the paper with Faith's address from the pad and handed it to John, who'd been watching TV and scarfing down room service while they'd waited for the background check. "Here's the address. Let's get moving."

"You should let me do this myself," John said, rising from the couch, "in case it gets ugly."

"Sorry," Finn answered shortly, "but no way. This is personal."

"I ain't gonna hurt her," he argued, "but I'm in a better position to pressure her than you are, man. No emotional attachment. No guilt. I'll be real nice at first, and if she doesn't cooperate I'll threaten her with the police. I'll have her crying like a baby . . . she'll give me the ring to avoid any trouble."

Finn somehow doubted that. "John, if I wanted the police, I'd call the police. This can still be handled privately, and that's how I want to do it."

John sighed, giving up. They left the suite and rode the elevator down in silence.

Larry was waiting for them in the lobby, having coffee and reading the newspaper. "No sign of her," he reported.

"We've got her address," Finn told him. "Have the valet bring up the car."

There were more people in the lobby than there had been earlier, some checking in, some checking out, others on their way to breakfast or business meetings.

"That's Finn Payne," said a woman's voice, and heads began to turn.

"Are you sure?" asked the guy with her, craning his neck to see. He caught sight of them quickly, hefting a camera onto his shoulder.

"It *is* him," the woman exclaimed, for everyone in the lobby to hear.

John moved to position himself between his boss and the two reporters, but it was too late.

"Excuse me," called the woman, teetering rapidly toward them on high heels. She was wearing far too much makeup for this hour of the morning, a crisp blue suit and clunky jewelry. "Excuse me! I'm Katie Binford, Channel 8 News! May we speak with you for a moment, Mr. Payne?"

Finn sighed, wishing he'd remembered to slip on his sunglasses before leaving the elevator.

"Sorry, no interviews. We're in a hurry," John growled, but Katie was having none of it, ignoring the big man as she would a gnat.

"Mr. Payne, may we speak with you a moment?" she repeated, thrusting a microphone close to Finn's face and giving him the charming, practiced smile of a consummate media mannequin. "Please? Surely you won't deny your fans a moment of your time?"

Finn stopped, though he didn't want to. He made it a point to always be polite with the media, and friendly to his fans—they were the ones who made it all possible, after all.

Them, and the ring, which he didn't have anymore.

He had a brief image of this same reporter cheerfully doing a story on his untimely death. *Rock star Finn Payne was found dead this morning . . .* A surge of panic at the thought made his heart pound, but he gave the woman a lazy smile. "Sure," he said, "but I'm in a bit of a hurry, so . . ."

Katie got right to the point, blindsiding him in the process. "Channel 8 received a tip about a supposed 'black magic' ritual held on the roof of the Ritz-Carlton this morning, and rumor is that you were found alone at the scene." The cameraman stepped back, panning out to include Katie and Finn together in his shot. "We've already got film coverage of the site itself . . . a pentagram, candles, melted wax. Is this rumor true? Do you know anything about this . . . this devil worship ceremony?"

The way she said "devil worship" reminded Finn that he was in Atlanta, Georgia, the heart of the Southern Bible Belt. A scandalizing tale about rock stars and devil worship would make for a great story for the local yokels.

Luckily he'd had plenty of practice dealing with the press, and kept his face impassive, slipping on his sunglasses. "That's quite a rumor," he said mildly. Larry and John shot each other a glance, then looked as one toward the front desk, where Herve Morales was nervously watching. As soon as the weasel saw them looking at him, he slid down the counter and out of sight.

"I don't know anything about it," Finn lied, then followed it with a truth. "And I don't recommend anyone practicing devil worship or black magic rituals," he added calmly, giving the reporter her quote.

She wasn't quite ready to give up. "But your music . . . it's known to be very dark, isn't it? In fact, they call you the Prince of Darkness, don't they?"

He nodded, knowing his years in the music scene were well documented. "I'm an artist," he said, "who sometimes finds inspiration on the dark side." He turned a wry smile on the camera. "That's all."

"Do you actually believe in this type of thing," she persisted, "or is this some kind of publicity stunt to promote your new CD?" She gave him a cheerful, upbeat smile, urging him to tell her all his secrets.

Finn said nothing, *this close* to revealing on camera that Katie could use a breath mint after her morning coffee. But he knew better than to feed the sharks when they smelled blood in the water, and turned away. "Excuse me, but I'm running late."

Larry held the door open for him as John

brought up the rear, using his body to block the camera shot.

"Finn! Finn! Can we get your autograph?" Two other young women rushed up, ignoring both John and Larry until the guards stepped in their way, then the women just tried to dance around them. "I was at the show at the Athenian last night," one of them gushed, "you were amazing! I still have the ticket stub in my purse; will you sign it for me?"

"No problem," he said, refusing to give the news crew any shots of him looking nervous or concerned. As far as he was concerned, it was business as usual, and that included signing autographs.

"Are you staying here?" the woman asked eagerly, digging frantically into her purse. "I'm in room 428. Could I buy you a drink later?"

"Don't be so pushy, Tammy," her friend said with an embarrassed look.

"Why not?" Tammy answered, with a flirtatious little laugh. She was pretty, but could use a better dye job—her roots were showing, dark beneath the blond. "How often do you get to meet a rock star? Carpe diem, I say." Ignoring her friend's advice, she leaned in closer, handing Finn the ticket stub. "I think we could have a really great time together, if you know what I mean." Her fingers covered his, deliberately, lingering during the handoff of the card.

"Thanks," he said, taking the pen John offered and scribbling his name on the ticket stub, "but I don't have a lot of time to myself when I'm on tour." His standard excuse, one he'd used a million times.

A couple in their midthirties joined the two women, and so did an elderly woman who proclaimed her granddaughter his biggest fan. A few minutes later he'd signed a few autographs and posed for a few pictures, and when the black SUV John and Larry had rented the day before pulled up, they were able to escape without drawing any further attention.

"What's all this about a pentagram and candles on the roof?" John asked as soon as the car doors were closed. He was in the driver's seat, while Larry was in the back. "I thought you went up on there to look for the girl . . . What were those reporters talking about?"

Finn just shook his head, unsure how much to tell them. "Call my attorney," he instructed Larry, who was in the backseat, "and tell him to contact the Ritz with a complaint about one of their employees talking to the media. Mention that creep at the concierge desk by name."

"Herve Morales," supplied John.

"That's him." He had no sympathy for opportunists who got off by sticking their noses into other people's business. What happened on the roof was between him and Faith, and needed to stay that way.

"What about the girl?" Larry asked. "You going to report her to hotel management?"

"No," he said sharply. "Not yet."

John shook his head, and Larry made the phone call to Finn's attorney as they drove. Finn watched the countryside speed past, thinking about what to say to Faith when he saw her next, and how he was going to get the ring back. He'd try calm persuasion first—despite her dirty trick on the roof—but if he had to get tough and threaten to have her arrested, then so be it.

Resolved, he still couldn't help but wonder: How deep in darkness was she steeped, and why did he even begin to care?

Finally the GPS led them to a shady, narrow street in an older neighborhood, forty minutes north of Atlanta. Tiny homes, wedged tightly together, lots of trees.

John tried one more time to get him to keep a

low profile. "Larry and I can handle this, Finn—
you should stay in the car. If she stole your ring,
we'll get it back, one way or another. No need for
any personal drama. Those news vultures could be
anywhere, and you don't need the bad publicity."

"I'm going to talk to her alone."

"But, Finn—"

A sharp look cut John's argument short. "I
know you two are paid to look out for me, but I
told you, this is personal. She's not going to admit
to anything in front of you."

"Is this about the ring, or the girl?" John dared
ask, but Finn just shook his head.

"It's okay either way," Larry offered, speaking
up from the backseat. "We ain't just your body-
guards, man . . . you know that."

"Yeah," John agreed gruffly. "We're your friends."

Finn couldn't help but smile a little at that. "I
know." John was about as subtle as a bulldozer,
and Larry wasn't the brightest bulb in the pack,
but they always had his back. "I'm just going to
go in there," he said wryly, "and be my charming
rock-star self. If she makes a run for it again, you
guys will be out here to catch her."

John sighed but subsided, leaning back into
his seat, while Larry gave him a grunt he took as
agreement.

A moment later, Larry said, "Dark blue Volvo, in the driveway on the right."

Finn saw it, too, noting the faded paint job and the bumper sticker that read, "All who wander are not lost." The house, like the car, had seen better days, and could use a new coat of paint, though there were flowers on the front porch, and cheerful curtains in the windows.

Larry pulled up behind the Volvo, blocking it in with the SUV. Before it was in PARK, Finn was out of his seat and on the way up the walk. The door had a peephole, and he faced it directly as he rapped sharply with his knuckles.

A moment later the door opened, and disappointment made his heart plunge; it was a young black woman, plump, wearing a pink robe and pajamas.

"Can I help you?" she asked, giving him an arch look.

"Who is it?" said a little boy, scampering up behind the woman. Unlike her, he was white, with curly brown hair, and looked about four—

"Breakfast is ready," sang out a voice, and there was Faith, with plates in her hands and a growing look of shock and horror on her face.

Her reaction speared him to the core, and he wasn't sure why. All he knew was that he didn't like that look—he much preferred the soft, smiling looks she'd given him last night.

Ruthlessly he reminded himself *why* she'd been giving him those looks—she'd wanted something, and she'd gotten it, which meant she was smart enough to continue lying about it today.

"Hello, Faith," he said calmly.

Her panicked gaze fluttered between the woman who answered the door, the boy, and him. She blinked, and her face began to clear, smoothing itself to calm, but there was no mistaking how pale she'd gone.

"Finn," she acknowledged stiffly. "What are you doing here?"

"We need to talk."

"No, we don't."

"I think we do," he insisted quietly, "unless you want me to call . . ." He hesitated, glancing down at the boy, who stared at him, wide-eyed, from behind the black woman. "We need to talk, Faith," he repeated. "Privately."

"C'mon with Auntie Dina," said her friend to the boy. She took him by the shoulder and steered him gently toward the other room, obviously knowing when to make herself scarce. "We're gonna go eat breakfast together while Mommy talks to the nice man."

"Dina, I—"

"If you want me to stay, I will," Finn heard the black woman murmur. "But maybe you should talk to him, hear what he has to say."

Faith looked like she'd rather poke her eyes out with a stick than listen to anything he had to say, but after a moment's hesitation, she gave a jerky nod.

"We'll be right here in the kitchen," Dina said loudly, with a warning glance over her shoulder at Finn. Her glance lingered a moment, boldly, as she took him in from top to toe. One dark eyebrow quirked upward in frank appreciation, and then she was gone, taking the plates from Faith's hands on her way out.

He stepped inside and closed the door behind him, not waiting to be invited in.

She glanced nervously toward the kitchen. "I don't know how you found me, but you need to leave," she whispered furiously. She reminded him of a cornered kitten, hissing to keep danger at a distance.

"I need the ring back," he said flatly. "I know you took it."

She shook her head, crossing her arms. "I don't know what you're talking about. I told you I didn't steal your ring."

"Then what were you doing up on the roof?" he challenged.

Her chin went up. "What I do in my own time is my own business."

He said nothing, staring her down.

"I'm sorry about throwing flour in your face, and locking the door, but you were scaring me." Her lips firmed. "Just like you're scaring me now."

"It was mostly salt," he answered flatly. "And it stung like hell."

"I said I was sorry."

"Why don't I believe you?" he asked. "Could it be because you've done nothing but lie to me since the moment we first met?"

Color rushed to her cheeks, staining them bright pink.

"You're a pretty good actress, at least you were last night." He stated it frankly, as though it didn't matter. "You got what you wanted," he went on, "and then you couldn't get out of there fast enough."

"I told you—"

"I caught you up on the roof performing a conjuring spell." He gave a disbelieving laugh. "You think I don't know who you were conjuring?"

She stared at him stonily, refusing to answer.

"Look," he said, striving for a reasonable tone.

"I don't care why you took it, and I'm not out to make trouble. I just want it back." He raked a hand through his hair, his ring finger feeling very naked. "The ring is important to me. I need it."

"So you've told me," she said coldly, not giving an inch. "But *I've* told *you* I don't have your ring. You need to leave my house."

"Give me the ring, or I'll call the police."

Fear flickered in her eyes, but she took a deep breath and called his bluff. "Go ahead," she said. "Call the police. I'll tell them you're a stalker. I'll tell them you followed me here all the way from the Ritz and barged into my house."

"Who do you think they're going to believe?" His temper, already strained, was beginning to fray, but he kept his voice low, not wanting the kid to hear. "I'll tell them all about how you lied your way into my hotel room using a false name, and lied to your boss to get the evening off."

Her face was white, but her expression stayed defiant. "So? Since when is lying or having a good time illegal?"

Her flippancy made him angry. The sweet, sexy girl he'd been lulled into thinking she was last night was no more. He'd gone out of his way to be nice to her, but now it was time to rethink that strategy.

"You have no proof I stole your ring—none at all." Her voice was shaking, just a bit. "I didn't steal anything, and you can't bully me into saying I did."

"Faith," called Dina, from the kitchen. "I think you need to see this." The TV volume went up. "Your friend here is on the TV."

Distracted, she glanced toward the kitchen.

"Look, Mommy!" Her little boy ran into the living room, going straight to the television and turning it on.

Dina bustled in right behind him, snatching up the remote. "Channel 8 News," she said, shooting Finn an awestruck glance.

Sure enough, there was the woman reporter who'd accosted him at the Ritz-Carlton that morning. *"While Mr. Payne denies any involvement in the strange incident on the roof, it is surely no coincidence that something like this occurs while the rock-and-roll Prince of Darkness is himself a guest of the hotel."*

Faith made a choked sound, raising a hand to cover her mouth. Her eyes were glued to the screen.

"Finn Payne is a rock-and-roll legend," the reporter went on, *"well-known for his penchant for the morbid and the macabre."* There was a brief clip from his Highway to Hell tour, where he'd used videos of

flames for a backdrop, and then there was his face on the screen, speaking into the microphone. "I'm an artist," he heard himself say, "who sometimes finds inspiration on the dark side." The camera cut away, back to what's-her-face. *"An homage from a group of fans, perhaps, or a publicity stunt gone awry? Either way, the implications are chilling."*

"Chilling?" Dina turned her questioning gaze on Finn. "What's she talking about? What's going on?" She glanced toward her friend. "Faith, you okay?"

Faith was still pale, but composed. "I'm fine—why wouldn't I be?" she asked, resting both hands on her son's shoulders and giving Dina a significant look over his head.

Dina took the hint, but the glance she gave Finn wasn't quite as friendly as before.

"Reporters," Finn said to her, with a wry smile and a shrug. "Always looking for a story."

"What's rock and roll mean?" Nathan twisted his head to look up at his mom, and it was then Finn noticed that an area on the back of his head had been shaved. At the base of his skull was a thin red scar.

"Music," said Finn, before Faith could answer. "Rock and roll is music. Lots of guitar and drums."

"Oh." The kid looked him in the eye. He was

cute—brown-haired and brown-eyed, just like his mom. "Like Michael Jackson?"

He bit back a smile. "Yeah, like Michael Jackson, although I don't get compared to him too often."

"Do *you* play the guitar?"

"I do—" he answered, but Faith interrupted him.

"Go back into the kitchen, Nathan," Faith said to him gently, "I'll be right there."

"You promised to take me to the park today, Mommy," the boy said, with a shy glance toward Finn. "Don't forget."

"Don't start pestering your mama about the park already," Dina scolded. "Mommy worked all night last night. She's tired. I'll take you this afternoon."

Faith shook her head. "No, Dina, you've done enough. Go home and take a shower." To the boy she said, "We'll talk about what we're going to do today later. If you're through with your breakfast, then go get dressed."

Nathan shot Finn another glance. "Is he coming to the park with us?"

"No," Faith answered shortly. "He's leaving now." She shot him a wary glare, the cornered kitten replaced by a lioness, protecting her cub.

Finn, however, was not afraid of lions.

"I'd love to come to the park," he said to Nathan, with his best grin. Giving the boy a conspiratorial wink, he added, "Do you like to play softball? I have a bat and a couple of gloves in the car."

Nathan's face lit up, and though Finn felt a twinge of guilt at the lie, he didn't let it bother him.

The boy was the key, he was certain of it.

Chapter Thirteen

"Master, you must come." Nyx stepped from the shadows, bowing low.

"Must I?" Samael asked idly, swirling the water of his bath without opening his eyes. His head rested between the breasts of a voluptuous water sprite, cat-eyed and green-haired, who bared pointed teeth at Nyx's intrusion. "Has Hell finally frozen over?"

Nyx lowered his eyes. "Apologies, my lord. The imps are causing trouble."

"The imps are always causing trouble." A frown of irritation appeared on Sammy's brow. "They're imps."

"They're inciting the ethereals, my lord. Storm clouds are gathering."

"Damnation," Sammy roared, thrashing himself upright. His anger frightened the sprite, who shrank away, hissing. In an instant, she'd slipped beneath the bathwater and was gone. "Do you not lead my army of demons?" Satan demanded angrily. "Are you not my second-in-command?"

Nyx drew himself up, wings poised for extension. "I am," he stated proudly. "Tell me what you would have me do, Great Shaitan, and I will do it."

Samael stared angrily at him for a moment, and then his anger seemed to subside. "Oh Nyx," he said ruefully, "would that everyone I dealt with were so obedient."

The demon preened beneath his praise, eyes glowing red with pleasure.

"Fetch Thamuz," Samael said shortly, and within moments it was so, Nyx disappearing like smoke, then reappearing with a struggling imp clutched tightly in the talons of one hand.

"Let go of me, you filthy soul-eater!" the imp squealed, ashy gray arms and legs flailing. Its voice matched its size, which was that of a child. A thin, wizened child, leathery with soot.

Nyx released him disdainfully, with a shove toward the man in the bath.

The imp froze at the sight of Samael, who regarded him coldly.

"I understand your people have been causing trouble, Thamuz," he said, in a voice tinged with ice. "Care to enlighten me as to the problem?"

The imp's knobby knees quite literally began to shake. "I . . . I know of no problem, Your Eminence," it squeaked, voice shaking as well.

"Do you remember what I did to you the last time you lied to me, Thamuz?"

Bulbous eyes blinked rapidly in fear. "It's Selene, O Great One," it blurted. "My people enjoyed working with her, and many find themselves with nothing to do now that she's gone." The imp swallowed, its face gone a nastier shade of gray. "She provided a great many opportunities for us," it babbled sickly, lifting long-fingered hands in a shrug.

"Can you not find your own 'opportunities'?" The water in the tub began to bubble and steam, reacting to the force of Samael's anger. "I created you to breed your own amusements, not wait for them to be handed to you like sweets to children."

Thamuz bowed his head.

"Tell him everything, carrion eater," growled Nyx. "Now."

Sammy cocked an eyebrow, waiting.

"There are rumors," blurted Thamuz in a rush.

"But I would not trouble the Dark Lord's ears with such nonsense."

"Go ahead," the Dark Lord said mildly. "Trouble me."

The imp seemed to shrink, wrapping its knobby arms around itself. "I myself give it no credence, of course, but there are whispers that you are no longer"—Thamuz closed his bulging eyes and cringed, as though expecting a blow—"quite as committed to the welfare of your people as you once were."

Sammy looked at Nyx, who shook his head, mutely denying anything to do with such rumors.

"Don't be ridiculous," Samael snapped at the imp. "Who would dare claim such a thing?"

"Not I, my lord. We heard it through the ethereals—those who roam the skies with Ashtaroth, Demon of Darkness."

"Did you now?" The water in the tub steamed and bubbled, the only sound in the otherwise deathly quiet chamber. "I'm told that *you* are the ones inciting the ethereals, and yet you claim it to be their fault. Who shall I believe, I wonder?"

"We didn't start it, Great Master, I swear!" Thamuz's voice had risen to a squeak. He kept his eyes on the marbled floor, small body shaking.

A low growl came from Nyx. "There is more, Satanic Majesty. This piece of beetle dung has not told you the half of it."

In a flash, Thamuz turned and bared sharp teeth toward the tall shadow at his back, hissing like an angry cat. "Speak," Samael said sharply. "Or I will let Nyx do as he wills. He likes nothing more than to eat imps like you for breakfast."

Nyx bared teeth of his own, black and pointed.

Thamuz turned back toward the tub, his flash of anger quickly defused by his craven nature. "It was not our fault, O Great One," he whined. "The boy is slippery, and hard to control, but we will get him back."

"Boy?" Sammy cocked an eyebrow, puzzled. "What boy?"

"The boy Selene gave into our keeping," the imp said, bulbous eyes blinking earnestly. "Your son."

For a moment there was silence, broken by a harsh laugh. "My son? I have no son, and never will." *All these eons, and no woman he'd ever slept with had ever quickened with new life. A by-product of his once angelic—and therefore sterile—state, he supposed.* "And if I did, I would certainly not need you or your kind to keep him safe," he sneered, angry at the imp's presumption.

Thamuz's face, ashen with fear, suffused

slightly with color at the insult. "Of course not, Dread Lord," he said quickly, accepting Sammy's disdain as his due.

"Where is this boy?" Despite the impossibility of his paternity, Sammy was curious. What manner of child was this, to be used as a pawn in yet another of Selene's twisted games?

"Alas, my lord." Thamuz hung his head, voice cracking. "The child escaped his guard . . . we've sent trackers to find him, but they've yet to return." Swallowing hard, he hastened to add, "There's no need to worry . . . the boy is mischievous, and easily bored; it's just a game to him, a challenge . . . He's run off before, but we've always been able to find him and bring him back."

"I'm disappointed in you, Thamuz." Samael leaned back, resting against the cushions the water sprite had dampened. "Your people seem to have grown not only weak, but delusional under your guidance. How could you possibly believe that this troublesome child has anything to do with *me*? Selene has played you for a fool, as she has so many others. Perhaps it's time to appoint another lieutenant, one who's not so gullible, and one who can control the spread of ridiculous rumors."

The gray head snapped up, bulbous eyes wide. "No, Master, please!" He fell to his knobby knees on the tiled floor, wringing sooty, long-fingered hands. "The lying bitch . . . no wonder you've banished her! I'll call back the trackers and leave the child to his fate, Most Evil Lord."

"Damn you," Samael snarled, eyeing the imp balefully. "I care nothing about the child—let me hear no more of him! I care only that storm clouds gather within my realm, fueled by false rumors, spread by your people! I won't have it, do you hear?"

Thamuz lowered his knobby head to the tiled floor, abasing himself before the tub. "I hear and obey, Satanic Majesty! I will punish those who spread these lies! I will spear them on the tines of my own pitchfork and roast them on a spit! I can control my people, I swear it!"

"There are many of you," Samael said thoughtfully, his tone all the more dangerous for its softness. "Perhaps too many, each of you willing to gut the other like a fish for the sheer joy of it. Don't make the mistake of thinking that since I've granted you some limited measure of authority, Thamuz, that you're indispensable."

The imp lifted his head to look at him fearfully, his pallor intensifying. The dark circles beneath his eyes stood out like bruises.

"You are my creature!" Sammy's sudden shout

echoed loudly throughout the tiled chamber, now thick with steam. "Do not, for an instant, ever think yourself beyond my reach. The fires of Hell are kept stoked those such as you, but I can just as easily cast you into them. Imps burn quite well, I've learned, particularly when they've been skinned first, inch by inch, with a very blunt blade."

"I am your creature, my lord," Thamuz whispered, lowering his eyes in surrender. "These rumors shall become anathema, and my people will find other ways to apply themselves to mischief. Forgive us."

There was a silence, which Thamuz wisely kept. He quivered with the effort of remaining still, an unnatural state for an imp.

"You must earn my forgiveness," Sammy said crisply. "Go to Ashtaroth, and bid him come to me. Immediately."

"Ashtaroth?" The imp's childish voice broke on the name. "But I have no power over Ashtaroth! The ethereals do as they please."

"True," Sammy agreed mildly, "but their quicksilver nature leaves them open to influence, as well you know. Someone's been whispering lies in Ash's ears, or the ethereals would not be so restless, nor so foolish as to repeat baseless rumors."

He lifted his head to stare sternly at the imp. "The only darkness allowed to roil within Sheol is the darkness I command. The ethereals are under my domain, and you will remind Ashtaroth of that. Go as my emissary, and bid him come to me and state where his true allegiance lies."

Thamuz swallowed, his Adam's apple as knobby as the rest of him. "He is unpredictable, Master," he whined, "and he is hungry. He will kill me for my insolence, smother me in Darkness . . ."

The Lord High Prince of the Underworld shrugged. "Then so be it. If he kills you for your insolence it will be only what you deserve, and I will send another in your place. And another, and another . . ." He closed his eyes, leaning his head against the wet cushions with a sigh. "There are many of you," he repeated, "but there is only one of me—do not forget that."

It was two full hours before the Dread Demon of Darkness, called Ashtaroth, answered his summons.

Sammy was waiting, confident he would not be ignored. He'd chosen his most formal of throne rooms for this audience, the one in the center of his temple, the chamber he fondly liked to call his Unholy of Holies. It was grandiose, overwrought even, with plush red velvet on the walls, and huge Swarovski-crystal chandeliers. Thirty-eight columns of pure gold lined the chamber, all of which reflected the light from the glittering crystals above. His throne, solid gold and pillowed in red, sat on a raised dais, and he lounged at his ease in it, calmly watching as dark billows of fog began to roll in from the far side of the room, like smoke preceding a fire. The fog became a coiling, shifting mass, thickening and writhing until its blackness was near absolute. As it thickened, it oozed its way steadily toward the center of the room, where it stopped, as though an invisible wall blocked its progress.

"Mossst High," came a rasping voice from the center of the Darkness. "We are sssssummoned."

"Yes, you are," said Samael, Lord of the Abyss. "And you took your fucking time about it, too."

The blackness before him roiled and boiled, but came no closer. He stared into it steadily, and soon, like flickers within a flame, twisted faces became visible within it, leering from the darkness to gaze at him curiously before they disappeared, to be replaced by others.

"I understand your people have been spreading rumors about me, Ashtaroth. What have you to say for yourself?"

"There are whissspersss that SSSamael the SSSeducer has himssself been ssseduced," rasped the Darkness, "by the humansss he once ssswore to dessstroy."

Sammy's eyes narrowed, sparks of anger threatening to kindle into flame. "You've been listening to Selene, who even now, I assure you, is regretting her weaving of that particular web of lies, and to the imps, who—like the cockroaches they resemble—have the intelligence of insects."

"We have ssseen thisss for oursssselvesss, when you allowed the human female, Nicki Ssstyxxx, to meddle in our affairsss. Losst sssoulsss belong to the Darknesss, but you have let her guide more than one lossst sssoul into the Light."

"You dare question me?" Samael asked, in a deceptively quiet tone. He rose, slowly, to stand before his throne. "You think to mount a challenge, demon? Who released you from the chains that bound you beneath the Valley of Gehenna?"

The Darkness didn't answer.

"Who has kept you alive all these eons, providing you with an endless supply of the broken, the lost, and the damned?"

The faces within the roiling mass of black smoke moved faster now, agitated, as they pressed against and blended with one another, mouths outstretched, eyes wide.

"All those negative feelings of guilt, remorse, and depression, all those hopeless, despairing souls that you need to survive—do you think you have a snowball's chance in Hell of continuing to get them without me? Who will supply them? There is no one more qualified to sow the seeds of discord among humans than I, he who sowed them first. If I choose to let one or two human souls go free in order to serve my own ends, what is that to you?"

"We are legion," rasped the Darkness, "and we are hungry. You do not feed usss asss often asss you onccce did."

"Boo hoo," Samael mocked, completely unconcerned. "You will eat what I give you to eat, whenever I choose to give it."

A hissing, moaning sound came from the blackened, swirling mass called Ashtaroth.

"You would still be bound beneath the earth, ravenous and alone, if it were not for me. Do not forget it."

"True," rasped Ashtaroth. "But we hunger, both for lossst soulsss, and for proof you have not abandoned usss. If what you sssay is true, then ssset the ssseal on your word through blood ss-sacrifice, and give usss the child."

"The child?" Sammy's eyes narrowed to slits. If Ashtaroth knew of his bargain with Faith McFarland, then he was being watched, which he would never tolerate. "What child?"

"The child who essscaped the impsss, and now hidesss within the Canyonsss of Dessspair. It isss sssaid he isss your ssson, protected and ssssheltered amid the ssshadows."

The Lord of the Abyss laughed, but it was a bitter laugh. "A lie, begun by your dear friend Selene, and spread by the clacking tongues of the imps. The very idea that a child of mine exists is ridiculous, as is the idea that anything could possibly be alive and sheltered within the Canyons of Despair, for it is the abode of the Basilisk." His smile was thin, and very cold. "If such a child existed, he's long dead by now. If his soul still wanders within the canyons, you are welcome to it."

Crossing his arms, he took a step toward the wall of Darkness. "I give you a final word of warning, demon: Be careful of listening to whispers, lest I be tempted to teach you a lesson. I am the only link between your world and that of humankind." He shook his head, glaring at the entity. "You should know by now that I have no love for mortals. They are foolish, and vain—their ridiculous penchant for virtue must be kept in check, lest it overrun the world like a sickness. I am all that stands between the darkness and the light . . . anger me, and I could easily step aside, let the Lightbringers win." He shrugged, turning to stroll back to his throne, where he seated himself. "I make no bones about enjoying the warmth of human flesh from time to time—as I did with Nicki Styx—but do not endanger your existence by thinking me weak."

The Dark boiled before his eyes, seething and twisting. A tinkling of crystal came from the chandeliers above, evidence of the coiled power within the room, and then just as suddenly, stopped. The eddying billows of black, oily smoke began to slow, and quiet, subsiding to ripples, as though the beast within were a chained leviathan beneath the surface of the deep.

"Forgive usss, Infernal Majesssty," came the rasp of a thousand voices, "we are your ssslavesss."

Chapter Fourteen

"Go and get dressed, Nathan."

Faith made her tone as no-nonsense as possible. She turned her son in the direction of his room and gave him a nudge, never taking her eyes from Finn.

Softball? The man was insane.

"What's the harm?" Finn asked with an innocent grin. "I have some time on my hands today, and I'd love to spend it in the park with you and your son." Turning to Dina, who was standing by, he said, "I don't think we were actually introduced earlier." He put out his hand. "Finn. Finn Payne."

Dina, clearly aware of undercurrents in the

room, shook his hand. "Dina Tate," she answered cautiously. "I live next door."

"Nice to meet you, Dina."

He kept that megawatt smile firmly in place, obviously confident Dina, being female, would prove no match for it, and her increasingly dazzled expression proved him right.

Alarmed at how easily Finn had overcome her friend's defenses, Faith said loudly, "Thank you so much for returning my wallet, Mr. Payne, but we wouldn't want to keep you from anything."

"Mr. Payne?" Finn arched an eyebrow in her direction. "Last night you called me Finn."

Heat flooded her cheeks. Surely he wasn't going to reveal her sexual proclivities in front of her son . . .

"In the gift shop at the Ritz, remember?" He was toying with her, and from the gleam in his eye, he was enjoying it. "Where we met. When you lost your wallet."

Avoiding Dina's knowing gaze, she concentrated instead on getting rid of him.

"Finn," she acknowledged stiffly. "Thank you again, but I'm sure you have a lot to do today. Drive carefully on your way back to Atlanta."

"Let him come with us to the park, Mommy."

Nate tugged at her hand, looking to Finn. "After we play softball, can you teach me how to play the guitar?"

Mortified, she gave Nate another nudge toward his room, more definite this time. "Go and get dressed," she repeated. "We'll talk about it later."

Nathan was a compliant child, and though he made a face, he didn't argue. "Okay." Still clutching his stuffed dog, he went toward the hallway. "But softball would be fun . . . I'll be careful," he added hopefully, over his shoulder. "I promise."

Taking her cue, Dina moved toward the door. "I'll, ah . . . I'll just head on home, then. You guys work it out and let me know about the park, okay?"

"Thanks." Faith shot her a grateful look, wishing she could throw her arms around her and beg her to stay, but knowing she needed privacy to deal with Finn.

"Very nice to meet you," he offered as Dina scooted past.

"Nice to meet you, too." The look she threw Faith told her there would be plenty of questions later.

"It's not going to work," Faith told him flatly, as soon as the door closed. "You can't just waltz in here and charm your way into my life—"

"Why not?" he interrupted. "That's what you did, isn't it?"

She bit her lip, looking away.

"All I want is the ring, Faith." He took a step toward her. "Give it to me, and I'll be gone."

"Please," she whispered, turning away. "I don't want any trouble." She rubbed the back of her neck, not having to pretend the weariness that made her whole body ache. "I didn't steal your ring. Please just go away, and leave me alone."

"You're dabbling with forces you don't understand," he murmured urgently. "I know what you were doing up on the roof. I know all about the pentagram, all about the ritual. You may think that ring is the way to get what you want, but you couldn't be more wrong."

"I don't know anything about the ring," she denied, shaking her head. She didn't, really—all she knew was that the Devil wanted it.

"It's evil," he said flatly. "It has a spirit attached to it; a spirit you'll have no way to control."

"A spirit?" Her mind reeled, but she refused to let it go there. She had to focus, and get Finn out of her house.

And then suddenly, she knew just how to do it.

"You think your ring is possessed?" She tipped

her head, eyeing him speculatively. "Just wait until the media hears about that."

A muscle flexed in his jaw.

"The cops are going to love this story," she said, hating herself with every word, "and so will the reporters. You show up here like a stalker, claiming I stole a ring that's possessed by an evil spirit, on the day you get accused of practicing black magic on the roof of the Ritz-Carlton Atlanta. What would the tabloids pay for the inside scoop on that, I wonder?"

There was a silence in which she refused to look away from those piercing green eyes—so angry, so frustrated.

So undeserving of what she was doing to him.

"So go ahead, call the cops." Inside she was quaking, sick to her stomach, but she stood up straight, crossing her arms across her middle. "Call the cops, because I swear, if you don't get out of my house right now, I'll call them myself."

The look he gave her was ominous. "You should know," he murmured, keeping his voice low, "that I'm a pretty good poker player. Lot of time on the road between concerts." He smiled, but it was a cold smile. "I recognize a bluff when I see one."

Her chin went up, and she looked him squarely

in the eye, refusing to look away until he did. *What she was doing was for Nathan.*

"Luckily for you, I'm not the kind of monster who would ruin a kid's life by letting his mom make a fool of herself in the tabloids, even if she is a lying, scheming, manipulative bitch. You may have won this hand, but the game is far from over," he said, and left.

Shaky, nauseous, and curiously bereft, Faith sank down on the couch and covered her face with her hands.

Damn her to Hell. How dare she look so scared and vulnerable while busy lying through her teeth. How dare she still touch something in him after he knew her for a coldhearted, opportunistic . . .

Finn strode down the driveway, fuming. He heard a woman's laugh, and looked up to see Faith's friend Dina leaning against the car, talking to John, his security guy. The fact that she was still in a robe and pajamas didn't seem to bother her a bit, as she was obviously flirting, and John was obviously enjoying it.

Without a speck of guilt for ruining his friend's fun, he clipped, "John, would you mind waiting for me in the car?"

"I'll, ah . . . sure," he answered, moving reluctantly to do as he was asked. "Nice talking to you."

"Name's Dina," she supplied, "and it sure was." Definitely flirting, pink robe, fuzzy slippers, and all.

John's grin was ear to ear until he saw the look on Finn's face. He got in the car and shut the door without another word.

"May I ask you something?"

"Depends." Dina gave him a wary look.

"What's wrong with Faith's son?"

She pressed her lips together, saying nothing.

"I saw the back of his head," Finn stated, impatient. "I saw the scar."

She sighed, and looked away. "You should ask Faith about that."

"I'm asking you."

She passed a hand over her face, lower lip trembling. She hesitated, then said, "Nate has brain cancer. He had surgery last month."

Of course.

"I'm sorry to hear it," he said, pushing back any thoughts of sympathy. She'd lied to him, over and over. "Does she need money?"

Dina looked at him like he was crazy. "Of course she needs money. She's a single mom with a sick kid to raise." Shaking her head, she added,

"But don't be getting any ideas in that department; Faith ain't the kind to take handouts. I've tried to help her out before, but she won't have it." She shrugged, shaking her head. "That's why I babysit for her—so she don't have to pay for it."

"I can help her," he said. He was gambling that Dina seemed like a person who could smell bullshit a thousand miles away, so it would be better not to spread any. "Tell her to do the right thing, and I'll make it worth her while."

Dina frowned, cocking her head. "The right thing?"

"She took something from me, and I want it back. I'll pay for it."

Shifting her hands to her fuzzy pink hips, Dina eyed him balefully. "You sure you got the right girl? Faith isn't like that."

Oddly enough, he wanted to believe her, and held her gaze, trying to decide if she was telling the truth. "Maybe you don't know her as well as you think."

Her eyebrows went sky high. "I've known Faith for almost six years, and she is *not* a thief." Something flitted across her face, but was quickly gone. "She told me this morning she was in trouble, and if that's so, I'm willing to bet you're at the heart of it."

Finn blinked at her directness.

"You're the first guy she's been with in a long time," she told him bluntly. "I know you're a big star and all that, but she's just a small-town Georgia girl with a full-time job and a sick son to raise. You've got nothing to offer her but trouble. It would probably be better if you just moved on down the road."

Nothing to offer her? He was Finn-Fucking-Payne, king of the goddamn rock-and-roll universe; he had more money in the bank than most people could spend in a lifetime. And this young woman, a total stranger who lived in a crackerbox duplex in Marietta, Georgia, was telling him he had nothing to offer.

Finn sighed, and looked away.

Sad thing was, she was probably right. He had nothing but his money and his music, and if he didn't get the ring back, he'd have neither.

"Ask her about what happened on the roof this morning. And while you're at it, remind her that stealing is stealing, whatever the reason." He opened the car door, ready to get in. "Ask her if whatever she's doing is worth selling her soul for."

She glared at him, all earlier friendliness gone.

John leaned across the front seat to make eye contact with Dina, obviously having overheard bits of their conversation. "Finn just wants her to do the right thing, that's all. He's missing a ring—"

"A ring?" Dina's expression turned scornful. "Faith wouldn't steal nobody's ring." She shot both men a look of disgust. "She's got enough on her plate right now—she's not going to risk going to jail over some celebrity pretty boy's ring."

Celebrity pretty boy. That's what he was, wasn't he?

"If she had some fun with you last night, all well and good, but if she don't want to see you today she must have a good reason for it." She stepped back, ready to dismiss him. "You guys get on out of here."

"Look, we came all the way out here without involving the cops," John said to her hastily. "Finn's tried talking to her, and now we're asking you to talk to her," he urged. "All he wants is the ring back."

Dina pressed her lips together, staring at John, who nodded encouragingly.

"I'm not the enemy," Finn said to her quietly, but didn't know how to elaborate.

There was a silence between them, in which she searched his eyes for the truth of his statement, and apparently found it.

"You really think she took it."

"I do."

"You care about her at all?"

"Enough that I don't want to see her go to jail."

"That's it?"

He said nothing, letting his silence speak for itself.

She stared at him. "Just as well," she murmured. "You'd have broken her heart."

He shrugged. "Maybe she'd have broken mine."

An eyebrow quirked, and for the first time, she smiled.

"Maybe she would've, at that." She turned away, heading up the walk. "Probably do you good to be taken down a peg or two."

Chapter Fifteen

"I don't care what he said, Dina, it isn't true." Faith shook her head stubbornly, keeping her eyes on Nathan as he played on the swings. The afternoon sun was warm, and she was on high alert, yet still so tired . . . the fitful napping she'd done on the couch while Nate watched cartoons earlier wasn't nearly enough. "Yes, I got carried away last night and did something I shouldn't," she agreed, "but it was purely physical, very spur-of-the-moment. I didn't take his ring. As far as all that talk about whatever was going on up on the roof, I don't know anything about it."

No way was she going to involve Dina in any of this. All she had to do was wait until tonight, until Nate fell asleep, to call up Satan and get rid of the ring. Then everything would be back to normal.

Only better, because Nathan would be healthy again.

Dina sighed, shifting her weight on the bench. "Nobody could blame you for going a little crazy last night, girl . . . that man is *fine.*"

Faith smiled a little, despite herself. Odd how she could admit that, yet still wish she'd never laid eyes on him.

Wish she'd never met him, and never felt his hands, gentle on her skin.

"His driver seemed kind of nice, too," Dina mused. "Lots of muscles."

With a laugh, Faith got up to push her son on the swings. "Just your type," she teased.

"You know it," Dina agreed complacently. "You sure you're okay? It ain't every day a rock star shows up on your doorstep. It'd be okay if you had something more to tell me."

Faith pretended she didn't hear, reaching out to grab the chains on Nathan's swing. "Ready, Superboy?"

"Ready!" he shouted, smiling hugely as she pulled him back as far as she could, and let him go, wishing he could fly like that every day, no worries.

"I think he liked you," Dina said loudly, ignoring the fact that she was being ignored. "I think you liked him, too."

Faith shook her head, giving Nate another push. "It doesn't matter, Dina." Another push, and then another. "It's over."

"Okay." Dina closed her eyes and leaned back on the bench, basking in the sun. "Whatever you say."

A moment or two later, her cell phone rang. Wishing she'd left it at home, she ignored it, knowing it would go to voice mail. A minute later, it rang again, causing Dina to raise her head and give her a questioning look. She ignored that, too, but when it rang a third time in as many minutes she knew she was going to have to answer it or turn it off.

"It don't *sound* like it's over," teased Dina, from the bench.

Faith gave Nate a final push and then stepped back from the swings. "I've gotta get this, baby," she told him, "it could be work."

Nervously she turned away from Dina, pulling the phone from her pocket to check the caller ID. The number was unfamiliar, and she was tempted again to leave it unanswered, but followed up her earlier bravado with Dina and defiantly pressed the RECEIVE button.

"Hello?"

When a man's voice—all too familiar—said, "I know what you did last night," she nearly dropped the phone.

"Mr. Morales?" she asked, recognizing the accent, and the sneering tone, in an instant.

"Your boyfriend came to the front desk looking for you this morning," her boss said smugly. "I think you have some explaining to do."

She closed her eyes, refusing to go into panic mode. "Excuse me?"

"You know what I'm talking about." Herve's voice turned hard. "I checked with everyone, and no one saw you anywhere in the hotel after you showed Mr. High and Mighty Rock Star to his suite. The front desk was empty this morning when the next shift came on, and you never even bothered to clock out."

Shit. How could she have forgotten about the time clock?

"Well," he asked impatiently, "do you have anything to say for yourself?"

"I—"

"You know I could fire you over this, don't you?" He sounded way too happy at the prospect. "I understand your son is ill. What would you do for health insurance then, hm?"

She literally *felt* the blood drain from her face.

In the background, children were laughing, Nathan among them. "Mr. Morales, please, I can explain—"

"I'll bet you can," he said, in an oily tone that made her skin crawl. "But I'd prefer you do it in person. Your next shift is when, Monday night?"

Blinking back tears, she nodded, then realized he couldn't see it. "Yes," she said, keeping her voice steady with an effort.

"Good. Monday nights are always slow. You can come into my office and put that pretty little mouth of yours to good use. Ten-thirty, shall we say?"

She bit her lip on the impulse to tell the nasty creep what he could do with his job, his office, and his hateful, sneering words.

"Do we understand one another, Miss McFarland?"

Unfortunately she understood him far too well, the scumbag.

"Unless you'd prefer I start the termination paperwork right now, of course."

"No," she said hastily, willing herself to calm. By Monday night she'd know whether Nathan was going to live or die, and the biggest part of her ongoing nightmare would be over. "Ten-thirty, Monday night. I . . . I'll be there."

All she had to do was keep Herve pacified until Monday night. Once she found out Nate was healthy, she'd no longer be at anyone's mercy, and she'd be free to find another job.

And if she found out differently, nothing was going to matter anyway.

Six hours later Faith was exhausted, damp from getting splashed during Nathan's bath, stuffed with chicken nuggets that neither of them should've eaten, and busy reading *Cat in the Hat* for the umpteenth time.

"Mommy?" Nathan interrupted the tale of Thing One and Thing Two by asking a question. "What's a rock star?"

Faith's heart plummeted. She'd hoped he'd forget about Finn's unexpected visit; she'd certainly been trying to. "That's, ah . . . that's a person who's famous because of their music," she answered, as honestly as possible. No question who Nathan was asking about, and she was too tired to dodge.

"Oh." Nathan flipped the page backward a time or two, tracing a hand over the pictures. "He was nice."

She closed her eyes briefly, and spoke the truth. "Yes, he was."

"I like his name." Nate twisted around to peer up at her. "It sounds like a fish."

That made her laugh, just a little. "Like a fish, except with two N's. F-I-N-N." They'd been working on Nathan's reading skills. He loved books, and was eager to read them on his own. In her opinion, he'd be reading at a first-grade level before he was five.

If he lived that long.

A shudder rippled through her.

He turned a page, tracing his fingertip over the increasingly unstable goldfish from the *Cat in the Hat*. "I'm better now, Mommy," he said softly. "You don't have to be so worried about me all the time. I can play softball."

Faith smiled down at brown curls covering her son's head. "We'll play softball tomorrow," she answered. "I promise." She didn't own a glove or a bat, and didn't have the money for them, but in cases like these, that's what credit cards were for.

"You're a girl," he said, a bit dismissively for someone who hadn't played much softball. "You throw like a girl."

"Hey!" she protested, but only halfheartedly. She *did* throw like a girl. While she prided herself on many things, sports was not one of them.

She resettled Nathan against her, kissed him

briskly, and went back to reading *Cat in the Hat*. It wasn't much longer before his head started to droop; he'd been up late watching TV with Dina the night before, and the afternoon at the park had worn him out. When he fell asleep, head pillowed on her arm, she wanted more than anything in the world to join him, but knew she couldn't.

She had miles to go before she slept.

Easing from the bed, she put the book on the bedside table and covered him with the blanket, letting her eyes linger on his face—so perfect, so small. Before she turned out the light, she picked up his favorite stuffed dog and tucked it in next to him; he grabbed it and pulled it close, never waking.

Then she picked up her shoes from the floor beside the bed and crept from the room, checking him one more time by the gleam of the nightlight before closing the door. She stood there a few seconds, resting her head against the doorjamb, gathering her nerve. *Could she do it?*

She had to do it.

Slipping on her tennis shoes, she went into her bedroom and got down on her knees beside the bed. The thought entered her mind briefly that she should pray—ask God to help her, throw herself on His mercy as she had so many times when she was a child. But she was no longer a child, and God's mercy had done her no good when her mother died, or when Jason left, or when Nathan got brain cancer. Instead she bent and reached beneath the bed to get the grocery bag she'd stashed there earlier in the day. Inside was a box of white candles, a lighter, a loaf of bread, a bag of flour, and a bag of salt. Next to it lay the black book the Devil had given her. Missing the most important ingredient, she took everything to the back door, and went outside into the darkness.

There was quick rustling in the azalea bushes— a mouse or a snake—and a dog barking in the distance. The moon shone high and round, and after a moment on the back steps, Faith's eyes adjusted. There was Nathan's swing set, over by the pecan tree. Beneath the tree, in a spot marked by a flower pot, was the ring, wrapped in tinfoil to keep it clean. She dug it up by hand, breathing a sigh of relief when she found it just as she'd left it.

Casting a guilty glance over her shoulder, she could see lights inside Dina's house, and knew her friend was still up, watching TV. It was risky to do what she was about to do in the open, but she didn't want to do it anywhere *near* Nathan, so the concrete slab on the other side of the garden shed would have to do. It wasn't a high place, but it was hidden, and could be hosed down when she was finished.

She rounded the shed and nearly tripped over Nate's bicycle, which she hadn't let him ride since his surgery.

Could she really do this? Could she really sell her own soul to save her child's life?

Dashing away unwanted tears, she never saw or heard the figure that crept up behind her. A hand over her mouth, an arm like a steel band around her middle, and a sour, sulphurous odor like that of brimstone . . . those were the last things she knew before spiraling into darkness.

Chapter Sixteen

Finn stared at her as she slept. Her son looked very much like her; same hair, same fine-boned features. The boy was turned toward her, even in sleep. He was wrapped in his own blanket, and clutching a stuffed dog.

"You're sure you didn't use too much?" he murmured to John. "It's been almost five hours. They didn't even wake up during the boat ride to the island."

"They're fine," John assured him. "Just a teeny bit of ether for her, a fraction of that for the boy. I checked their heart rate and their blood pressure every fifteen minutes—you saw me." He looked up from his magazine. "Don't worry . . . kids this age can sleep through anything. Once they're down, it takes a bomb to wake them up."

Finn frowned, still staring. He'd had to make a choice, and he'd made it, but that didn't mean he liked it. It went against his very nature to put a kid at risk—particularly a kid as fragile—and as cute—as this one.

"I was a medic in the corps," John reminded his boss gently. "I know what I'm doing."

Just then, Faith took a deep breath, beginning to stir.

"Question is," John murmured, rising from his chair beside the bed, "whether you do." He didn't wait for an answer, leaving the room and closing the door softly behind him.

Finn sighed and ran a hand through his hair, knowing that what he was doing was absolutely, positively, certifiably insane, but damned if he knew what to do differently.

Damned if you do and damned if you don't, he thought, and smiled grimly at the irony.

He was still smiling when Faith opened her eyes, and for a moment—just a moment—she smiled back at him with a look of such joyous wonder on her face that his heart clenched. Then the look was replaced by one of horror, and his heart gave a thud of disappointment.

"Shh . . ." he said, raising a finger. "Don't scream. You'll scare your son."

He had to give her credit—she kept her cool. Breathing fast, she looked at the boy sleeping next to her, then back at him, terrified and wary.

"He's fine," Finn whispered, "only sleeping. No reason to scare him. No one's going to hurt him, or you, I swear."

She sat up, fear replaced by fury. "How dare you touch my son!" she whispered angrily, a hushed hellcat in jeans and a T-shirt, white tennis shoes stained with red Georgia clay. "Where are we?" Her hair was a mess, and she wore almost no makeup, yet the sight of her made his groin tighten. "How did we get here?"

"You're in the British Virgin Islands," he told her calmly, taking the seat John had so recently vacated. "I brought you here on my private jet."

Her jaw dropped. "You did *what*?"

Finn knew it would be easier to just keep talking, so he kept his voice low and told her everything. "You gave me no choice. As soon as it was dark you were going to call up the Devil, and I couldn't let that happen."

Her face, already so pale, went dead white.

"We're old acquaintances, he and I," he said, leaning back in his chair. He met her gaze, unsmiling. "Where do you think this all comes from?" He gestured toward the room they were in; a big bedroom with plush draperies and carpet, heavy teak furniture, fantastically carved and gleaming with polish. "All my talent, all my money, all my fame . . . he gave it to me in return for my soul." Faith said nothing, but he saw her lip tremble. "I know he's offered you your heart's desire in return for the Ring of Chaos, and I"—his eyes flicked to the sleeping boy—"I know your heart's desire." He leaned forward again, resting his elbows on his knees. "Let me offer you an alternative."

He watched her throat as she swallowed, admiring her ability to remain calm. There was no explosion, no high drama, but Finn wasn't fooled; there was a lot going on behind those chocolate brown eyes. She was furious, she was frightened, and if he knew her at all, she was busy thinking of a way to run like hell.

Except this time she had her child with her, and nowhere to go.

"There's a patio on the other side of those curtains," he murmured, with a lift of his chin. "Get cleaned up, and come outside so we can talk in private."

She looked down at the boy, touching his shoulder, adjusting his blanket. "I'm not leaving him."

Finn stood, dismissing her statement as an excuse. "I've told you, no one here would hurt a hair on his head. He's only here because you are."

She stroked Nathan's hair, and her touch roused him enough that he took a deep breath, turning on his side. He tucked the stuffed dog beneath his chin and went right back to sleep.

"There's a bathroom through that doorway." Finn turned away from the look of tenderness on her face. *She'd been tender to him once.* "Join me outside when you're ready."

Before stepping through the curtains, he made sure to squash any unrealistic hopes she might have had. "There's nowhere to go, Faith, nowhere to run. I've taken the book and your supplies. It's one o'clock in the morning in the middle of nowhere, and no one here is going to help you."

The ring was still in her pocket. She couldn't believe it, but there it was, still wadded in tinfoil. They'd taken her bag, but they obviously hadn't searched her pockets, which made Faith feel marginally better, until she realized once again that she and Nathan had been *kidnapped*, and a part of her had been secretly hoping to be rid of the damn thing.

"Oh my God," she moaned, staring at herself

in the bathroom mirror and not liking what she saw. A crazy person; wild-eyed, frantic, and in dire need of a brush. Her toiletry bag was by the sink, and in it were her things: brush, toothbrush, makeup—pretty much the contents of her bathroom counter. Furious as she was at the thought of someone in her house, actually handling her possessions, she was relieved to have her own stuff—anything familiar was good right now.

What was she going to do?

She splashed her face with water and took a few deep breaths, but it wasn't until she began to brush her hair that her mind began to work again.

Finn seemed to know everything. What if she threw herself on his mercy, begged for Nathan's life? Was there a real person inside that rock-star exterior? He had everything . . . how badly could he possibly need one ring?

And yet Satan had warned her not to ask him for it—to seduce the man and steal the ring—but she'd already done that, so would it be breaking the terms of the bargain to ask for it *now*?

Faith moaned to herself again, brain hurting. She had until Monday morning to fulfill her end of the bargain, which left her tonight and tomorrow night to perform the summoning ceremony.

Tonight was going to be a wasted opportunity, just like last night, unless she could talk Finn into letting her get the nightmare over with.

Nathan was still sleeping, and she couldn't resist checking on him again as she went past the bed. He was fine, breathing deeply, twitching like a puppy as he dreamed, and hogging the bed just like he did at home.

The curtains were raw silk, nubby beneath her fingers, and behind them were French doors, leading out to a moonlit patio. There was Finn, sitting in a lounge chair, staring up at the night sky. She took a deep breath and stepped outside, and he turned his head so their eyes met. The scent of the sea washed over her, and somewhere out in the darkness, the crash of waves sounded like faraway cannon.

"You look better," he said. "Come and sit down. Have something to drink." There was an ice bucket on a table next to him, holding chilled bottles of water. He opened one for her and held it out.

"You have to let us go," she said. "Please."

Finn said nothing, merely gesturing for her to take the bottle.

So she did, in large part because she had little

choice. She was exhausted, vulnerable, and in the middle of nowhere, so she took it, sat down, and drank.

"Nathan seems like a nice kid," he said thoughtfully, after she'd had a few swallows. "I'm very sorry to hear about his cancer."

Against her will, her eyes filled up with tears. She dashed them away, refusing to let her tenuous hold on her emotions slip.

"Thank you," she managed, not caring how he knew. "That's why you have to let us go—he has an appointment at the radiologist Monday morning."

"I can help you with Nathan," he said. "I can get him all the care he needs."

Incredulous now, she stared at him. "You don't even know us." She was doing everything she could for Nathan, and then some. The idea that she wasn't made her defensive, and the idea that she'd entrust his care to a stranger was ludicrous. "He *is* getting all the care he needs, or at least he was, until you stole him right out of his bed! You were crazy to bring him here; he could've been hurt, you could've bumped his head! He's on medication—"

"Steroids to reduce swelling," he interrupted. "Least invasive form of treatment for brain stem glioma. I have a copy of his entire medical history."

"That's confidential," she said stupidly, stunned he'd invaded her privacy to such an extent.

He looked away, staring toward the sea while she blinked back tears of worry and frustration. "It's amazing how little patient confidentiality matters when there's money involved."

His jaded tone sparked her temper. "What am I supposed to tell him when he wakes up in a strange place?" she demanded. "Did you think about that?"

"Tell him you're on vacation." Finn turned back to her with a shrug. "The island is beautiful. Take him down to the beach in the morning and let him play in the sand. Let him be a kid."

Now she was the one to look away, furious he was able to so calmly rearrange her life. "On vacation," she repeated. "With you."

"Why so hostile?" he asked her curiously. "I thought we had a connection last night. Did I do something during the course of the evening to offend you?"

Last night? Had it been only twenty-four hours ago that they'd lain naked in each other's arms, breathed each other's breath, touched each other's skin?

"I'm sorry," she replied, looking down at the flagstones beneath her feet. "But surely you know by now that last night was just a means to an end." She risked a glance at his face, shadowy in the moonlight. "And I can't say I'm too thrilled with the way you've behaved since."

He gave a snort of disbelief. "The way *I've* behaved? You lied to me, stole from me, threw salt in my eyes, and tossed me out of your house."

"I might not have done some of those things if you'd just left me alone," she said hotly, knowing she was wrong to blame him for any of it.

"That's bullshit and you know it," he said calmly.

"You abducted us!" she spat, in a loud whisper. "I'd say that tops whatever I did!"

He shook his head. "I could've called the police right from the beginning, but I didn't, and do you know why?"

She looked away, taking another sip of her water.

"Because you told me about your life, and about your son, and I didn't want to get you in trouble at your job."

Turning her head, she tried to see his eyes, but they were in shadow. "Even after I figured out what you were up to on the roof"—his voice hardened—"I didn't go to the cops, sure that if I explained to you about the ring you'd do the right thing." A breeze set the shadows dancing over his face, rustling through the palms surrounding the patio. "But you were dead set on your deal with the Devil, and I had to wonder why—what was so important that you'd risk selling your soul for it?" He leaned forward, so she could see him fully, in the light. "And then I saw Nathan, and I knew."

There was a pause. "I don't blame you, either, if it comes to that—if I had a child—I'd do whatever it took to save him."

Faith blinked, not sure where this was going. Why was he being so understanding? He'd kidnapped them, for God's sake—

"He told you he'd heal Nathan if you got him the ring, didn't he?"

She nodded, unable to deny it.

"There's a reason he's called the Father of Lies, Faith. He lays out a deal that makes you believe he's the only way out, but there's always another way out."

"And you know this how?" she asked him coldly. "You've told me twice now that you and he are old friends, so why should I believe a word you say?"

"Fair question," he answered softly, leaning back in his seat. "You'll just have to trust me, I guess."

There was a silence between them, filled with only the rustle of the wind in the palms and the faint *boom* of the ocean.

"If you give me the ring back," he said, "I'll pay for whatever medical treatment Nathan needs— no matter how many specialists, tests, or special treatments it takes. I did some research, and there are some promising new types of treatment being tested at a clinic in Switzerland . . ."

"Clinical trials?" she interrupted softly. "My son is not a guinea pig."

"But it's okay for him to be used as a pawn?"

"Of course not."

"Then don't let him be. Take him out of the equation." Finn rose, pacing to the edge of the patio, where he stood, looking out into the darkness. "You're *assuming* the Devil will deliver on his promise to get rid of your son's cancer. He might, but whatever happens, I can guarantee the results won't be what you expected." He turned, facing Faith where she sat. "I'm living proof that no matter what you think, the Devil doesn't always keep his promises."

Despite herself, Faith couldn't help but wonder at the grim note in Finn's voice. She looked at him, dark-haired and lean, so self-contained and so damn arrogant. What did he know of desperation, or of the sheer, mindless panic that accompanied the thought of losing a child? He had everything, and she had nothing, and she wasn't going to give up the one slender chance she had to save her son's life.

He met her gaze evenly, letting her take her time with an answer.

"What kind of promise did he make you?" she challenged, genuinely curious. "What's your story?"

Unbelievably he smiled, and once again she saw the diabolically handsome look that had been last night's undoing. "Come for a walk with me on the beach, and I'll tell you."

Chapter Seventeen

Bone of my bone, flesh of my flesh.

Sammy held his hands toward the fire, looking closely at his fingers, the beautifully fashioned, perfect fingers of an angel, created in the image of the One.

He'd just come from the Hall of Mirrors, where he kept track of those who'd been foolish enough to bargain with him. There he'd seen—and reluctantly admired—Finn's latest move, that of using Faith's child to win back the Ring of Chaos. After all these eons, he still found it a bit puzzling, the drastic lengths humans would go to in order to protect their young.

Everything he'd once known of parenthood

had been stripped away in an instant, so long ago that many of the details had grown blurry in his mind. He'd been so sure as a young fledgling, offered the universe, that his Creator would keep him safe, and yet it was the One who'd punished him to eternal damnation.

One hand giveth, and the other taketh away. He flexed both of his carefully, then laid them on the arms of his chair.

His thoughtful sigh drew the attention of his companion, a night black hellhound who lounged at ease on the carpet before the fire. It cocked one of its three heads at him, ears sharply pricked, while the second head yawned, and the third closed its eyes. "It's just you and me tonight, Ajax," he told the hound. "Perhaps we'll go hunting tomorrow, eh, boy? The imp population definitely needs thinning."

The hound opened its jaw in a pleased pant, revealing razor-sharp teeth. Its yellow eyes remained fixed on its master.

"Good boy," Sammy told the dog idly, and took a sip of his wine.

"Do you think it's wise to go after the imps?" A woman's soft voice made him pause, cup halfway to his mouth. "It's not their fault they're easily bored and prone to mischief." She stepped into the firelight, nudging the hellhound aside as she slipped to her knees before him.

"Persephone," he murmured. "My darling bride." They both smiled at the inside joke, for though legend claimed the supposed Goddess of Spring to be his bride, she'd never been more than his lover, nor had she ever wanted to be. A true child of nature, she was fey, elusive, and delightfully amoral. "How've you been, my sweet?" He reached out to stroke her hair, a warm and vibrant shade of gold, and touched the petal-soft, peach-tinted skin of her cheek. She was naked, as she always was when she came to him, her body lush and full, generous in its curves.

"I am well, beloved prince." She took his hand and buried a kiss in it. "Would that you were, too."

"Beloved, or well?" he murmured sardonically, taking another sip of wine. He wasn't surprised to see her, for despite the ancient myth, Persephone was free to come and go in the Underworld as she pleased, regardless of the season.

"Both," she answered softly, transferring her kisses to his bare knee. He was, after all, in his private chamber, where he preferred being naked to being clothed. "You are lonely." A second kiss, this time on the other knee. "You are sad."

Her hands, small and soft, caressed his ankles and massaged his calves, stroking, easing.

"I don't deny it," he replied, knowing it would be useless to do so. One of Persephone's greatest gifts was that of empathy; she was attuned to nuances, and always eager to please. In all the time they'd known each other, she'd never been wrong about his moods, and adapted to them easily: a rough coupling here, a gentler one there, with no aim other than mutual pleasure.

Today she seemed determined to go slowly, stroking her clever little hands up and down his legs, squeezing and rubbing the tension from the long muscles of his thigh. "My poor darling," she breathed, pomegranate-stained lips following her hands, trailing their way upward. "Let me make it better."

And so he did, leaning his head back against his wooden chair and closing his eyes. Her kisses were hot against his skin, her tongue tracing delicate trails all leading to one destination, and by the time she reached it he was hard, and growing harder. She didn't rush, however, nuzzling and licking at the sac that held his balls, breathing deeply of his scent before taking them one at a time into her mouth, rolling them gently upon her tongue as though they were fruit, bursting with juices.

He made a purely male noise of contentment, happy to let his body overrule his brain, and happy to let her take the lead in telling it what to do, at least for the moment.

She took his hardness in her hand, stroking and squeezing, much as she'd done to the muscles of his thigh. Up and down she stroked, rasping and gliding her palm gently along the column of flesh, still lapping at his balls, in no hurry to leave them. His cock jerked and strained as she stroked and squeezed, the sensitive ridge near the tip becoming ever more sensitive. She knew the instant he could stand it no longer, and took him in her mouth, engulfing him in heated pleasure.

Down, down he went, groaning aloud as she began to bob her head to the same rhythm her hand had already established. She sucked and pulled, her lips locked to his engorged member, every ounce of her concentration on him, where it belonged.

The fire crackled, but it was nothing to the inferno that arose inside his mind, the one where no deep thoughts intruded and no decisions needed to be made, save when to release his barren, tainted seed.

Amid the flames flickering against his closed lids, a remembered image appeared. A dark-haired young woman with pink streaks in her hair, regarding him solemnly on a quiet rooftop. She'd put out a hand to touch his bare chest, and in doing so, had seared her name upon his heart.

His groan this time was of frustration, but it merely incited Persephone's talented tongue to work harder. Lust rode him now, and he didn't care if his hands gripped her head too tightly, or if he pushed himself too hard down her throat. She, like everyone else who entered his domain, was under his control, despite the liberties he granted them.

And when he came, in great, spurting bursts of pleasure, he held her there until she'd swallowed every drop. Only then did he allow her to climb naked into his lap, where she curled up like a kitten, licking her lips as though she'd just enjoyed a dish of cream.

"Thank you, my prince," she murmured, tucking her head beneath his chin.

"It was nothing," he replied truthfully, for that's all it was—nothing.

They sat in silence for a while, the crackle of flames and the reddish light they cast providing a small island of peacefulness and comfort amid the surrounding shadows and darkness.

"How's the whelp doing?" Persephone asked idly, trailing a hand across his bare chest.

Sammy stiffened. "The whelp?"

Persephone, sensing his tension, raised her head to look him in the face. What she saw there seemed to puzzle her, for a frown marred her lovely brow. "Don't tell me he's been causing trouble here, too? That's why I sent him to you, you know . . . so you could keep him in line. The child was forever starting fires in the forest and throwing stones at the birds; he's become far too much of a handful for me."

Sammy rose, unceremoniously dumping Persephone from his lap. She hit the stone floor with an exclamation of pain, which he ignored.

"What are you saying?" he asked, his voice low and tight. "What child, and why would you send him to *me*?"

"Because you're his father, of course," Persephone replied, exasperated. She was rubbing her hip, and missed seeing the terrible look that came over her lover's face. "One has only to look at him to know . . . that white-blond hair, those blue eyes . . ." Her voice trailed off as she raised her head again, regarding blue eyes far older, and far colder, than any child's could ever be. "Oh dear," she murmured, stricken.

Sammy kept his anger under control with an effort. "Are you telling me that I—that we—"

"Oh, the wretched little monster!" she interrupted, slapping her palm hard against the floor. "I told him specifically that he was not to explore the Underworld on his own, but was to come here, to you!"

"*Explore?*" he asked, nearly strangling on his own fury. "Don't you think you might have mentioned a word of this child's existence before you turned him loose in Sheol?"

She looked up at him, distracted, through a curtain of golden hair.

"Did I forget to mention him? I'm quite fertile, you know, particularly in the spring and summer . . . there've been so many children through the years that sometimes I forget to inform their fathers—"

Samael's roar of rage brought the three-headed dog leaping to its feet, barking furiously. "You *forget*?"

"I can't help it!" she exclaimed defensively, rising to her feet. "I have a lot on my mind! Nature doesn't run itself, you know! There are seasons to change and plantings to oversee and harvests to safeguard, not to mention dealing with natural disasters like hurricanes and mudslides and volcanic eruptions!"

"You—I—we—"

To her credit, Persephone didn't cower in the face of Sammy's rage, eons of volcanic eruptions perhaps having prepared her for his. "Yes!" she interrupted him, impatiently motioning the still barking hellhound to quiet. "You have a son, who I would've been quite content to raise on my own—as I have the children of so many others through the years. He could have lived happily as a forest sprite, or some other form of elemental, if he hadn't been such a spoiled, headstrong hellion, just like his father!"

In the silence that followed that pronouncement, Sammy found his knees curiously unwilling to hold his weight, and sank back into his chair.

"This is not acceptable." He stared into the red-gold heart of the fire, unwilling to believe what he was being told. "You speak of nature, but only an unnatural mother could be so careless with her offspring." As he said the words, he was forced to acknowledge the well of bitterness from which they sprang. So, too, had he been cast off and ignored; it made him view Persephone through new eyes, and they were no longer eyes that admired.

"You've always known what I am, darling." She shrugged a naked shoulder. "My world is untroubled by conscience. The beauty of a sunrise, the touch of the wind against my skin . . . these are the things that move me. Motherhood is neither a gift nor a burden; it merely *is*."

"Where is he?"

"How should I know?" Persephone asked, tucking wheat gold hair crossly behind her ears. "I saw him to the River Styx myself, and paid that bony excuse for a ferryman to bring him straight to you. I would've brought him in person, but he begged for a boat ride in the dreary old thing, and I was very busy ushering in spring at the time—the cherry blossoms were particularly lovely this year."

"Charon can never leave the river," Sammy answered shortly, his mind working furiously. "The child never arrived."

Persephone looked more annoyed than concerned. "But it's been weeks—months, even! Where could he possibly be?"

"Someplace he shouldn't," Samael answered grimly, damning himself for a fool. He'd heard the rumors, and discounted them as more of Selene's twisted machinations, designed to misdirect his subjects and weaken his authority.

"The incorrigible little beast! I'll take a willow switch to him, I swear it. Do you know where he is? Tell me."

He raked her naked form with a scornful gaze, unaccountably angry. "It's a bit late to worry about discipline now, isn't it? You abandoned the boy on the bank of the River of the Dead, and haven't concerned yourself with his whereabouts since!"

She shrugged. "He's at least nine years old, and quite big for his age. Quite resourceful, too, I might add—crafty as a fox and quick as an eel. He's hardly a babe in the woods."

"No," Samael agreed grimly. "He's a child, lost in the Canyons of Despair, and in all probability, he's already dead."

He rose, snapping his fingers for the dog. Naked, gilded by the fire, he looked down on Persephone from his greater height.

"Leave me," he told her, touching the petal-soft skin of her cheek one final time. "And don't bother coming back."

Then he strode away into the darkness, the hellhound at his heels.

* * *

Less than ten minutes later, Samael stood upon the ancient barge which comprised the whole of Charon's domain, receiving only the nod of a shroud-covered head when he asked about a certain blond-haired, blue-eyed child who'd been seen with Persephone. "So the boy was here, and you took him across, alone?"

It was important to verify Persephone's story. Between the imps and the ethereals, he couldn't afford to be caught off guard again. There'd been enough rumors swirling around the Underworld, and now he needed the truth.

"Has he been back since? Have you ferried anyone to the other shore, anyone at all?"

Charon, mute and impassive as always, shook his shrouded head in the negative.

Ignoring the moaning, weeping shades who cowered on the rotting, coin-covered deck, Sammy impatiently brushed away one who dared come too close. "Which way did he go when he left the barge?"

Charon lifted a bony finger and pointed westward, toward the Forest of Forgetting.

Swearing beneath his breath, Sammy leapt from the barge as soon as it reached the bank, snapping his fingers for the three-headed Ajax, whom he'd brought with him.

"Search out his trail," he ordered the hell-hound. "See if you can find anything that smells like cherry blossoms."

All three canine heads cocked quizzically.

"Flowers," he said shortly, then amended it to "Something that smells like Persephone."

The beast was off in a flash, while Sammy followed at a more sedate pace, wending his way past the blackened stones that lined the River Styx, through the rocks and toward a gray-green forest of stunted, oddly contorted trees.

When he heard a soft rustle of wings behind him, he was not surprised.

"Master?"

"What is it, Nyx?"

"You are disturbed."

"No shit," he answered grimly.

"What's happened?"

Sammy whirled, bringing his second-in-command up short. "Why? Did you hear of something happening?"

Nyx's red eyes flickered in what—in mortal terms—would've passed for a blink. "No, Satanic Majesty. I merely feel your agitation. We have always been attuned . . . I was created from your essence, after all."

Samael the Fallen gave a short bark of laughter. "There seems to be a lot of that going around lately. My condolences." He turned, and resumed walking.

"I don't understand," murmured Nyx, falling in step at his back. "Humor has never been my strong point."

With a sigh, Sammy filled him in on the day's developments, knowing that he would be unable to keep his trusted lieutenant in the dark for long anyway. "The rumors of a child of mine are true," he told Nyx. "He was on his way to see me, when—I suspect—he fell into that she-wolf Selene's clutches. She must've placed him with the imps and told them to keep him close, probably hoping to use him as a weapon against me at some point."

The baying of dogs rose in the distance, and Sammy picked up his pace, knowing Ajax had found the scent. "Clever, clever Selene . . . I'm afraid I may have underestimated her. By telling Thamuz's people that I was the one who wished him kept a secret, she kept him a secret from me as well." He shook his head, hearing the dog's baying grow louder as they entered the Forest of Forgetting. Here a light wind whispered constantly through the misshapen trees, like a million voices in a conversation never meant to be heard. They spoke of dreams and nothingness, of flowing water and endless skies, oblivion and absolution; all lies, of course.

"Forgive me, Master," Nyx said, "but all these eons, all these women . . . there has been none to bear you a son."

"True enough," Sammy returned, following Ajax's excited yelps into a nearby thicket. "But Persephone is no ordinary woman, nor even an ordinary immortal. She is a goddess." He stopped, surveying a clearing surrounded by spiderwebs, stretched between the trees like sticky traps for the unwary. "An amoral, conscienceless creature, much like myself." There was an area where the spiderwebs were broken and torn, an area much the size a nine-year-old boy might have made if he'd stumbled into them.

"I was right," Sammy murmured, half to himself. "This is Selene's handiwork, taught to her by the Weaver." It would be useless to seek out Ariadne and demand an explanation; she would speak of patterns and circles, and leave him to wonder at nothing, as she always did.

"Prepare yourself," he told Nyx crisply. "For we go to the Canyons of Despair."

"Your Infernal Majesty," Nyx replied, in a tone

betraying his trepidation. "That is the realm of the Basilisk."

"Do you think I'm unaware of that?" Samael asked sharply, over his shoulder.

"Of course not," Nyx soothed, "but if the boy went there, he is already dead. Nothing made of flesh can withstand its gaze without being frozen into immobility, easy prey for a creature such as the Basilisk. It is a single-minded hunter, one who kills without hesitation."

"That's all right," Sammy replied, smiling a grim smile as he looked one last time at the broken cobwebs. "So am I."

Chapter Eighteen

Finn was going to seduce Faith, the way she'd seduced him. Not only was there a sort of poetic justice in it, but he couldn't ignore the fact that Faith was a beautiful woman, and that he still wanted her. Why should he deny it? He'd seen how she looked naked, and known every lying, luscious inch of her.

He would again, before the night was over. The breeze, the beach, the moon . . . they were all going to help him get the ring back on his finger, where it belonged.

Holding out a hand to her, he coaxed, "You have nothing to be afraid of. Come on, let's walk on the beach."

He'd had a lot of time to think today, while

she'd been napping on the couch and playing at the park. She'd been under surveillance almost every minute since he'd left her house, and he'd had Bert digging into her past with a fine-tooth comb before they'd even left the driveway. He knew everything there was to know about Faith McFarland, including the fact that she had no family besides her son, and extremely limited resources.

"Let Nathan and me go home." She rose from her chair, ignoring his proffered hand. "If you let us go now, I swear I won't tell anyone what happened. If you don't, sooner or later someone will find us, and when they do, I'll tell them everything. Your career will be ruined."

He laughed at her valiant attempt to play her one remaining card. "I hate to be the one to point this out to you, but it's going to be your word against mine. My people will back me up. You lied to your boss in order to spend last night with me, as several witnesses can verify. Your house is locked up tight, no signs of a robbery or break-in, and your luggage is here. If I claim you came willingly, at my invitation, no one's going to believe otherwise." He cocked his head. "And when you go back to Atlanta, if you make any wild accusations, I'll simply explain to anyone who cares to hear it that we had a fight, and when I asked you to leave, things turned ugly. Do you think the cops are going to believe I'm so hard up for women that I have to kidnap them?"

She pressed her lips together, and he knew, for the time being, that he'd won.

"*When* we go back to Atlanta?" She eyed him suspiciously. "You're going to let us go?"

"Of course. You'll be home by Tuesday."

"Why Tuesday?" A note of pleading entered her voice. "Why not now?"

"Walk with me and find out."

"I don't want to leave Nathan alone," she demurred, glancing worriedly back toward the room.

"He's not alone," Finn said, knowing that both John and his housekeeper, Trina, were hovering over the boy like mother hens, fully aware of what he was doing and completely disapproving of it. He didn't tell Faith that, though, adding only, "He's being monitored through a security camera." Faith would meet Trina soon enough, and he didn't want her knowing she had any allies this early in the game.

The path was clearly marked with gravel and footlights, and he took it, knowing she'd follow. When the palms and plants surrounding him gave way to the wind and sea, gleaming with whitecaps in the moonlight, he stopped, and waited. The water was rough tonight, churning, matching his mood.

She came up to stand beside him, a few feet away, saying nothing.

"It's beautiful, isn't it?" The view was breathtaking during the day, sweepingly dramatic after the sun went down. He'd spent many dark nights walking this beach alone, writing lyrics and music in his head. "Look at the stars, how they go on forever."

He also wanted her to see their isolation—no lights, no bridges, no houses save his. He turned to see her reaction, but had to suppress his own at the sight of her; pale skin gleaming in the moonlight, the wind molding itself to her curves.

She was staring at the sky, and as he watched, she took a deep breath, inhaling the crisp, clean scent of the sea. When she let it out, some of her tension seemed to go with it. "Tell me about your bargain," she said, "and the ring. How did you end up with it?"

He walked on, toward the water's edge, and she followed, pacing him in the sand, a few feet apart.

"I was sixteen," he began, "and very stupid. I wanted to be a rock star, and was willing to do anything to make it happen." He had nothing to lose by telling her the truth, or at least some of it. She was as steeped in darkness as he was, regardless of her motives. "I was obsessed with bands like the Ramones and the Sex Pistols, filled with rebellion and aching for my shot at the big time." Seashells crunched beneath his feet. "I thought I could find it between the pages of an old book I'd found in a thrift store."

He felt her curious gaze on him, but kept walking, into the wind. "Initially I just thought it was someone's old sketch pad, filled with pencil drawings of demons and devils, and I had the vague idea that I could use some of the ideas for designing T-shirts." He smiled at the memory of that long-ago boy, desperate to make money any way he could, particularly if it might help get him where he was going. "But it turned out to be a journal . . ." He hesitated. "A grimoire."

"A grimoire?" She'd obviously never heard the word.

"A Book of Shadows," he said matter-of-factly. "A very old Book of Shadows."

She stopped walking, forcing him to stop, too. "I don't understand."

He faced her, knowing it best to speak plainly. "A book of spells and incantations, one of which was how to call forth a specific demon, and force it to reveal the hiding place of the Ring of Chaos."

She stared at him, but he couldn't see the expression in her eyes in the moonlight, and didn't really want to. "The Ring of Chaos," she repeated skeptically. "Are you a Tolkien fan, because that sounds very *Lord of the Rings*–ish to me."

He smiled, an ironic smile that didn't reach his eyes. "Where do you think Tolkien got the idea? The story is an old one, far older than his. The Ring of Chaos is one of several magical objects supposedly owned by King Solomon, hidden away among his treasures, a secret for thousands of years."

"King Solomon. As in *the* King Solomon." Her tone had turned sour. "The biblical king from the Old Testament."

"That's right." He made no apologies for the fantastical nature of the story. "Didn't you know that good old Sol could constrain demons and force them to perform magical feats? That how the Temple of Solomon was rumored to have been built, on the backs of demons and devils—it was his way of evening the scores between good and evil, forcing those who'd made the mistake of defying God into working for His glory."

"You're serious."

"Solomon was also rumored to have written a

treatise on demonic rituals—an ancient, obscure text called the Key of Solomon, which holds the secrets of demons and magic."

She was shaking her head, pushing windswept hair behind her ears.

"I didn't have the Key, of course, but there were bits and pieces of it within the journal. It took me six months, but I eventually figured out the summoning spell. I spent a lot of time at the library, putting the pieces together, doing my research." The library had always been a refuge—no matter what town they lived in when he was growing up, there'd always been a library. "I thought it was cool . . . a game, a challenge, and when it turned out to be true"—he turned away from her, looking out over the waves—"when it actually *worked*, I could hardly believe it."

The boom of the surf receded as he remembered that night, so long ago, in the basement of an abandoned warehouse where he'd been sleeping. He'd been living rough for about a year at that point, having run away from the dumpy old trailer where his mom and her latest husband lived. There'd been no room for him anyway, and they hadn't seemed to care—no one had come looking for him.

"The Ring of Chaos is possessed by a dark

spirit," he stated frankly, repeating what he'd tried to tell her earlier, back in Atlanta. "A spirit who longs for expression, but is trapped inside an inanimate object. As long as the person who wears it provides an outlet—whether it be art, music, poetry—it will conform itself to its owner's deepest desires, and endow them with a talent, a genius, far beyond what they would've had otherwise." He sighed, staring out over the waves. "As long as Chaos is allowed to express itself, the partnership works, but ultimately, the muse of Chaos is very hard to control. It's overwhelming, all-consuming—and why so many creative types come to a bad end. Van Gogh, Nietzsche, Edgar Allan Poe . . ."

"Wait a minute. You're claiming *they* wore the ring?"

He shrugged. "There's a fine line between genius and madness, and the ring is very old. Who's to know how many people have worn it?"

There was a silence between them, and he let it go on, giving her time to absorb what he'd said. He waited, staring at the surf, mesmerized by how the waves crested into themselves, spilling and tumbling onto the sand, over and over again. "I knew the risks but I didn't care." He hadn't cared about anything except becoming famous, regardless of the cost. "Eventually, I figured out the spell, and called forth the demon of Chaos." *How incredibly stupid he'd been.* "There was no fanfare, no thunder or lightning, no scaly-limbed creatures from Hell. Just a man who stepped from the shadows as though he was made from them." An involuntary shudder ran down his spine at the memory. *Those ice blue eyes, so cold.* "He said he knew where to find the ring, but if I wanted it, I'd have to give him something in return."

Finn no longer heard the crash of the ocean, didn't even see it.

"I—"

"Don't say anything," Finn cut her off sharply. "Let me finish."

It was surprisingly cathartic, for he'd never told the story to anyone. "I promised him my soul in return for the ring. I suppose he hoped I'd break under the pressure as so many others had, go crazy at an early age, drink myself to death, but as long as I wore the ring, my soul was my own." He glanced at her. "By sending you to steal it from me, he's changed the rules of the bargain. Apparently he's no longer willing to wait for my soul." He turned his head, eyeing her speculatively. "And he certainly seems eager to corrupt yours."

She winced, saying nothing.

His story was almost done, and he didn't feel the least bit bad about finishing with a half truth, or minor misconception. "Bottom line, I have until Monday morning to get the ring back, or my life is over."

Chapter Nineteen

"Over?"

The ring lay like a stone in the pocket of her jeans, and suddenly, Faith wished nothing more than to take it out and toss it as far out to sea as she possibly could. He was right, it was evil, and the longer she had it the worse the evil became. Her mind reeled at the story he'd just told her, and if she hadn't seen the very *face* of evil—on two different occasions—she wouldn't have believed him. How could she live with this man's death on her conscience?

She shook her head mutely, horrified by the weight she was expected to carry. The moon shone high over the water, so cold and distant, just like the stars, meaningless glitter in a vast void of darkness. She searched them in vain, desperate for help she knew wasn't going to come. *She'd never asked for any of this—she'd just wanted to raise her son, live her life, maybe meet somebody nice to share it with one day.*

But there would be no fairy-tale ending for her, because her life would be forever marred by blood on her hands. *Finn, or Nathan?* She bowed her head, understanding, for the first time, the lure of oblivion, for there were no decisions to be made when you were dead.

The crash of the waves, the buffeting wind— all become one with the pounding turmoil within her heart as Faith put her face in her hands, and let the tears come.

"Hey, now." Finn slipped an arm around her shoulder. "Don't cry." She hadn't the strength to refuse comfort, and leaned into him, sobbing. His heartbeat was against her cheek, vital, and alive. His arms went around her, firm and strong. She cried harder, envisioning Nathan, ill and silent in the hospital, too weak to lift his head. *What was she going to do?*

"Shhhh," he murmured, holding her close. He rested his cheek on top of her head and rocked her gently, saying nothing more, while the wind and the waves went on about their never-ending, uncaring business.

It was then she admitted, in her secret heart, to the feelings she'd tried so hard to keep at bay. She'd fallen in love with him last night, when he'd teased her over dinner about playing footsies under the table, when he'd kissed her and touched her and drawn from her emotions and feelings she'd forgotten existed. Finn was the one who'd been wronged. She'd lied to him and used him, put his life at risk and driven him to extremes, yet *he* was comforting *her*.

"I'm so sorry," she wept against his chest. He moved his hands to her shoulders, but she wouldn't let him pull away, winding her arms around his waist and keeping her cheek pressed against his shirt. "I never meant to hurt anyone, I never . . ."

His hand slipped beneath her chin, forcing her face upward. "Shh," he said again, gently, and bent his lips to hers.

She could taste the salt of her own tears, thick with guilt. She could feel her breasts against his ribs, the thump of his heartbeat. She opened herself fully to the kiss, knowing she shouldn't but helpless against his tenderness, his strength—the feel of him in her arms. He'd bared his soul, and asked for its return, but she had nothing to give him in that moment except herself.

Within seconds, tenderness was replaced by heat; his mouth slanted over hers, hot, demanding, devouring. She lost herself in an erotic exchange of lips and tongue, moaning deep in her throat at something she'd thought she'd never feel again. Desire unfurled, deep within her belly, blending with the crash of the ocean and the sharp, salty scent of the sea.

She pressed herself hard against him, stroking and touching the lean muscles of his back and waist. The bulge in his jeans was obvious, and she thrilled to the feel of it. More than anything, she ached to take him in her hand, hot and heavy, the way she'd done last night.

She tore her mouth from his long enough to whisper, "Please," not even sure what she pleaded for.

"Please what?" he whispered, breath rasping in her ear.

"Please . . ."

He stopped her reply with his lips, exploring her mouth more leisurely this time, rasping his tongue alongside hers in an erotic duel that would end only in surrender. She gave it, and it was then he pulled back, eyes glittering in the moonlight, and took her by the hand.

"Come with me," he murmured.

She nodded, numb yet burning, and let him lead her back toward the house, thinking only of how strong his fingers felt, wrapped around her own, and how the memories they made this night must last a lifetime.

The night wind cooled her heated cheeks, and whether the heat was from shame or desire, she couldn't tell.

She only knew that no matter what happened tonight, whatever ecstasy they shared, she could never give up the ring, not if there was a chance it could save Nathan.

But in the meantime, she'd show him with her body all the things in her heart, and try her best not to think about tomorrow.

He led her to a side door near the room where Nathan slept, which opened to reveal a beautifully tiled chamber in shades of blue and green, filled with potted plants: tall palms and delicate orchids, exotic bromeliads. Two of the four walls were carved from solid rock, creating a breathtakingly beautiful private grotto, overlooking the sea. A sunken spa steamed and bubbled in the center of the room, and a row of floor-to-ceiling windows, open to the roar of the surf, faced the beach.

"Wow." Dashing the last of her tears from her cheeks, Faith took a good look around and noticed an abundance of candles, already burning. On the tiled edge of the spa sat a tray holding a bucket of champagne and two glasses.

"Pretty sure of yourself, weren't you?" she asked, slanting him a glance. "What if I'd said no?"

He grinned, and gave her a shrug. "My housekeeper knows I like to come here and unwind after I've been on the road, that's all."

She shook her head at the shameless transparency of the lie, but found she didn't mind it. The night had taken on a dreamlike, fantasy aspect in which nothing surprised her. Her fears about Nathan's immediate safety had receded; she believed Finn's claim that no one would hurt him. He'd always been a very sound sleeper, and she doubted he'd wake until morning. That gave her a few hours to spend here, in this private paradise, with Finn.

"You should know"—he leaned in, lips brushing the tip of her ear—"I never use a bathing suit."

She smiled, enjoying the image he conjured. "Of course you don't." Her fingers brushed the front of his jeans, deliberately, and he surged against her hand. "You seem to have a real problem with constraint."

He laughed, and the sound of it made her feel bold, daring, almost happy. Not wanting to think, wanting only to feel, Faith drew back, grabbed the hem of her shirt, and pulled it over her head. Grinning, he did the same, and in moments they'd both toed off their shoes and shucked off their jeans.

"Last one in is a rotten egg," he said teasingly, and strode toward the water, giving her a mere glimpse of his cock, jutting from its nest of dark curls.

Denied that glorious sight, she admired the tight roundness of his ass as he walked away. Hesitating only a moment over whether to remove her bra and panties, she did, having no idea whether she'd have any dry clothes to wear in their place.

Finn lowered himself into the spa until the water was above his waist, then ducked his head beneath the surface. He came up on the other side of the pool just as she reached the steps, wiping the water from his eyes and face. His dark hair, already short, looked just as good wet. "You're beautiful," he said with a warm smile.

Suddenly shy, she held tightly to the metal stair rail as she lowered herself into the warm, bubbling water. It swirled against her knees, her legs, the juncture of her thighs, the curve of her belly. "Mmmm." She dipped her knees so the water reached her chin. "This feels so good." Warm silk against her bare skin, soothing and caressing every hypersensitive inch of it.

"It's one of the main reasons I bought this place." He didn't rush her, staying on his side of the tub, swirling his arms easily through the water. He glided toward the tray and took up the champagne bottle, opening it with a *pop.* "You should see it in the daytime—the view is spectacular."

It sure is, she thought, admiring his back and shoulders. His angel-wing tattoo looked darker when it was wet. Seeing him in this steamy, tropical setting called to mind the Greek god Pan, with his love of music and his naughty penchant for seducing hapless maidens. *All he needed was a pair of horns.* A giggle escaped her as she realized that for once, she was happy to play the role of hapless maiden.

Hearing her giggle, he turned toward her smiling, glass of champagne in hand.

She caught her breath at the picture he presented, wet, naked . . . temptation itself. She'd become a shameless wanton, and she didn't care.

Besides, it wasn't *she,* it was he, and a woman

would have to be dead not to feel wanton in this situation.

She moved toward him, taking the champagne.

"Wait," he said, raising a finger. He picked up the second glass and offered a toast. "To tonight," he said, looking directly into her eyes. "No more talk of bargains or promises, no pressure." His voice lowered to a more intimate level. "Just you"—they clinked glasses—"and me."

Faith rolled the champagne on her tongue before swallowing, wanting to savor each drop and every moment. His eyes, dark green and slumberous, remained on hers over the rim of his flute.

"Do you like my private Eden?" he asked huskily, watching her closely.

"It's magnificent," she acknowledged, but she wasn't talking about the room. She was talking about him, and the paradise she knew she could find in his arms.

He smiled again; she was lost. Completely, utterly lost.

Another sip of champagne, and then another, and then her glass was empty. She didn't protest when he took it from her, setting it beside his on the rim of the spa. She didn't pretend coyness when he took her hand, drawing her to the side of the pool where a tiled bench ran beneath the surface. He sat, pulling her onto his lap, and she gasped at the rough rasp of his thighs beneath her bare bottom.

"I like the way you smell," he murmured, warm mouth to her ear. Easing her back to his chest, he cupped her breasts in his hands, while his cock, hot and hard, pressed against the small of her back. "Like flowers. So fresh and pretty."

She closed her eyes, putting her hands over his, willing herself to think of nothing but the here and now. His body felt so good. The champagne went straight to her head, while blood rushed to her nipples, making them hard.

He squeezed them gently between his knuckles, eliciting a gasp. One hand slid downward, over her belly, smoothing itself over the curls between her legs. She laid her head back against his shoulder and moaned as his fingers brushed the hard little bud he found there. Everywhere her skin touched his she seemed to prickle, forcing her to writhe and twist in his arms, but it was a mock battle, never meant to be won. His breath came hot on her neck as he moved his fingers over her delicate folds, rubbing, stroking, and touching. Catching the lobe of her ear in his teeth, he nipped it gently. Her hair was damp, clinging to her shoulders as she lost herself in sensation.

Finn's hand was doing something to her that was indescribable, and she raised her hands to the back of his head, holding on to him like a lifeline. His rock-hard maleness nudged her between the thighs, and she shifted to allow him easier access, unable to help it.

He slid into her, and then there was no outside world, only bliss. She exploded, her body spasming in intense pleasure. Speared, overwhelmed, and overloaded, she gasped and shuddered, while her mind whirled and spun.

Drowning, she was drowning, and she never wanted it to end.

Chapter Twenty

The Canyons of Despair were well named, for it was a place of emptiness and desolation. Wind-scoured rocks the color of rust, deeply scored with dry gullies, several yards wide and hundreds of feet deep. No life, no movement, only the howl of wind, rising and falling like the moans of a thousand souls, lost in misery and anguish.

Even Sammy, standing on a cliff top looking down over the canyons, felt the hopelessness the sound of the wind evoked. How to find one small boy—or the remains of one—in such a place?

He hadn't let himself think about why he even bothered. If he cared to delve deep enough into his own psyche—which he didn't—he knew it had something to do with the anger he felt over his own fate. The Heavenly Father who had supposedly known and loved him had turned his back and left him to make his own way in the wilderness, and he would not do the same to his own son, even though he'd never laid eyes on him, for to do that would make him no better than the One. There was nothing sentimental or maudlin about his decision; a human would probably be grieving the loss of what might have been, but he was neither human nor divine, and made his own rules.

The boy was merely a loose end, which needed to be tied up.

"Perhaps we should've brought the hellhound," said Nyx, at his shoulder.

Sammy shook his head, his eyes scanning the barren landscape. "The boy lived among the imps. The scent of brimstone would've wiped out any trace of his life above ground, leaving nothing for Ajax to track." He turned his face to the underground sky, sullen and gray with ashen clouds. "Besides, I don't want to lose the hound to the Basilisk."

"Where to begin?" Nyx asked. "Shall I take to the air? The boy's remains could be in any of these gullies."

Sammy ignored the familiar pinprick of jealousy over the fact that his second-in-command could fly, while he could not. "Yes," he answered shortly, "and pay particular attention to areas of shadow. Ashtaroth specifically mentioned the shadows as a hiding place."

He watched as Nyx spread his night black wings and launched himself into the air with one powerful, pistonlike thrust of his legs. In flight, the Soul Eater was a thing of macabre beauty, a silent reaper, a supernatural raptor who glided above the canyons without a sound. *Yea, though I walk through the valley of the shadow of death, I shall fear no evil . . .*

King David was a fool, who obviously knew not of what he spoke. If he'd seen Nyx—wings outspread, eyes glowing—his biblical royal bowels would've turned to water.

Sammy's reflections were interrupted by a familiar little *chirrup* from the rocks to his right. Turning toward the sound, he smiled. "Ichor," he said, "I thought I might find you here."

The yellow lizardlike creature slipped from beneath the shadow of a flat rock, and scurried to his master's feet. Yellow-green eyes, full of reptilian intelligence, peered up at him from the dusty ground.

In an instant Sammy knew what he must do. Let Nyx seek the boy, while he would seek much larger prey, one who knew well how to hunt within these dry and barren canyons. Predators often took their prey to their private lairs, to be consumed at leisure; it was as good a starting place as any.

"Clever little creature, aren't you," Sammy crooned, crouching to scratch Ichor beneath his scaly chin. "Tell me, where would a giant lizard like your cousin the Basilisk be found?"

Ichor *chirruped* an answer, half closing his eyes in bliss at the touch of his master's hand. As Sammy straightened, he roused his lizardly self and scurried away, clearly confident he would be followed.

And followed he was, through a narrow defile between high rocks, across a dry creek bed and over ridges made of stone. The terrain was treacherous, but Sammy welcomed the challenge, his hobnailed boots made for hiking, the physical exertion helping to ease the turmoil in his mind; turmoil he'd been unable to quiet since Persephone's casual mention of a son. The certainty with which he ruled his Underground world had been rocked, and he didn't like the feeling.

With knowledge came power, and he wasn't about to give up one iota of his. He'd find out what had happened to the boy before anyone else did and regain the advantage, and with it, his equilibrium.

Following the agile little lizard, he soon found himself at the opening of a large cave, overhung with stones that looked as though they'd been stacked there by the hand of a giant.

Ichor, at his feet, looked up at him without making a sound, and it was this that warned Sammy that the Basilisk was near. With a flick of his fingers, he dismissed his pet lizard, who vanished beneath a rock as though he'd never been. Then, armed only with his power and his wits, Sammy stepped boldly toward the cave.

"Ho, there!" he shouted, knowing himself safe. "Come out, come out, wherever you are!"

A slithering sound, scales against rock, was his answer. The Basilisk was his own creation, and he'd dealt with it before. An experiment gone slightly awry, if truth were told, for the creature's very nature had been its undoing; its stare rendered its victims completely immobile, and what fun was there in that? He'd created it during the Greek era, when legend and mythos had reigned supreme, but found he preferred to watch his victims squirm on the pyre of their own guilt and evil ambitions, not seek heroic death during some pointless, supposedly glorious adventure. It always ended so predictably: grown men, reduced to helpless deer in the headlights. He'd become bored with the creature long since, loosing it into the canyons a millennium ago and leaving it to its own devices.

Now it slithered its way from the cave like the monster it was: half lizard, half snake, with the fully maned head of a lion. Its face was not feline, but avian, sharp-beaked as an eagle, with the piercing, pitiless eyes of a hawk. Two-legged instead of four, using sharp claws to drag its long, snakelike body forward over the hard-baked ground and out of the cave.

"Long time no see," Sammy said lightly, knowing the creature had no idea what he was saying. "Eaten any small children lately?"

The Basilisk cocked its head, its great golden eyes staring him down. Its beak opened, and raucous sound emerged, somewhere between a squawk and a roar. The coarse hair of its mane stood on end in a fierce display, clearly designed to intimidate.

Knowing himself immune to the hypnotic quality of the beast's gaze, Sammy merely cocked his head in return and stood his ground.

In a flash, the Basilisk lunged, beak snapping.

Twenty yards away from where he'd stood just a second before, Sammy laughed as the beak snapped closed on empty air. "Yoo-hoo," he said, lifting the middle finger of his right hand in an obscene gesture. "I'm over here."

Another raucous croak issued forth from the creature's throat, this time tinged with rage. It gathered its lower body into a snakelike coil, obviously readying itself for another spring.

His plan was to draw the creature away from its den so he could search it without distraction, but the plan was momentarily interrupted as a clatter arose in the rocks above the cave, drawing the beast's attention. Its head swiveled sharply toward the sound, and one of the rocks—much to Sammy's amusement—tumbled down the incline to strike the Basilisk squarely on the head.

It flinched, blinking owlishly, only to flinch again as a second rock hit it, much closer to one of its eyes. A third rock struck it in quick succession, and it was then that Sammy realized that the rocks weren't falling: they were being *thrown*.

"Hey, blondie!" came a shout. "What are you, an idiot? Get the hell away from that thing!"

Sammy, for the second time in less than an hour, found himself at a momentary loss for words.

The Basilisk, hearing the taunting voice, immediately began a pursuit, despite the hail of rocks that were now showering down on it.

"You! Yeah, you! Have you forgotten how to run? Put one foot in front of the other, and do it fast!" The voice was now coming from a different direction, echoing off the high canyon walls. "I can't keep it distracted forever, you know!"

Sammy caught a quick glimpse of movement, high and to his right. A dark head, ducking behind a boulder. "Yo, pretty boy! Move it!" A wiry arm, gray with ash, was outlined against the sky just for a moment, as another rock sailed through the air.

An imp, likely one of the trackers who'd been sent after the boy, and obviously ignorant of the fact that the man he insulted was no ordinary man.

Sammy narrowed his eyes and stayed put, watching as the Basilisk clawed its way lithely up the side of the canyon in pursuit of its rock-throwing prey.

He caught the flash of movement again, and his

suspicions were confirmed by the next shouted insult. "What's it gonna take, meat sack . . . a burning brand up your butt? Get the hell out of here!"

If he'd been in a laughing mood, he would've been amused by the imp's cheekiness. Curse and stones continued to rain down, and as he watched the Basilisk climb, he grew thoughtful—imps were hardly known for their good deeds, and it was a measure of how lax Thamuz's rule had obviously become if one sought to save a stranger from the Basilisk. It should've been cheering the beast on, not drawing it away.

A dark shadow passed overhead; Nyx, scanning the area over which he stood. Sammy knew the instant he saw the imp, for Nyx's eyes glowed a brighter shade of red as he banked, flying in a tight circle. The Basilisk saw nothing except that which it was focused on, which was the small dark-haired form scampering among the rocks, continuing to shout and throw stones.

"Shit for brains!" the imp yelled, and Sammy wasn't certain whether that particular insult was meant for him, or the lizard.

It hardly mattered, though, as with a flick of his wrist and the point of a finger, he sent Nyx plummeting toward the impudent little beast who'd interfered with his plans. A moment later, there was both a startled squeal and an outraged roar as both the imp and the Basilisk registered Nyx's sudden snatch-and-grab. His great black wings flapped as he gained altitude, clutching the struggling imp with both hands, leaving the Basilisk to screech angrily at the unexpected loss of its prey. Obviously unwilling to give up its dinner, and too stupid to know that it would never catch Nyx, it took off in the same direction, and disappeared over a ridge.

Take the imp back to the temple, and chain it, Sammy told Nyx silently, within his mind. *I'll deal with it later.*

He would make an example of it, along with Thamuz. Imps had but one job, which was to torment lost souls, not save them. For that, and for failing to recognize its own master, it would pay.

The Basilisk, its screeching growing farther and farther away, had obviously forgotten him, so Samael the Fallen walked on silent feet into the lizard's den, where he found nothing but ancient armor, rusted swords, and broken lances, remnants of long-ago days and the foolish mortals who'd once owned them. No fresh bones, no bloodstains; the boy wasn't here, and never had been. A few greenish-yellow marks showed where some of Ichor's brethren had met their demise, but nothing to help him in his search for the boy.

Undaunted, he went back outside to resume his search, looking first under the rock where Ichor had disappeared. His old friend was still there, safe in the shade.

"Well?" he asked the lizard. "What of you? Have *you* seen a blond-haired, blue-eyed boy anywhere in these canyons?"

Ichor shook his reptilian head in a clear negative.

Sammy sighed, looking up at the ashen-colored sky, scudded with clouds. It would take Nyx some time to return, so for now he was on his own.

"Gather your people," he told Ichor. "Ask each and every one of them if they've seen any sign of him, and report back to me."

Ichor scurried away to do his bidding as Sammy rose, and began his search anew.

"Damn those imps!" he snarled savagely to Nyx, several hours later. "How could they have lost him?"

The search of the canyons had been fruitless. Now, several hours later, having bathed the dust of the place from his face and body, Samael the Fallen was absolutely furious. He strode up and down the marble floors of the inner temple, having had no luck soothing his temper with any of the objects that normally eased his eye and magnified his powers.

The All-Seeing Eye of Horus saw nothing, the Chalice of Caradoc reflected only the face he saw every day in the mirror, and Stone of Clarity remained opaque.

All these magical treasures, hoarded and used only for his own benefit through the centuries, now benefited him nothing.

"If there is anything left of the boy, Ichor's people will find it," Nyx asserted stoutly. "They will scour every inch of the canyons, including cracks and crevices where we could never fit."

"I should *not* have to rely upon reptiles," Sammy answered tersely, tossing the Stone of Clarity back onto the pile of treasure that filled one corner of the room. "The imps were charged with his care, and even though I knew nothing of Selene's original plan, they failed in their efforts, and have thus failed me. Fetch the one we caught in the canyon."

Heads were going to roll, and he would start with the one who'd dared call him pretty boy.

A few moments later, Nyx reappeared, grasping a struggling, swearing imp. "Think you're tough, do you?" it screeched, doing its best to squirm from Nyx's hold. "You look like a flying monkey from *The Wizard of Oz*, minus the uniform!"

Sammy, who'd seated himself in a golden chair that had once been the throne of an ancient prince of Crete, looked up sharply at that, wondering how in Hades an imp would know anything about modern-day cinema.

"Shut up," he told the imp harshly, unwilling to listen to any more of its screeching. "Abase yourself before me."

The imp, whom Nyx had abruptly released at the sound of Sammy's voice, straightened itself to its full height, which was somewhere in the area of Nyx's waist. Brushing its sooty arms in an exaggerated manner, as though brushing off dirt, it shot the soul eater a nasty look before turning toward the throne.

"Abase this," it said calmly, and made a very rude gesture, directly in the Prince of Darkness's face.

It was then that Sammy saw the imp's eyes; pale blue, almost unnaturally so. The ashy gray skin that should've been leathery and wrinkled was smooth and unlined, and the hair that he'd taken for dark was merely dirty, sooty, and matted with filth.

For a moment—just a moment—his breath caught, though he schooled his face to impassivity.

"Boy," he rasped, in a voice gone suddenly rusty. "What is your name?"

The boy eyed him narrowly, but didn't hesitate.

"Cain," he said. "My name is Cain."

And that, Sammy thought, *is why I saw nothing during my search, for what I sought was merely a reflection of myself.*

Chapter Twenty-one

Laughter woke Finn in the morning. Lifting his head from his pillow, he listened, hearing a little boy's voice drift through the open window.

"Hurry up, Mommy! Look, there's the beach!"

His room was on the second floor, overlooking the garden and the sea. Faith's was on the first, and he'd taken her there himself at three in the morning. The clock by his bed showed 7:45 a.m., so neither of them had been asleep long.

Rolling over, he stretched, smiling at Nathan's excited chatter as it faded—something about a sandcastle.

"Nice sound, isn't it?" A woman's voice made

him jump. "When are you going to have some children of your own? This place could use a little life."

"Trina," he groaned, catching sight of his housekeeper, standing right beside the bed. "How many times have I asked you to knock before you come in?"

"Probably just as many times as I've asked you to sleep with some drawers on," she returned, unruffled. Trina was in her sixties, leathery and tan, her silver hair worn straight and simple, a shorter version of how she'd worn it back in her hippie days. "Now get up and tell me what's going on with our houseguests."

Giving her a baleful look, Finn threw back the sheets and rose from the bed, uncaring if his nakedness made her uncomfortable. She did what she always did, and averted her eyes, but other than that, showed no signs of retreat.

"I told you last night," he said, scooping up his jeans from the floor beside the bed. "It's complicated. Just do whatever needs to be done to keep them fed and happy, while staying as far away from them as possible."

Trina crossed wiry arms over her middle. "Are you kidding me? Did you see that little boy?"

She shook her head, clearly refusing to be put off so easily. "He's been sick—a mother knows these things—and he's adorable, far more adorable than you or your goons, so if I'm expected to choose sides, I choose his. I want to know why you brought them here, and what your intentions are toward his mother."

"My *intentions*?" Finn yanked up his jeans, exasperated. "What is this, an inquisition? You're not *my* mother, you know."

"Thank goodness for that," she answered sharply, "or I'd take you over my knee for acting like such a spoiled brat. You can't just drag women to your lair like a caveman, you know, especially a woman with a small child. You couldn't choose a more vulnerable human being on the face of the planet."

There was a brief stare down, but neither of them was truly angry. It wasn't the first time Trina had tried to run his life, and since she did such a great job of running his house, he forgave her much. She cared about him, and he, her, and damn it all—he knew she was right.

With a sigh, he shook his head. "Everything's going to be fine. There's no need to worry." The troubled look on her face sparked a few feelings of guilt, but he squashed them. "You heard the kid—he's having a great time."

Her face cleared slightly, so he pressed his advantage. "It's just for a couple of days, and no one's going to get hurt, I promise. I'd just rather you avoided Faith as much as possible. She's, ah . . . she's very manipulative."

Trina gave him a world-weary look, clearly not buying it. "*She's* manipulative?"

"Trina . . ."

"All right, all right!" She threw up her hands. "But I sure as hell hope you know what you're doing. There's something about this one—she's not your usual type, and there's not a thing about her that says groupie—not with those battered old tennis shoes."

With a sigh, Finn decided to avoid Trina as much as possible himself today—there was only so much nagging he could take, and his conscience was doing a good enough job without her.

"It'll be fine," he repeated. "Now how about some breakfast?"

"Fresh fruit, muffins, and orange juice in the kitchen," she said, turning to go. "Help yourself, unless John and Larry ate them all."

"Why do I keep you again?"

"Because nobody else would put up with you. Left you some sunscreen on the bedside table; take it down to the beach. That boy's as pale as milk, and so is his mother."

By the time Finn made it to the beach, there was a sloppy-looking pile of sand that was evidently supposed to be a sandcastle, and on their knees beside it were a windblown Faith and a very wet, sandy little boy who—when he saw Finn coming—jumped to his feet and cried, "Hi, Finn! Look what I made!"

Before he quite knew what was happening, Nathan had run up and grabbed him by the hand, dragging him toward the pile of sand. Faith rose to her feet, smiling but wary. She was still wearing the same clothes she'd been wearing yesterday, jeans and T-shirt, but the jeans were rolled up to the knee, and she was barefoot.

"That's, ah . . . that's a pretty impressive castle," he said to Nathan, who beamed at his praise. "Did your mom help you with that?"

Faith's lip twitched at his attempt to be tactful.

"She helped some," Nathan answered excitedly, "but I did most of it myself. This place is cool—is this really where you live, all the time?"

He looked down into the boy's face, so open, so trusting. "Yep, it is. You like it?"

"It's awesome," Nate said worshipfully. "Thanks for letting us come visit."

"You're welcome." He grinned at the boy, who grinned back. "Gone swimming yet?"

"Mom won't let me." He shot his mother a disgusted look. "She says it's too dangerous."

Arching an eyebrow, he glanced at Faith, who hastened to defend herself. "I don't have a bathing suit," she said, "and he can't go in by himself. Look how high the waves are; he doesn't have his floaties."

"Floaties?" Finn had never heard the term.

"Those dorky things you wear on your arms," Nate told him disgustedly. "I have to wear them when we go to the pool." The look he shot his mom was dark. "Not that we go to the pool that much."

"Nathan!" His outspokenness embarrassed her, he could tell, her pale cheeks flooding with color.

"That reminds me," Finn said smoothly, reaching into the back pocket of his swimsuit. "I brought you some sunscreen."

Faith took it gratefully, while Nate rolled his eyes.

"Maybe your mom would feel better if I went in the water with you," he suggested. "You could hold on to me."

The boy's face lit up. "Can I, Mom? Please?"

Looking alarmed, Faith glanced from Nathan to Finn, then back again.

"It'll be fine," he reassured her. "I'll be right there with him."

"Yay!" Nathan didn't wait for his mom's approval, tugging Finn toward the water.

"Hang on a minute." Dragging his shirt over his head, he tossed it to Faith, forcing her to catch it. She did, and when he caught her looking at his bare chest, he gave her a wink.

"Whoa," Nate said, behind his back. "Is that a tattoo? Is it real? Can I touch it?"

"It's real, and yes, you can touch it."

"I want one! Mommy, can I have one?"

"Absolutely not," Faith said promptly. "No tattoos, unless they're washable."

Finn looked down at Nathan and shrugged. "Not much fun, is she?"

Nathan laughed up at him, and something squeezed inside his chest. He seemed like a great kid; no shyness or inhibitions. *What would his child have been like, if he'd had one?*

He'd never know, since he had no intention of having any.

"She's not too bad," Nathan said loyally, in his mom's defense. "She just worries too much."

"Somebody has to," Faith murmured, reaching out to touch his curls.

"Let's go, kiddo." Finn found himself curiously eager to get wet. "Last one in the water has to eat worms."

"Worms!" shouted Nate, gleefully, as he took off running.

"Hold his hand," Faith yelled, as they raced toward the water. "Don't go in too deep!"

Too late, Finn thought, as a wave broke over his knees. Nate's small hand grabbed his big one without a shred of self-consciousness, and dragged him in deeper.

Two hours and half a tube of sunscreen later, all three of them were wet, sandy, and relaxed. The haphazard pile of sand had been refashioned by the scraping of seashells into a fairly decent-looking sandcastle, and Finn, having been man-handled, splashed and dunked by a boy one third his size, was feeling more laid back than he'd been in months.

"Your nose is pink." He brushed sand from his

hands, observing Faith critically, and thinking she looked rather cute that way.

"Yeah? Well, you have seaweed in your hair," she returned, looking as relaxed as he felt. Her own hair was wild, blowing in the wind that set the waves crashing, and she was smiling.

"Do you realize that this is the first time I've seen you in the light of day?" he asked, reaching up a hand to find the piece of seaweed, then tossing it away.

Her smile faltered.

"The sunshine suits you. You should get out in it more."

Nathan was throwing shells down by the waterline.

"Not a lot of time for that." Faith sighed, watching her son with an eagle eye. "Between work and doctor appointments . . ." She trailed off, settling herself more comfortably in the sand. "It's been a while."

"It must be tough, having to raise a kid all by yourself."

She shrugged. "It has its drawbacks, but I wouldn't trade being Nathan's mom for anything in the world."

"Tell me more about his father."

She shot him a glance from the corner of her eye. "Why?"

"Why not?"

Her lips thinned, but she didn't evade further. "His name was Jason, and I haven't seen or heard from him in five years. He's not a part of our lives."

"What happened?"

"Oh . . ." She shrugged again, wrapping her arms around her knees as she watched Nathan chase seagulls across the sand. "Same old story, I guess. He claimed he loved me, but when I told him I was pregnant, everything changed." She rested her chin on a knee, not looking at him. "He didn't want kids, pressured me not to go through with the pregnancy. Told me I had to choose between him and the baby." Now she turned her head and looked at him, deliberately. "I chose the baby."

He said nothing for a moment, well aware of her point.

"Did you love him?" Why the answer mattered, he had no idea.

Tucking a strand of hair behind her ear, she shook her head. "I thought I did, once, but he was childish and selfish and irresponsible— everything I didn't need in a man. It hurt when we split, but I got over it." She turned her head to keep an eye on Nathan. "Besides, I had a new love, and more important things to concentrate on."

"What about your parents?" Changing the subject, he found himself genuinely curious—according to Bert's report, she was the only child of deceased parents, but the report hadn't included details. "What happened to them?"

She made a noise of exasperation. "Wow. You're being awfully direct today."

He shook his head. "I've been up front with you from the start, about everything. Why stop now?"

It was her turn to be silent. A few moments later, during which they both watched Nate dipping his toes in the ocean, she spoke again. "My mom and dad had me late in life. Dad died of cancer when he was sixty-eight, and I was twenty-one. My mom never got over it. She went into a depression, spent the next few years as a virtual recluse, and passed away just after my twenty-fourth birthday." Her voice was steady, but he saw the gleam of tears in her eyes. "One night she just went to sleep, and never woke up. It was her heart, ironically enough."

"I'm sorry," he said softly, not knowing what else to say.

She sent him a grateful look beneath her lashes, swallowing hard in an effort to keep her emotions under control. A deep breath or two later, she asked, "What about you? Your parents must be awfully proud of all your success."

He gave a snort of laughter. "Hardly."

"What do you mean?"

"My mom's an alcoholic, and I never hear from her unless she needs money," he told her bluntly. "As far as my father goes, I never really knew him—not entirely certain she did, either. He left when I was small. I never heard from him again."

"That's terrible!"

He shook his head, not wanting or needing her pity. "Can't say as I blame him." A seashell near his foot caught his eye; he picked it up and threw it toward the water, as far out as he could. "You haven't met my mother."

"I'm not sure I want to," she huffed, but quickly backtracked. "I'm sure she's not as bad as all that."

He quirked an eyebrow at her and said nothing, which pretty much said it all.

"Finn!" Nathan's excited shout drew their attention. "Look! A shark!"

"A shark?" Faith was on her feet in an instant, but Finn only laughed.

"It's a dolphin," he shouted back, getting to his

feet. Heading toward the boy, he pointed out to sea. "Look, there's another one."

"Where? Where?" Nathan was so excited, he was jumping up and down. "I can't see! Pick me up! Let me see!"

He did, surprised it felt so natural. Nate's skinny little arms went around his neck; he didn't weigh much. The guilt he'd been staving off since yesterday reared its ugly head again—what if he was wrong about the clinic in Switzerland? What if Faith's deal with the Devil was the only way out for the kid? "Look, out there beyond where the waves are breaking." Forcing himself to live in the moment, he raised his free hand to point out where more than one fin was breaking the surface. "There's three or four of them, I think. They travel in groups, called pods."

"Wow," Nathan breathed, against his neck. "Can we swim with them? I saw some people on TV once, they went swimming with the dolphins."

"Those were tame dolphins," Finn told him. "These are wild."

"Oh." Nate was disappointed. "Can we feed them?"

He shook his head. "They don't need us to feed them; they're getting their own food, see?"

Ahead of the dolphins, a glittering shower of

small fish broke the surface, scattering like dia-
monds flung across the water.

"Did you see that, Mommy?"

Faith had come up beside them. She had an odd
look on her face, but he couldn't tell what it meant.

"I see them," she said. "That's not something
you see every day."

"Dolphins are good luck," he said lightly, "did
you know that?"

"Are they?" She didn't seem to want to look
him in the eye. "For whom, I wonder?"

Chapter Twenty-two

Nate obviously liked him, and that worried her. When he'd seen the dolphins, it had been Finn he'd called out to, not her. He was usually a bit shy around men, since there were so few of them in their lives; Dr. Wynecke, Dina's occasional boyfriend, the mailman—that was pretty much it. Yet this morning, when he awakened in a strange room in a strange bed, he hadn't seemed the least bit worried once she'd explained they were at Finn's house, and that he'd slept through the trip there.

Kids were so adaptable, so accepting. Why couldn't she be that way?

Finn's hair was spiked and sticky with salt water, and there was sand on his chest and shoulders from Nathan's hands. Finn didn't seem to mind holding him, even looked natural doing it—something she'd never expected to see, and it made her heart hurt. She swallowed, feeling as if she'd missed something that might've been important, had it been allowed to develop on its own.

But it couldn't, because they had to get out of here—now, today. It had been a lovely, idyllic morning, but it wasn't real. Reality was doctor appointments, bills to pay, and a bargain to keep if she wanted her son to live.

"I think the dolphins have the right idea," Finn said, his voice breaking into her thoughts. "I'm starving. Anyone else?"

"I'm hungry, too," Nate said, "but can we come back down here after?"

"We'll see," Faith said, before Finn could answer. She reached out to touch his knee, unable to help herself. "I don't want you to overdo it."

"Mommmm," her son said, rolling his eyes in exasperation. "I'm not a baby anymore."

"Obviously not," Finn told him staunchly, "but Mom's in charge. What she says, goes." He put

Nate down, turning toward the house. "Let's go raid the kitchen, shall we?"

Nate took off running, obviously still full of energy.

"Thanks," she said to Finn as they followed at a walk. After what he'd just told her about his own mom, she was pleasantly surprised by the show of support.

He glanced at her, scooping his shirt from the sand as they passed the sandcastle. "For what?"

"For backing me up with Nate. A couple of months ago I wouldn't have worried so much, but now . . ."

"Have you given any more thought to what we talked about last night? The clinic in Switzerland?"

She shook her head, looking away. It was a lie, of course. She'd thought about it, even though she'd tried hard not to. Not quite ready to spoil the day just yet, however, she took the easy way out and changed the subject. "Nathan!" she called. "Slow down and wait for us. You can't go in the house all sandy like that!"

Finn didn't press her, for which she was grateful. "There's an outdoor shower on a side patio," he said. "We can rinse off there."

Not only was there a shower, but three big, fluffy towels were stacked on a lounge chair nearby. "Your invisible housekeeper is awfully efficient," she told him. "There was a big tray of food outside our door this morning. I can't believe Nathan's already hungry again."

"He's a growing boy."

And I'm going to keep him that way, she vowed silently to herself.

"So where is everyone?" She tried to keep the question casual, but if she was going to find a way out of here, she needed to start somewhere. Maybe if a member of the staff knew that she and Nathan were here against their will, they could be talked into helping her. "Surely this place doesn't run itself."

He shrugged. "They're around." Lowering his voice so Nathan couldn't hear, he added, "But they're not going to help you, Faith. I pay them very well, in large part for their discretion."

"Please," she murmured, touching his arm. "You can't mean to go through with this—you can't keep us here. Time is running out." She shot an anxious glance toward Nate, who was distracted by the little lizards in the bushes surrounding the patio. "There's only one night left, and if I don't . . ."

She couldn't bring herself to finish.

"He's a liar, Faith. Who are you going to believe, me or *him*?" He didn't need to say who "him" was, and she was relieved he didn't. He looked down at her, green eyes intense, compelling. "There's still time to fix this; give me the ring and I'll start making calls right away. We can both get what we want."

How she wanted to believe him. How she wanted to think that somewhere out there lay the answer to all Nate's problems—some doctor, some treatment. That her son could live, that Finn could live, that maybe even the three of them . . .

"No," she said, firmly. *No time for fantasy, when reality was staring her in the face.* "I'm not going to take a chance on my son's life."

"Is mine so unimportant?"

"Of course not."

"Why are you being so stubborn about this? I can show you the research about the clinic in Switzerland, you can interview the doctors, the former patients . . ."

"Stop it." She raised a hand to her head, not wanting to hear any more.

"Faith." A note of pleading entered his voice. "Be reasonable."

"You didn't see what I saw," she whispered. "You didn't see what he showed me."

There was a silence between them, broken only by the splash of water from the outdoor shower as Nate turned it on, full force. "This is cold!" He giggled as he stood beneath it, letting it run over his head.

"I want to do as you ask, Finn. I . . . I care about you . . ."

"Save it," he clipped, turning away. He grabbed a towel and headed down a garden pathway that led away from the house.

"Finn!" Nathan saw him leaving. "Where are you going? I thought we were going to get something to eat!"

"I'm not hungry anymore," Finn tossed over his shoulder. "The kitchen is right through that door. You guys go ahead without me."

"But Finn—" Nate ran after him, soaking wet, before she could stop him. "You said you'd show me how to play the guitar, remember?"

He paused, and that was all the time needed for Nathan to catch up. The lump already in Faith's throat got larger as she watched her son grab him by the hand, urging him to stop. He looked down at the boy, then bent so they were almost eye-to-eye. "I'll be back," she heard him murmur. "I just need some time to myself right now, okay?"

For a moment Nate looked like he might cry.

"Go with your mom," Finn told him gently. "I'll see you later on this afternoon."

"You promise?"

Faith had to turn away at that point, unable to bear the hopeful note in her son's voice.

"I promise," Finn murmured, and then she heard the crunch of gravel as he walked away.

The kitchen was huge, gleaming tile floors and granite countertops. It was empty, but someone had obviously been there recently; the air smelled of fresh-baked blueberry muffins and ripe straw-berries, both of which sat on a table by a window overlooking the sea. Three place settings, and a big pitcher of orange juice.

"This is a pretty house," Nate said. "I wish we could live here."

"Do you?" She smiled down at him, glad to see his spirits had revived after Finn's abrupt depar-ture. "As soon as I win the lottery, we'll buy one just like it."

He shook his head, moving toward the table. "Uh-uh. I want this one. I want you to marry

Finn, and then we can all stay here and live happily ever after."

The cheerful, matter-of-fact comment stole the breath from her lungs. "There's no such thing as happily-ever-after," she replied, more harshly than she intended. "It's only in fairy tales."

"You read me fairy tales all the time," he said, unconcerned by her denial. "Oo, muffins! Can I have one?"

"Nathan." She had to nip this in the bud. "We're just here for a visit, and Finn is just a friend. Nobody's going to marry anybody."

"Why not?" He took a seat at the table, regarding her curiously. "Don't you like him?"

She swallowed, uncomfortable. "Of course I like him, but that doesn't mean I want to marry him."

"*I* like him," he said, reaching for a muffin. "And he likes you, I can tell. He's always smiling when he looks at you."

"He's just being nice," she said, wishing he'd talk about something else.

"Nope." Crumbs flew as Nate talked around a bite of muffin. "You're not paying attention, Mommy."

"Don't talk with your mouth full," she said automatically, reaching for a strawberry.

"He thinks you're pretty," her son said.

"Enough," she scolded, appalled at how pleased she was at the thought.

"But you *are* pretty," he insisted. "And besides, I don't want you to be lonely if . . ." He trailed off, taking another bite of his muffin.

"If what?" A cold finger of foreboding trailed her spine.

Nate just chewed, looking at her.

"If what, Nathan?" She didn't like this, not one bit, but she had to know what he was thinking.

He finished his bite and swallowed. "You know, Mommy," he answered simply.

"Nate." She was out of her chair and on her knees beside his before she knew what was happening. "Nothing is going to happen to you." His little arms were so slender, his chest so thin. She gripped him tightly by the shoulders, forcing him to look her in the eye. "I'm not going to let anything happen to you, I swear."

"It's okay, Mommy." The look in his chocolate brown eyes was wise beyond his years. "The angel told me not to be afraid. He said he'd be there for me, whatever happened."

Her heart skipped a beat. "What—" She licked lips gone suddenly dry. "What did you just say?"

"The angel. He came to me last night while I was sleeping, and told me not to be afraid."

Faith sank back on her haunches, stunned.

"He had long brown hair, like a girl's, and his face was all bright and shiny." He nodded his head, warming to the topic. "I'm pretty sure he had wings, but it was hard to tell, because he was so bright. I think I heard them flutter, though." Taking another bite of his muffin, he regarded her calmly, obviously serious about what he was saying.

What was she supposed to say? Deny that angels existed, and take away what had clearly been a comforting experience? Or agree with him, and acknowledge the possibility that if demons existed, so did angels?

She felt a flash of anger, and looked away so Nate wouldn't see it in her eyes. If angels existed, then where was God, and why had He let this happen to them?

Silent, shaken, Faith got to her feet and slid back into the chair opposite Nathan's. "That sounds like a nice dream, baby," she murmured faintly.

"It wasn't a dream," he stated emphatically. "Well, it kind of was, but it wasn't; it was real, I know it was."

She didn't want to argue. "Either way, it sounds really nice."

"It was," he agreed. "Can I have another muffin?"

One more muffin and a big glass of orange juice later, Nate gave a jaw-cracking yawn, his energy level obviously beginning to flag.

"Time for a nap, I think," Faith said lightly, determined to behave as normally as possible under the circumstances.

"But Finn said he'd be back. He said he'd teach me how to play the guitar."

"Later," she replied. "He said later. Right now, I think we could both use a little rest, don't you?"

Another yawn sealed the deal, so she got up from the table and held out a hand. "C'mon. Let's find our room."

They left the kitchen and entered a hallway that went both left and right. A quick peek to the right revealed an empty dining room with a table large enough for twelve people and bright, abstract paintings on the walls. They turned around and went the other way as Faith tried to mentally picture the way the house looked from the beach. If she was correct, the guest room they'd awakened in this morning would be just a few doors down.

An open door at the end of the hallway proved her correct, and with a sigh of relief, she pulled Nate inside, then closed and locked it behind them.

"Let's get you out of those wet shorts," she said, both relieved and irritated to see a familiar SpongeBob backpack at the foot of the bed, right next to her own battered suitcase. In no time she had him changed and tucked beneath the covers with his stuffed dog, his earlier protests forgotten as his eyes drooped shut. Within minutes, his breathing was deep and even.

While he slept, she took a much-needed shower, leaving the door open between the bedroom and bathroom, and changed into clean clothes of her own: her favorite white T-shirt and khaki cargo pants. The ring was still in the pocket of her jeans, wrapped in foil, and though she briefly considered hiding it somewhere in the room, she couldn't bring herself to leave it, so she slid it into a side pocket of her cargos, making sure the Velcro tab was securely closed.

"Time to find a way out of here," she murmured to herself, touching Nate's chest on the way to the door to make sure he still breathed. Old habits died hard when you were a mother, and she'd been doing that since he first came home from the hospital as an infant, so tiny and helpless.

Reminding herself that although he was no longer tiny, he was still helpless, she unlocked the door and slipped into the hallway.

There was no sound, nothing, but she knew the house wasn't as empty as it looked. She flitted through it, her sneakers making tiny *snick*ing sounds on the tile floors. Most of the windows faced the beach, and all the rooms were beautifully decorated in varying shades of blue, beige, and gold. One thing that struck her was the absence of personal photos or mementos; the house looked like a designer showplace, without the finishing touches that would've made it a home. When she found the front door, she was elated, until she realized it was dead bolted, with no key. A couple of side doors were the same way, the only one unlocked being the kitchen door she'd used earlier. A staircase with a wrought-iron railing led upward, but she saw no reason to go that way, refusing to give in to her own curiosity. She wanted *out*, not up, and she felt enough like a voyeur already, creeping around all by herself.

A rumbling noise froze her in her tracks. She listened, hard, and then realized what it was—thunder, low in the distance. Glancing out a nearby window, she saw dark clouds on the horizon, where the ocean met the sky. It was still sunny out, but obviously wouldn't be for long.

Worried that Nathan would hear it and wake to find her gone, she headed back toward the guest room to check on him.

Opening the door as quietly as she could, she peeked in, and found the bed empty.

Her son was gone.

Chapter Twenty-three

"I don't care whether you like it or not, you will do as I say," Samael the Fallen said implacably. "Get in that tub and wash. You stink."

They were in his private bathing chamber, where the air was thick with steam, the oversized tub filled and ready.

"Yeah? Well, you don't smell so good yourself," Cain returned defiantly. "And I'm not doing it."

He'd known his son for less than an hour, and found him stubborn, rude, foul-smelling and completely, utterly fearless. If it weren't so irritating to his nose and ears as well as his psyche, he might've felt some stirrings of pride over the fearlessness, but his short stint as a father had already left him ready to strangle the boy with his bare hands.

"Your time among the imps has soiled your mind as well as your body," Sammy said, restraining his temper with an effort, "if you think to challenge *me*."

Cain shot him a cold look from ice blue eyes. "And who do you think you are," he asked mildly, with a self-possession he'd never have believed possible of a nine-year-old, "the fucking prince of Persia?"

Nyx stepped forward, saving his master from the sin of patricide. "You are addressing His Satanic Majesty, Son of Morning, Prince of Darkness, and Lord of the Underworld. Keep a civil tongue in your head, or I shall beg his permission to rip it from your throat."

Those blue eyes, so disturbingly like his own, flicked briefly over Nyx, then back to Sammy. "You're . . ." For the first time, the boy seemed to have no ready reply. "My mother said . . ." He looked away, swallowing hard. Then he squared his small shoulders in a gesture that Sammy reluctantly recognized, and opened his mouth to say more, but was forestalled.

"Nyx is correct in listing some of my titles," the Great Shaitan said quietly, "but I believe it might be best if you just called me Father."

They stared at each other for a moment, Sammy once again getting the feeling that the boy was far older than his years.

"Mother claims you're all-powerful," Cain said, "so I suppose that means I have to do what you say."

"Your mother is a wise woman," Sammy lied.

"No, she isn't," the boy replied, calling him on it. "She's silly, and vain, and way too nice for her own good." Then, surprisingly, despite the tenseness of the moment, he smiled, displaying teeth that looked astonishingly white against the sooty grime that covered his face. "Which is why I usually get my way."

"Well, you're not getting it today," Sammy said, resisting the pull of that megawatt smile for all he was worth. "So get in the tub."

Cain shrugged, stepped out of his grubby loincloth without a shred of modesty, and did as he was told, though his expression showed him clearly not happy about it.

"Nyx will be your instructor for the next few days," Sammy said, knowing his lieutenant would prefer to be boiled in oil than to babysit, but not caring. Now that he'd found the boy, he had no idea what to do with him, and needed some time to think. "You are to do as he tells you without argument, and go nowhere without him."

Cain's attempt to give him a sullen look was spoiled as he picked up a bar of Sammy's favorite clove-scented soap and took a sniff. "That smells good," he said, and immediately rubbed it in his hair, smearing the bar with sticky black goo.

Inwardly Sammy sighed, knowing that particular bar was ruined. His tub was going to need a thorough scrubbing, too; the water was already turning gray. "It's made especially for me by the dryads of Eternia," he said wryly, "and it's not meant to be used as shampoo."

"What the hell is shampoo?"

A heathen. The child was an ignorant heathen.

"Shampoo is what Nyx will use to wash your mouth out if you don't watch your language," he returned, watching with interest as Cain scrubbed dirty, soapy hands over his face and head. "You're too young to use profanity."

Cain ignored the reprimand, dunking his head beneath the water. When he came up, scrubbing slightly cleaner hands over his face, Sammy watched with interest as his features were revealed.

A straight nose, much like his own. Persephone's chin, though the shape could change as the boy grew older. The eyes, of course, were unquestionably his, and the hair—well, it was still too filthy to tell, but if it matched the boy's eyebrows it would be blond.

In a corner of the tub, behind Cain, a curious water sprite emerged, wrinkling her pretty nose at the dirty state of the water in which she found herself. Her cat-eyed gaze flicked curiously over the boy, then toward her master, who gave an almost imperceptible nod. Silently she slipped beneath the surface and emerged a few moments later holding aloft a beautiful bottle made of iridescent glass. She placed it on the tiled rim of the tub, where it made a slight *click* as she put it down.

Cain whirled at the sound, quick as an adder, and snatched the sprite's arm before she could withdraw. Alarmed, the sprite's eyes widened, and she bared pointed teeth in a snarl.

"Whoa," Cain breathed. "What are *you*?" The very male appreciation in the boy's tone was unmistakable.

Sammy, who'd been about to interfere, said

nothing, merely watching as the sprite took Cain's measure. Slowly she pulled her arm from his now slackened grip, allowing her snarl to fade. Once free she withdrew to a corner, cocked her green-haired head curiously, then favored the boy with a slightly coquettish smile before slipping, once again, beneath the surface.

Cain, dark runnels of dirty water dripping from his hair over his nine-year-old neck and shoulders, gave Sammy another one of those megawatt smiles. "I think I like baths," he said cheerfully. "Can I take another one later?"

Beside him, Nyx gave a low chuckle. "Oh, he is definitely your son," he murmured, giving His Satanic Majesty a red-eyed wink.

Sammy scarcely knew how to feel about such a statement, much less respond, so he turned and strode from the chamber. "Watch him until I return," he snapped, "and make sure you keep the horny little devil on a tight leash."

"What do you want, Gabriel?"

Unsettled, Sammy had gone to one of the few places that always managed to give him some measure of peace. He visited the Sistine Chapel often, privately admiring Michelangelo's *Last Judgment*, which held a rather good depiction of him in the lower right-hand corner. The chapel was closed at the moment, of course, as he'd never been able to abide crowds, so when he heard a footfall, feather-light, and smelled the scent of sandalwood, he knew who it was without turning.

"The artist seems to have made you a bit pudgy," said Gabe, coming up beside him. "Everywhere except where it counts."

Turning his head, Sammy glared at him. "A bawdy joke from one so innocent. Careful the One doesn't strike you down for your blasphemy."

Gabriel shrugged, examining the painting closely. "There's nothing blasphemous about the human body," he said mildly. "I was merely pointing out that he's given you a penis the size of a peanut. And your head . . ." He shook his own, brown-haired and shining. "That head, though handsome, is not nearly large enough to contain your colossal ego."

"If you're trying to provoke me, it's not going to work."

"Ah. Lost your sense of humor somewhere in the darkness, I suppose. 'Blessed are those who can laugh at themselves, for they shall never cease to be amused,'" Gabriel quoted. "One of the unrecorded Beatitudes."

Not for anything would he show his amusement, so Sammy turned away, strolling toward another fresco. Gabriel followed, for all the world as though they'd come here to offer their joint opinion on man's conception of the heavens.

"I never took you for a Catholic," Gabe said idly, as they perused scenes from the life of Moses. "Yet here you are at the Vatican. Something to confess?"

"Your sarcasm is wasted on me," Sammy returned, though it wasn't. "I enjoy beauty in all its forms, whether it be in a chapel, in a field, or in the arms of a woman. You, on the other hand, are limited by the narrowness of tunnel vision. You see everything as black or white, good or evil, with no shades of gray."

"I am limited by nothing," Gabriel replied, "save my love for you."

"Careful, Gabriel," he mocked. "The church frowns on such things."

"You know exactly what I mean, and don't pretend you don't."

"*Love,*" Sammy scoffed, peering into the eyes of a painted saint, virtuous and pure. "How can you believe in love after all these years?"

"I needn't experience it physically to know it exists. I see in the wondering eyes of a new mother or the steady, peaceful gaze of a faithful spouse. Surely you remember our early teachings, Samael. 'And there remain these three: faith, hope, and love . . . and the greatest of these is love.' "

"More platitudes? What do you want from me, Gabriel?" Sammy's anger, temporarily set to simmer, began to boil. "Why do you keep showing up to annoy me when I've warned you to leave me alone?"

His old friend shrugged. "You demanded your way with Faith McFarland, and I gave it. I said nothing as you shamelessly used her love for her terminally ill son to get what you wanted."

Privately relieved to think of something—anything—other than his own recent paternity issues, Samael watched as Gabe leaned in to better examine the cherubic version of the baby Moses, rescued from the bulrushes.

"I haven't interfered while you turned her into a thief, made her pander her body for gain, or had her kidnapped," Gabe went on. He turned, facing Sammy directly. "The least you can do is offer me an explanation, even if it's all lies."

The lies were right there, on the tip of his tongue, as they always were. He could tell Gabriel anything he wanted, pull the puppet strings just to watch him dance. Eyeing his erstwhile brother narrowly, he considered it, then did the opposite.

"My methods may not be yours, but I'm doing what's best for Faith McFarland, whether it seems so or not." His chin went up a notch. "She was in danger of becoming a dried-up spinster. What kind of mother would she be if she allowed no one to get close? And"—he smiled, as though at a private joke—"if I can get something I want in the meantime, it's nobody's business but my own. Finn Payne is mine, and has been for some time."

"You don't like him very much, do you?"

Sammy rolled his eyes at the stupidity of the question.

"You don't like him because he reminds you of yourself, and because *she* likes him."

Anger stilled to cold, freezing him before a colorful fresco of Moses' journey into Egypt.

"The dark-eyed girl, the one you claim not to love." Gabriel continued to stroll along the north wall of the chapel, wisely keeping himself out of reach. "She likes his music, plays it in that quaint little clothing shop of hers all the time. Great taste in fashion, by the way." He paused, holding out his arms so that Sammy would notice his shirt. "Levi's button-down, circa 1965."

"You bastard," Sammy said, in a tone only a fool would ignore.

"You're jealous of the musician," Gabe stated, ignoring away. He shook his brown head chidingly. "How very petty of you."

Samael took a deep breath, astounded and furious at the depth of Gabriel's daring. No one had called him to task for thousands of years, save one small slip of a girl who vexed him even now, when she wasn't here.

"Ah, well." Gabe gave a fatalistic sigh, shrugging his shoulders. "Let's go have a glass of wine and talk about it, shall we? I know a wonderful little restaurant down in the piazza. The olive oil they use in their dishes is extra virgin, just the way you like it."

Despite himself, Sammy burst out laughing. The sound echoed within the chapel, rising as Gabriel joined him. It was a commingling of sound not heard for millennia, and for a moment—just a moment—it was as though the past had never been.

"So you like Italian food, do you?" Sammy asked wryly, when he could trust himself to speak again.

"I'm often offered food and drink by humans unaware," Gabe replied, brown eyes twinkling. "But standing on a street corner with my hand out becomes tiresome after a while. I prefer pasta." He turned his back on Samael and walked toward the door of the chapel. "You can pay."

"Pasta will make you fat, much like your head already is."

"Touché, my friend, touché." He glanced over his shoulder to make sure Sammy followed. "But try to be more original in your insults next time, will you?"

Chapter Twenty-four

The loud whining of the band saw vied with the voices in Finn's head, the ones that told him to let Faith and Nathan go home. He could put them on the boat, call up the pilot on the mainland and tell him to ready his private plane, and have them back in Atlanta long before nightfall.

But then they would be gone, and he would be spending a lonely, sleepless night before the Devil showed up to gloat, and he wanted neither of those things. How and when would the end be for him? he wondered. Suicide, Satan had said; pills would be easier and less messy than a gun. Drowning maybe—Trina would never forgive him if he left a mess in the house.

The wood beneath his hands was mahogany,

almost the exact shade of Faith's hair. He'd been saving it for something special, and now he knew what it was: a dolphin, riding the crest of a wave. Nate would like it; it would be something to remember him by.

He'd discovered something about himself in the last twenty-four hours, which was that he truly wasn't the badass the world—and he—had thought he was. Here he was, actually considering letting them go, accepting his fate and letting the Devil put him out of his misery. His plan to seduce Faith had backfired, because he was the one who'd been seduced . . . the way she'd felt in his lap, naked and gasping, the way the water had swirled around her breasts and shoulders, entangling both of them in her hair.

The way Nate had laughed up at him on the beach, so small and trusting, his hand in Finn's, tugging him toward the water.

Finn turned off the saw and moved toward the bench that held his carving tools. It was then he heard thunder, grumbling and rumbling, quickly followed by the patter of rain on the workshop's tin roof. Afternoon thunderstorms were common in the islands, so he paid it little heed, focusing instead on how best to bring out the grain of the wood.

When the door to his workshop flew open, he was so deep into the carving that he narrowly missed slicing his thumb open.

"Nathan?"

It was Faith, soaking wet and frantic.

"Is Nathan in here with you?" She looked around his workshop, wild-eyed. "I've looked everywhere—have you seen him?"

He stared at her, mind working. He had no idea where Nathan was, but he wasn't worried, not with Trina and John on the job. "Maybe I have," he said slowly, "and maybe I haven't." It was pouring outside, wind whipping through the palm trees.

Her face paled. "What are you saying?"

He shrugged, dropping the knife and the partially carved dolphin onto his work bench with a clatter.

"You took him, didn't you?" Her expression, so worried, turned furious. "Where is he? What've you done with him?"

"Give me the ring," he said calmly, "and I'll tell you."

She flew at him, so quickly he barely had time to put up his hands to stop her. Enraged, she tried to claw at his face, but he had her by the wrists. Surprised at her strength, he tried his best to keep her from hurting him without hurting her. "He's just a little boy," she cried, and kicked him hard in the shins, while he struggled to get her under control. The workshop was full of sharp knives, saws, and pieces of wood—if she took it in her head to use any of them, he'd end up bloody, he had no doubt.

"Stop it," he hissed, grunting as she landed another kick on his shins. "I don't want to hurt you."

"Oh no?" she snarled. "Then what are we doing here? How could you use a child—" her voice broke on a sob, but he hardened himself against her tears, recognizing an opportunity when he saw one. It could still work—if she gave him the ring, if the doctors could help Nate . . . they could both go on living, and maybe she'd come to forgive him.

Spinning her so her back was to his front, he kept tight hold of her wrists. "Give me the ring," he said urgently, in her ear. "That's all I want."

"Bastard," she spat. "You horrible, heartless bastard! Where is he?"

He said nothing more, letting her struggle until she realized the futility of it. Her head sagged, wet hair covering her face. He could feel her heartbeat against his arm, racing like that of a trapped bird.

"Please," she whispered, "don't do this," but he forced himself to be made of stone; hard and unyielding. Mercy was no longer a quality he could afford to show, not when Fate had placed her in the palm of his hand, and time was running out. It didn't matter if her body fit him perfectly, didn't matter if her hair smelled like flowers and her skin was soft as silk . . .

His own heart was pounding, the breakfast he hadn't even touched threatening to rise up and choke him. She'd been ready to believe the worst of him when she'd found Nathan gone; now he'd give her good reason to.

"I never told you exactly how I got the ring, did I?" he asked, low in her ear.

She was crying, jagged sobs that made her body shake.

He held her tighter, thinking of that night so long ago, when Satan had opened the door to Hell, and he'd walked right in. "I got it from a guy named Mike Gilliam—a small-time musician who could play the drums like nobody's business; he was a madman with the sticks. He was on his way up, part of a band called Dead Man's Hand." Her sobs went on, but he refused to listen, casting back in his mind to that long-ago time. "They were playing in some crummy little bar in Ohio, on the verge of being picked up by a major label. I hitched my way there, claimed I was a fan, offered myself as a roadie. No pay, just beer and sandwiches, and maybe somewhere to sleep when they were on the road. I'd set up and take down his drum kit, screen the girls who were always hanging around the backstage door, pick the prettiest ones for him and slip 'em inside."

She wasn't fighting him anymore, and despite her tears, he knew she was listening.

"Back then, the ring was his—I didn't know how he got it, and I didn't care. It was taking him higher and higher, and the band along with him. I could see it happening, right before my eyes. The venues got better, the girls got prettier, and the money was rolling in, hand over fist. One night, after a show, he got so drunk he passed out— wasn't the first time, and it sure as hell wasn't the last. I stole the ring right off his finger, even though I knew what was going to happen to him when I did. The Devil told me, you see."

She looked up at him through her wet hair, saying nothing.

"Yes, Faith," he said gently, "I did the same thing to him you did to me, and guess what?"

She didn't answer.

"Two days later he was charged with the assault and rape of a minor; he thought the girl he'd been with that night had stolen it, and beat the crap out of her to get it back. Turned out she was underage, and her parents had him arrested. His career hit the skids, and he never played another gig. Blew his brains out in an alley behind a bar less than three months later."

He smiled a cold smile, hating himself as much now for what he'd done as he had when it happened, using his own self-loathing as a way to convince her of his heartlessness.

"That's not going to happen to me," he told her firmly. "I'm not going to end up like that."

"Are you going to beat me up, too?" she spat scathingly. "Is that how this works? Patterns repeating themselves, over and over?"

He was honestly shocked, glad she couldn't see his face. "I've never hit a woman, and I never will, but you're going to give me the ring back, one way or another."

No, he'd never hit a woman, because he'd seen what it had done to his mom. He had a vague memory of her being kind and loving once, when he was very small, but between the alcohol and the lowlife boyfriends she'd chosen because of it, he also had memories of lying in his bed, listening to her shriek and cry, hearing the thud of fists against flesh.

It had been his fault that girl had been beaten

up, just as it was his fault that Mike had killed himself. No need to tell Faith of the guilt that gnawed at him over it—he'd already revealed enough of his dark side.

"Where's my son?" she asked, low and frightened.

"Where's the ring?" he returned implacably.

She bowed her head, and he knew he'd won. "It's in my pocket," she whispered, "on the right-hand side. Go ahead and take it."

He let her go, stepping back.

She turned to face him, eyeing him fearfully.

"You have to give it to me," he said. "I'm not allowed to take it a second time."

A mixture of expressions crossed her face: surprise, a flicker of hope, then, worst of all, a contemptuous sort of understanding that made him want to crawl under a rock.

"You lied to me last night about your life being over, didn't you?"

He shook his head. "Not really. It's just a matter of how long it will take."

"You tried to make me feel sorry for you, so I'd sleep with you, so I'd lo—" She caught herself before she said the word. "So I'd think you were a nice guy, and give you back the ring."

Saying nothing, he merely watched her.

"You never had any intention of calling any clinic in Switzerland, did you?"

That one caught him by surprise. "No! I mean, yes . . . of course I did! I meant what I said about that."

"Save it," she clipped, repeating the phrase he'd used with her earlier. Her eyes were hard as agates, her mouth bitter. "You're a liar." Reaching into her pocket, she pulled out a silvery wad of tinfoil and threw it at him.

He ducked, but it hit him in the temple, narrowly missing his eye.

"Take your fucking ring," she spat, "and give me back my son."

Slowly, as though he were an old man, he stood up straight. The wad of tinfoil had rolled to a stop over by the scroll saw; he went over to it and picked it up, peeling it away to reveal the ring within. As though in a daze, he slipped it back onto his finger, feeling none of the triumph he'd felt the first time he'd put it on, so long ago. It was cold, as cold as the place where his heart should've been, as cold as the look in her eyes.

"You're right," he told her woodenly. "I'm a liar." Walking toward the door, he found he couldn't look at her anymore. "I don't know where Nathan is," he admitted, "but we'll find him, and then I'll send you home."

Her shriek of rage warned him, and he turned just in time to see her snatch up his carving knife and run at him. For an instant, just an instant, he was tempted to let her use it, and that instant cost him a cut on his arm when he raised it to block.

His hiss of pain brought her up short, her face gone white. She stared at his arm, where blood was already welling, then at the knife in her hand. It fell to the floor with a clatter.

"Faith—" He reached out to her, heedless of the blood, not even feeling the cut, for it was nothing to the pain in his heart.

"I could've killed you," she whispered, horrified. Then her face hardened. "And if anything's happened to my son, I will."

Chapter Twenty-five

The wind was picking up, and so was the rain, lashing his face like needles. The short dash to the house left him soaked. Faith was right on his heels as he went through the kitchen door, sticking to him like a burr.

"Trina," he shouted, not bothering with the intercom system. "John! Larry!"

Striding through the kitchen door and into the hallway, he heard answering footsteps on the stairs, and looked up to see John hurrying down them, gun drawn.

"Put that thing away," he snapped, not wanting Faith any more on edge than she already was. "Where's Nathan?"

John reached the bottom step and looked at them, obviously baffled. "I haven't seen him . . . I thought he was napping."

"You were supposed to be watching him," Finn ground out.

Slipping his gun back into its shoulder holster, John answered. "He was with his mom. I didn't think I needed to."

Faith made a despairing noise, somewhere between a whimper and a groan.

"Trina," Finn shouted again, not wanting to turn around.

"I'm right here," she said mildly, coming through the door to the dining room. "What's all the shouting about?" Her breath caught on a hitch. "You're bleeding!"

He looked down to see blood dripping from his arm, splashing on the tile floor. "It's nothing," he told her shortly. "Have you seen Nathan?"

Trina's eyes went from him to Faith to John, then back again. She shook her head, looking worried. "I was working in the front garden until the rain started . . . Since then I've been reading in my room."

"Where's Larry?"

"In the garage, I think."

Not bothering with introductions or anything

else, Finn headed for a nearby side door, punched in the alarm code to release the dead bolt, and entered the garage. Larry was on the other side of the SUV, wearing headphones and buffing the hood with polish. John slipped past him, already scanning the place, looking for Nate.

"What's up?" Larry saw them, tugging his earphones from his ears. The faint sound of Mick Jagger singing "Sympathy for the Devil" came through into the air.

"My son," Faith said urgently, pushing past him into the garage. "Is he in here?"

Larry shook his head, shooting John a look. "We were both in here most of the morning. John just went into the house a few minutes ago."

"Put that down and help me look for him," his partner growled, checking corners, even under the car.

"Spread out," Finn ordered quickly. "Trina, you take the upstairs, Larry the downstairs, and John, you take all the outbuildings. Faith and I will take the gardens and the beach."

"The beach?" Her face, already so pale, turned even paler. "But it's storming out. Surely he wouldn't go down to the beach!"

The dolphins. Nate had wanted to swim with the dolphins. Finn's blood ran cold at the thought, but he didn't voice it aloud. "Get moving," he said to his team, and moved to hit the garage door opener. Wind and rain came in with a *whoosh*, wetting the concrete floor. He didn't wait for it to open all the way, just ducked beneath it and took off running, knowing Faith would be right behind him.

Wet palms slapped against him as he ran down a little-used path by the side of the house, scanning the bushes between the trees. "Nathan!" he shouted, wondering if he'd be heard above the storm. It was still building, thunder rumbling overhead, sky the color of lead lit by flashes of lightning. "Nate! Are you out here?"

"Nathan!" screamed Faith. "Where are you?"

It was hard to see in the driving rain, but he didn't let that stop him. Pushing forward, he led Faith through the foliage until they reached the sand dunes behind the house. The beach lay before them, wild and stormy, the waves having grown higher and rougher since this morning. The sandcastle was gone, devoured by the elements and the rising tide.

"Nathan," Faith shrieked, but Finn could barely hear her above the crash of the waves, the howling of wind and rain. She ran past him, scanning the beach frantically for any sign of the boy.

Flotsam and jetsam littered the sand, disturbed by the storm. An oddly shaped piece of it made his heart stop, until he recognized it for what it was: driftwood, dark with age.

"Faith!" he shouted. "He's not here! Come back!" but she ran on, soaked and frantic, to check out the driftwood for herself. He followed, but only to draw her back, away from the water's edge, so they could start searching the jungle-like foliage that surrounded the house. When she fell to her knees beside the driftwood he thought she'd stumbled, and as he reached her he saw what she'd seen. Nestled beside the wet log was a sodden stuffed animal—the dog Nathan had clutched in his arms while he'd slept, all the way from Atlanta.

The keening sound he heard wasn't coming from the wind or the waves, but from Faith herself as she snatched up the dog and stared at it, limp in her hands.

Never in his life had he felt so helpless; never had he felt the weight of unbearable, crushing guilt as he felt it now.

"Nathan!" she shrieked again, rising to search the waves with her eyes, frantically scanning the dark, raging water for any sign of her son. Finn did the same, desperate for a glimpse of a little head, a little body, anything to grab, to reach, or save.

But there was nothing, just the wind and the waves and the sound of Faith's sobbing—a sound he'd never forget as long as he lived. Pulling himself together, he took her by the arm. "C'mon," he said, "let's go back to the house and call the coast guard."

"No," she screamed, pulling away from him. "I'm not going anywhere until I find him!"

"Faith . . ."

"Leave me alone," she shouted. "I hate you! This is all your fault! If you hadn't brought us here, he'd be home with me—" Her voice broke, and she bent over double, clutching the sodden stuffed dog to her chest.

He said nothing, because there was nothing he could say. There was nothing he could do to make it up to her, nothing he could do to fix this. Instead, knowing she would put up a fight but doing it anyway, he reached out and grabbed her by the shoulders, pulling her to him. He wrapped his arms around her, wishing he was as dead as she wanted him to be, having nothing to offer but the comfort of his body, a flimsy and useless shield against the cold, uncaring world.

She didn't fight him, though; all the fight seemed to have gone out of her. Her face buried against his chest, the dog between them, she wept as though her heart were broken; which, of course, it was. He put his lips to her hair and closed his eyes, fighting back tears of his own. He had to be strong for her now, whether she wanted him to be or not. "We'll find him," he said, tightening his arms around her. "Faith, baby, sweetheart . . . don't cry . . ." He barely knew what he was saying, just knew he'd do anything to make it better. "He must've just dropped it. We'll find him."

"Finn!" Far away, barely heard above the storm, someone was calling his name. He lifted his head and saw John, waving frantically at him from the dunes.

Faith heard him, too, and looked up, her face ravaged.

"He's here." John waved them in, pointing toward the house. "He's up here."

They both took off at a run. Finn had only one thought in his mind: *Let him be okay.* If he still believed in God, he'd pray for it, but since he didn't, he just kept repeating it over and over in his mind, hoping it would be enough.

"We found him in the pump house," John said urgently, as they got closer. "Trina's with him now."

"How is he? Is he all right?" Faith was ahead of him, and missed the glance John shot him over her head.

"He's . . . ah . . . he seems a little woozy."

"Woozy?" she asked sharply, pushing past him toward the house. "What do you mean, woozy?"

John fell into step beside him, avoiding Faith's eye. "Confused, I guess you could say. He . . . um . . . when I found him, he thought I was an angel or something."

Finn would've laughed at the uncomfortable look on John's face, except there was no laughter left in him.

"Where is he?"

"We put him in the guest bedroom, where he was before."

They hurried there, Faith bursting through the kitchen door and running all the way to the guest room he'd put them in when they arrived last night.

There was Nathan, lying on the bed with Trina sitting beside him, looking worried. She rose, making way for Faith, who rushed to the bed.

"Nate." Faith leaned over him, touching his head, heedless of the water that dripped from her clothes, her hair. "Nate, wake up."

His eyes fluttered open, and Finn breathed a silent sigh of relief.

"Nate, it's Mommy," she said to the boy gently. "Where've you been? You scared me to death."

"Don't be scared, Mommy," he told her drowsily. "I told you not to be scared. It's pretty there, with lights and music, and lots of flowers."

She sank to the bed, her hand never leaving him. "Where, sweetie? Where did you go?"

"To Heaven," the boy said simply. "The angel took me, and then he brought me back."

There was a deathly silence within the room, as if no one dared breathe. Above their heads came a low rumble of thunder, as if punctuating Nate's statement.

"It was just a dream," Faith whispered, smoothing her son's hair, as she must've done a thousand times before. The gesture was already so familiar to him—so heartbreakingly familiar. The doorjamb was against his shoulder, and Finn was grateful for it, as his legs seemed unwilling to hold him without support.

Nate said nothing, his eyes drifting shut at the touch of his mom's hand.

Finn stepped back, into the hallway, beckoning John to follow. Trina joined them, closing the bedroom door quietly behind her. The three of them moved down the hall and into the living room. Larry was already there, sitting on the couch and looking incredibly guilty.

"Is the kid okay?" he asked, without preamble.

"I don't know," Finn answered tersely. "What the fuck were you guys both doing in the garage, anyway? Didn't I tell you to keep an eye on him?"

Larry eyed him uneasily, but John was the one who spoke up. "Sorry, man. We let you down."

"You sure as hell did," he returned, running a wet hand through his wet hair as he turned to the window. Outside the storm was still raging, wind whipping through the palm trees, rain spattering hard against the windows. Lightning flashed in the distance, illuminating the horizon, followed quickly by another roll of thunder. He couldn't get the image of Nate out of his head, so small and so helpless. *What was all this talk about angels?*

"What was he doing in the pump house?" he wondered aloud. "It's barely big enough to hold the generators." When you were on a private island, you had to have your own generators.

"Maybe he thought it was a playhouse," Trina offered, in a subdued voice. "The bigger question is why he was outside at all."

"He was looking for Finn." Faith came into the

room, heedless of her wet clothes and hair. She looked like a china doll who'd been left out in the rain, her face white, brown eyes huge in it.

"Trina, get Faith a blanket." Finn didn't move from where he was standing, afraid to shatter the eerie sense of calm that seemed to surround her.

Trina went to do as he asked without saying a word, which should've worried him, but he was too worried about Faith and Nate to care.

"He thought you might've gone down to the beach to watch the dolphins without him," Faith said numbly. "I'm afraid he might've had a seizure while he was out there."

"A seizure?"

Trina was back, gently draping a blanket around Faith's shoulders. He wanted to do it himself, wanted to wrap her up in it and hold her tight, but he didn't dare move.

"The doctor warned me it could happen," she said, staring at the floor. "If the tumor"—her eyes squeezed shut at the word—"if the tumor grew. Seizures, hallucinations . . . it's all happening."

Stillness be damned. He couldn't bear seeing her like this, and was at her side in three strides. The blanket was already slipping, and he caught it, wrapping it around her as he led her toward the couch. Just as on the beach, she didn't try to fight him, but let herself be led, like a lamb to the slaughter.

"Larry," he clipped, "go start the boat. We're going back to the mainland."

There was a silence, during which nobody moved. He glanced up to see Trina, John, and Larry looking at one another, but Trina was the one who spoke up. "Do you really think that's a good idea? Those seas are looking pretty rough, three or four feet at least. A bumpy ride in an open boat . . ." Her voice trailed off.

She was right, dammit.

"Call the coast guard, then," he said, feeling Faith tremble beneath his hands. "Get them to send a helicopter."

John looked doubtful, but went into the kitchen to do as he asked.

"You should both get out of those wet clothes," Trina said briskly, apparently deciding she'd been quiet long enough. "You'll be no good to anyone if you get sick. Finn, you need to let me see to your arm."

He'd forgotten about the cut. It seemed so long ago that he and Faith had stood in his workshop, facing off over the ring. *The goddamn, cursed ring.*

"It's nothing," he told her brusquely, keeping his arm around Faith's shoulders. Her docility frightened him; up to now she'd fought him tooth and nail, and now she acted as if he were invisible, despite the fact that he was right *there*, heart in his throat.

"Faith," he murmured, squeezing her gently. "It's going to be okay. I promise it's going to be okay."

She finally looked at him, eyes swimming with tears. "You can't promise that," she said simply.

"I'm so sorry," he said urgently, desperate to wipe the hopeless look from her face. "I'm so sorry about all of this. I never meant for it to happen, I swear."

"I know." Her forgiveness made him feel even worse. "I guess, in a way, I should thank you."

Beginning to fear that she'd snapped completely, he shook his head. "Why?"

"Because now, if Nate"—her voice caught on a sob—"if Nate goes to Heaven, I'll be able to follow him there."

Larry and Trina were still in the room, but they might as well have been on the moon for all he cared.

"Nate's not going anywhere," he told her fiercely. "We're going to get help for him." He didn't even notice his use of the word "we." "He's going to be all right."

John came back into the room and dropped a bomb into the emotionally charged silence. "The coast guard says all flights are grounded—it's not just an afternoon thunderstorm, it's a tropical depression. They're clocking wind bursts of sixty miles per hour on the mainland. Another fifteen, and we'll be looking at a category one hurricane."

Chapter Twenty-six

A storm was brewing in the underground skies above Sheol, and the time had come to unleash its fury.

"Thamuz!" the Prince of Darkness thundered, "Come forth!"

For this audience, Samael had chosen the Throne of Tears, high above the Chasm of Lamentation. The weeping and wailing of the damned, far below, were the perfect backdrop for the screams that came from the throat of the blackened imp being dragged toward him by four of his own kind. Thamuz's own private guards, all laughing and cackling with unholy glee at their former ruler's plight.

Secretly he'd always despised the imps, having

created them only out of necessity. *So many souls to torture, so little time.* They'd been born of the fears of the humans they now tormented, plucked from the nightmares of the evil and the damned, long before they died. Serial killers, child molesters—the Great Shaitan had no real need to seek his victims among the innocent, for there were so many humans who weren't.

"You have failed in your duty, Thamuz." Despite the din, the Wicked One's voice was heard by all, for the Throne of Tears amplified both sound and fury. Carved of black onyx and cushioned with spiderwebs, the back of it rose several feet above his head, depicting the giant horned head of a ram, eyes glittering with rubies the size of baseballs. The armrests were capped with human skulls, their empty eye sockets regarding both the gathered demons and the restless dead with an utter lack of mercy. "Your laxity put the life of my son at risk . . . If you cannot manage your own people, you are not fit to rule them. For your weakness, you shall be made an example of what befalls those who fail in their assigned tasks."

There was a collective gasp of surprise from the imps, followed by much muttering, for this was the first time Samael the Fallen had publicly acknowledged Cain's existence. He'd briefly considered having the boy beside him during this audience, but had decided against it; what was about to happen was not fit for the eyes of a child, no matter how precocious said child might be.

"You said he wasn't your son," the imp shrieked, struggling and flailing against those who held him. "You said Selene lied, and that it didn't matter that the boy escaped!"

Samael was not about to admit that he'd known nothing of the boy's existence, for lack of knowledge over something so important would most assuredly be seen as a weakness.

"It was a test of your cleverness, Thamuz," he lied. "A test which you unfortunately failed. You seem unable to tell truth from fiction. The fact remains that you lost a child you believed to be my son and heir. Worse, you took orders from Selene without checking with me first, nor notifying me after."

He steepled his fingers, looking coldly down from his throne. "Finally—as if I needed any further reason to kill you, which I do not—you allowed foul rumors to be spread about me—rumors that I no longer had a care for the good of my people."

"Punish Ashtaroth! Ashtaroth is the one who spread these rumors, not I!"

The Mighty Mephistopheles smiled, but it was a bitter smile. "Ashtaroth is made of grief and despair, while you are of flesh and bone. Which do you think burns better?" His laughter was cold, uncaring. "Snap, crackle, pop," he said lightly. "The breakfast of champions, as the humans say."

"No!" Thamuz squealed, snapping with razor-sharp teeth at the taloned hands that held him. "Please, Master! Give me another chance, I beg you!"

"Beg away," Samael answered, "by all means. And do so loudly, so that all my subjects may hear you."

Frenzied, gibbering, bulbous eyes rolling, Thamuz fought like a mad thing, but it did him no good.

"I hereby sentence you to be torn apart, limb by limb, then gutted, gelded, and spitted like the worthless piece of meat you are, roasted in the flames you were created to tend."

Demented laughter rose from the chasm, quickly replaced by screams of agony as the imps within the pit quelled it with their whips and pitchforks.

"All this shall be done while you still live," Samael added, giving specific instructions to Thamuz's guards. "Be sure to leave the head intact. It will be no fun otherwise." A quick flick of his finger, and dozens of imps scurried forth to do his bidding, swarming over themselves in an attempt to rend Thamuz into bits.

Another group rushed toward the largest of the already burning bonfires, thrusting their pitchforks into the flames, heating them until they were red-hot and glowing. Their cackles and squeals of glee grew louder and louder, drowning their former leader's shrieks of agony.

Watching, Sammy gave a bored sigh, knowing how important the spectacle was to his subjects, but also knowing he would be forced to do it again sometime in the near future. *And again, and again, and again . . .*

When the low rumble of thunder sounded, heralding the arrival of Ashtaroth, the Dread Demon of Darkness, it was almost a relief. Here, at least, was a challenge worth facing.

"Infernal Majesssty," came the rasp of a thousand voices, "we sssee you are disssspleasssed."

The gleeful shrieks of the imps turned to shrieks of terror as they cowered beneath the gathering darkness above their heads.

"I am," stated the Great Shaitan, "and well you know why."

"We are disssspleasssed alssso," spoke the Darkness, "for we are denied what is oursss by right."

"By right?" Samael remained seated, hands gripping the skulls that made up his armrests. "You have no rights but those I give you; I believe I made that clear the last time we spoke."

"Not ssso," came the voices, "for you promisssed usss the boy, a blood sssacrifice."

"Oh dear," Sammy said lightly. "I do hope you're not taking me to task for lying, since it is—after all—what I do best."

A rumble of thunder set the walls of the Underworld shaking. "Beware, SSSamael, SSSon of Morning, for asss we grow in numbersss, we grow in power." Several imps near the edge of the chasm lost their footing and fell in, shrieking.

"Staging a coup, are we?" Samael the Fallen smiled thinly, drumming the fingers of his right hand atop an empty skull. "I think not."

The bonfires surrounding the Throne of Tears blazed up, as if on cue, sending showers of sparks into the air to dance upon currents of heat, rising and twisting. Within the orange-red sparks, shapes began to form. Sinuous, writhing, growing and lengthening, reaching higher and higher, until each bonfire became a creature unto itself; towering serpents of flame that stretched toward the Darkness, illuminating the billowy, smokelike entity.

"Ssstop," commanded Ashtaroth, but the serpents did not heed him. They grew taller, thicker, casting their light over the quivering, abject imps, who moaned and whimpered their fear, covering their eyes. More sparks fell to the stony ground, and from them sprang more serpents, needing no fuel save that of Samael's anger, which grew apace with the flames.

A hissing began, growing louder and louder, though whether it came from the hellfires below or the Darkness above wasn't clear. Twisting, twining, burning, the flaming serpents rose higher and higher, their tongues licking and flicking at the clouds of darkness. They began to strike, mouths open wide, fiery furnaces feeding on the soul-filled mass of doom and gloom that was Ashtaroth.

"Noooo," came the legion of voices, "ssstop!"

But the serpents didn't stop, maddened into a feeding frenzy that lit the Underworld with hellish flame, driving back the Darkness, pushing it farther and farther away from the Throne of Tears, and the man who sat upon it.

Samael the Seducer, Ruler of the Abyss,

watched, smiling grimly, as Darkness was consumed by fire.

"Infernal Majesssty . . ." The voices were weaker now, far fewer of them than there'd been before. "Have mercccy on usss . . ."

"Mercy?" He laughed. "You seek mercy? You, who prey upon weakness and despair?" He stood, unaffected by the heat of the flames surrounding him, or by the shrieks and screams of the panicky, cowering imps, who were blinded by the unholy light that now lit the Underworld. Their bulbous eyes were used to bonfires, not conflagrations, and their charred, leathery skin was used to heat, not infernos. "Will the Lightbringers show you mercy, I wonder, if I step aside and allow them sway over humankind? World peace, the milk of human kindness, brotherly love and selfless sacrifice—*these* are your enemies, Ashtaroth, not I." He sneered at the shrinking, fragmented Darkness, torn asunder by the voracious, greedy flames. "How quickly you forget where true power lies."

"Forgive usss," rasped the voices. "Forgive usss."

Samael's face was hard, the line of his mouth bitter. "Forgiveness," he said, low beneath his breath, "has always been denied me. Why should I give it to you?"

"We have ssserved you well, Massster, and will do ssso again," pleaded the voices. "Pleassse do not dessstroy usss."

"So you acknowledge that I can?" he asked sharply.

"Yesss," rasped the Darkness. "We were foolisssh to think otherwissse."

A quick wave of his hand, and the flames burst into a shower of a million sparks, to fall on the hard ground surrounding the Throne of Tears, igniting the imps, who squealed and thrashed in agony before bursting into flames themselves.

"Little bastards," he muttered. "There were too many of you, anyway."

Turning, he resumed his seat upon the throne. The smell of charred meat offended his nostrils, causing them to flare.

"Abase yourself before me," he commanded Ashtaroth, "and hide these abominations from my sight."

The Darkness, or what was left of it, pooled itself around Samael's feet, eddies of billowy black ooze that covered the blackened corpses of the imps. "I will have no more insolence from you," he stated, "or you will be cast into the Void, forever hungry, forever denied the souls you would feed upon. Is that clear?"

"It isss, Infernal Majesssty," rasped the Darkness.

"Good." Samael the Fallen placed his hands once again upon the empty, eyeless skulls of his enemies. "And fear not, for you shall have your blood sacrifice. I have a very special tidbit in mind for you."

When he returned to his chamber, Cain was sound asleep in his bed, Nyx keeping watch over him like the angel of death—dark, somber, and silent. Now scrubbed clean, Cain's small form looked even smaller beneath the down comforter on the great four-poster bed.

With a flick of his wrist, Sammy sent Nyx back into the shadows from whence he came, wanting time alone with the child who'd turned his world upside down, and needing no witnesses.

Once Nyx was gone, he stepped closer, staring down at the boy whose head rested so trustingly on his pillow.

Awake, Cain was astounding in his impudence; asleep, he was breathtaking in his perfection. His hair was so white a blond as to rival the milky sheen of the sheets, his mouth a tender pink rosebud instead of a blackened slash, spewing profanities.

Without thinking, Sammy raised a hand to rub his chest, which seemed to ache in a way he'd never felt before. Realizing what he was doing, he snatched it away, but was unable to tear his eyes from the boy's face quite as easily.

What was he to do with this true child of perdition? He had no skills as a parent, and had never desired to be one. He'd seen the rise and fall of many human monarchies, and always—always— the worst betrayals came from within. Sons of an unpopular ruler were the first choice of a disgruntled people, and the first person to look toward when an assassin's blade or a poisoner's dart found a home within a monarch's breast.

It was then that Cain's eyes opened and looked sleepily into his.

"Are you truly my father?" he whispered, unmoving.

Sammy nodded, not speaking. He sat down on the bed, which had seen so much raucous iniquity, and thought only of lost innocence, and how, once lost, it could never be regained.

"I miss my mother," Cain said dreamily, his eyes glazed with sleep. "Will I ever see her again?"

Strangely unwilling to ruin the quiet peacefulness of the moment, Sammy replied only, "Perhaps."

"I'll bet she's mad at me," Cain murmured, his eyes already drifting closed. "But that's okay. I know she still loves me."

The poignant certainty of the statement was enough to make the angels weep.

Sammy sat there, unmoving, until the evenness of the boy's breathing revealed that he was once again asleep.

Then he lowered his head, hearing only the crackle of the fire in the grate, and wondered whether there was anything left of the angel in him.

Chapter Twenty-seven

The storm didn't let up, raging and howling around the house all afternoon. Nate slept through it, while Faith sat pale and red-eyed by his bed. She wouldn't eat, and just shook her head when he tried to talk to her, though Trina managed to get her into some dry clothes.

Finn eventually did the same, then returned to the living room where John and Larry were glued to the Weather Channel, watching and listening for any break in the storm. He sat with them as long as he could, then, to keep himself from checking on Faith and Nate for the umpteenth time, he prowled into the kitchen, where Trina had been baking cookies to keep herself busy. He could tell she was angry by the way she slammed the oven door as she took them out.

"Are you ready to tell me what's going on?" she asked, without preamble. "What's this about a tumor? What's wrong with that little boy?"

Finn stared at her, and some of his misery must've shown in his eyes, because despite her anger, she enfolded him in a hug. For a moment he let her; Trina was the only woman who ever showed him unconditional affection, whether it was scolding or crabbing or happiness to see him when he returned from the road.

"Her name is Faith McFarland, and Nathan has brain cancer," he told her bluntly, as soon as she let him go. It was the first time he'd said the words aloud, and didn't like how they sounded.

The blood seemed to drain from Trina's face, and before he knew what hit him, she'd drawn back her arm and slapped him, hard.

He stumbled back against the kitchen counter, hand to his cheek, taken completely off guard.

"Brain cancer?" She was absolutely furious. "You brought them all the way out here against her will, to the middle of nowhere, when he has brain cancer?" She advanced on him, and he held up a hand, unwilling to be slapped again. "Who the hell do you think you are?"

He had no answer for her. None that she'd understand, anyway.

Trina glared at him, hands on hips, waiting for an explanation. She looked like an avenging harpy, gray-haired and sharp-eyed, ready to rip out his liver and serve it for breakfast.

"What's going on?" John and Larry both stood in the doorway. "Who has brain cancer?"

"Nathan," Trina hissed angrily, keeping her voice down so Faith wouldn't overhear. "The little boy you helped Finn kidnap."

"Now wait a minute," John said, shaking his head. "You never said anything about the kid having brain cancer. I would never have—"

"Yeah," Larry broke in before John could say any more. "No wonder his mom is so pissed at us—she wouldn't even speak to me earlier when I asked how he was doing. I've got kids of my own, you know. If one of them was that sick, I'd kill anybody who pulled a stunt like we did."

Like I *did*, Finn thought, knowing they'd just done as they were told.

They were all glaring at him now. Unable to meet their eyes, he looked away. How was he supposed to explain why he'd gone to such drastic lengths? Any way you looked at it, he was an asshole—an irresponsible, selfish asshole.

"That's it, Mr. High and Mighty Rock Star," Trina spat, turning on her heel. "I quit. I've cleaned your floors and done your laundry and cleaned up your messes long enough. I've been here for you when nobody else has, but I'll be damned if I'm going to be party to something like this." She cast a final parting shot over her shoulder. "I hope you choke on those cookies."

John and Larry said nothing, but turned around and followed her.

Finn stared at their retreating backs, understanding completely. "Damned is right," he murmured. "More than you'll ever know."

It wasn't night outside, but the sky was dark with storm clouds. It was dark enough, and his studio would do, just as that smelly, dank basement had done when he was sixteen.

Finn stepped into the recording studio on the second floor and closed the door behind him. Nobody ever bothered him while he was working on his music, and nobody would bother him now, particularly under these circumstances. He was carrying a grocery bag—the one Faith had been carrying when John snatched her from her own backyard, on his instructions—and he put it down on the chair behind the mixing console. From it he drew everything he needed: flour, candles, incense, matches. He didn't bother with the bread or salt; there'd been enough sacrifice going on that weekend without it. His integrity, the respect of his friends, a woman's heart, maybe even a little boy's life. There was a small black book inside the bag, but he ignored it, having brought his own. All these years and he still had it, hidden behind a false panel in his closet. He'd never wanted anyone else to find it, but hadn't been able to bring himself to destroy it.

Now he needed it again, because he didn't want to wait until the Devil decided to show up on his own. Last night he'd chided Faith about letting Nathan be used as a pawn, and he was tired of being one himself—it was time to take charge of his own destiny, and do what needed to be done.

Taking the flour, he dribbled it on the floor in four straight yet intersecting lines in the partial shape of a star, leaving the fifth line unfinished. Putting the five candles at the five points of the pentagram, he lit them, and put the stick of incense in the center, along with the remaining flour. Then he went to the window and stood for a moment, watching the storm, listening to the rain lash against the glass. Slowly he drew the blinds and waited a moment longer for his eyes to adjust to the resulting gloom before turning around.

As he well knew, candlelight changed everything. His familiar studio was no longer familiar, the mixing console in shadow, the glass of the soundproof booth now a hazy mirror reflecting the flicker of flames. His favorite guitar was just a vague shape in the darkness, the drum set a series of black holes, the microphones spiked arrows pointing to nowhere.

Stepping to the center of the pentagram, he picked up the bag of remaining flour and drew a circle around all five points of the star, then drew the fifth and final line, sealing himself within the very center. The incense was next, which he lit from one of the candles. Its sweetish-sour scent made his nose sting, but he waved the fragrant smoke into all five corners of the pentagram until he was surrounded by a smoky haze, then stuck it into the melted wax of the candle.

Reluctantly he pulled the grimoire from the back pocket of his jeans, and began to read aloud.

"This place is protected, prepared, and sanctified for the presence of the One Most High, the Lord of Night, Son of Perdition." He paused, hating what he was about to do. "Samael the

Serpent, Samael the Black, Belial the Accuser. I invoke thee, O Wicked One, O Dragon of Darkness, Lucifer, Father of Lies."

Lightning flashed outside the windows, followed by a *boom* of thunder that shook the entire house.

"I invoke thee, Ruler of the Abyss, by this seal of sun and stars, by the power of moon and sky, to come forth."

He waited, unwilling to take the final step, even though he'd taken it before: *Open yourself to the Darkness, and embrace it within the very depths of your soul. Acknowledge Satan's power, and only then will his glory surround you.*

Closing his eyes, he steeled himself, but instead of Darkness, he saw chocolate brown eyes and windswept curls. Instead of lightning and thunder, he heard a little boy's laugh and a woman's sighs of ecstasy. He wanted to weep at what he was giving up, but grief would do him no good. All he would have left would be memories, the wishes and dreams of what might have been.

"Dear me," came a voice, laced with dry humor. "You've got it bad, don't you?"

Finn's eyes snapped open, and there was the Devil, leaning against the wall, arms and ankles crossed.

"Love," said Satan, "is such a cruel thing. Far crueler than any torments I could devise, wouldn't you agree?"

He said nothing, his mouth gone suddenly dry.

"Wouldn't it be wonderful if such a thing as happily-ever-after actually existed? If promises made under the white-hot influence of passion were actually kept, and desire never died?"

Beelzebub chuckled, pushing himself away from the wall to stroll the room as he talked. "Unfortunately there's always something in the way, isn't there? Greed, lust, secrets . . . always secrets. Does anyone ever truly know anyone, after all?" He touched the guitar, plucking a single note from the air. "Nothing to say, Finn? What's the matter, cat got your tongue?"

"I have the ring," Finn stated baldly, refusing to be toyed with.

Satan cocked a blond brow. "Do you, now? I must say, I'm surprised. I really didn't think Faith would let herself be seduced into choosing a sweet-talking pretty boy like you over the life of her son. Such an adorable little innocent—those brown curls, that smile, just like one of Botticelli's cherubs. Perhaps one of them will become his 'special' friend after he dies."

"She didn't choose me over him," he ground

out, wishing he could plant his fist into that perfectly sculpted face, but not daring to leave the circle until he had what he wanted. "She chose *him* over *me*."

"Aw," the Devil mocked, "how that must've hurt. Still, you got your true heart's desire after all—your life of selfishness, stardom, and rock-and-roll debauchery will continue. That's all that matters in the end, isn't it?"

The candles flickered, casting shadows high on the wall. Finn knew then that Hell itself couldn't be any worse than what he was feeling right now, right this moment. Nate lay downstairs, maybe dying as they spoke; Faith hated him and always would. Without them, the future lay before him as empty and meaningless as the past.

"I want to make another bargain," he said, and held out the ring.

"Tut, tut," the Wicked One said, shaking his head. "No take-backs. A bargain is a bargain."

"I want to make a new one," he repeated. "The ring, and my soul—here and now—in return for Nathan's life."

A sneer lifted one corner of the Devil's lips. "How noble of you. Are you really prepared to give up *everything* for one little boy . . . a boy, I might add, whom you barely know?"

"I know all I need to," Finn said. "He has his whole life ahead of him, and doesn't deserve to be used as a pawn in any of your twisted games. Neither does his mom. Take the ring, take my soul, and leave them both alone."

Satan smiled. Shifting his gaze to a point behind Finn, he asked, "What do you think, Faith? Should I do it?"

Finn whirled and saw her, standing in the doorway; he hadn't heard the door open, though the flicker of candles should've warned him. Her face was pale in the gloom, her eyes dark pits of shock and despair. As he watched, her chin went up in a gesture he recognized—her fighting spirit was back, and it made him fiercely, incredibly glad. She was going to need it to keep Nathan going.

"No," she said to the Devil, stunning him to his core. "I think you should take me instead."

She moved forward, and Finn put out a hand to stop her. "Get out of here, Faith. Don't interfere."

She ignored him, stepping over the flour and past the candles, to take his hand in both of hers. He could see her clearly now, could see the tears glittering on her lashes and the way her lower lip trembled. Holding tight to his hand, she turned her head and addressed Samael the Serpent, Father of Lies. "I'm the one who failed to live up to my end of the bargain. Take me, and leave Nathan and Finn alone."

"No," Finn said firmly. He grabbed her by the shoulders, and gave her a little shake. "Go back downstairs, right now—Nate needs you."

She looked up at him, her heart in her eyes, and he felt his own swell in response. "Promise me you'll do what you said," she whispered, "and get him the treatment he needs."

Finn found he couldn't speak past the lump in his throat. She was so beautiful, so selfless, when all around him was ugly and painful and useless.

"Promise me," she repeated, tears spilling down her cheeks.

Hardening his heart against her plea, he shook his head. "No. You're going to do it yourself. I've already left specific instructions for my accountant to set up a trust fund for Nate's medical expenses, and named you as executor. Take him to Switzerland, and get his treatment under way."

He would do this for her whether she liked it or not. He would do it for Nate, and for the future the three of them might've had together if he hadn't been such a reckless, selfish fool.

She shook her head, choking back a sob. Her fingers were clutching at his shirt, and she buried her face against his chest.

The scent of her hair filled his nose; so fresh and sweet, like all the flowers he'd never taken the time to stop and smell.

"I've been a coward," he told her softly. "I've spent my whole life running away from responsibility, looking for something I was never going to find. Let me, for once, be the man I should have been, the man I want to be when I look into your eyes."

She lifted her head, opening her mouth to speak, but he laid a finger on her lips.

"Let me do this, for you and for Nate. I love you, Faith McFarland. If you believe nothing else about me, believe that."

She stared up at him, and he looked into those chocolate brown eyes for the last time, seeing a future there that would never be.

Her hand came up to cover his, pulling his finger from her lips. "I love you, too," she said urgently, "and I'm not going to let you do this! Keep the ring. Stay with us . . . we'll find a way to make this all work."

"Oh dear," said the Devil, from the shadows, "I do believe you two dreamers are made for each other."

Finn turned his head to glare in the Devil's direction, and saw him coming closer.

"Give me the ring."

Before Faith could stop him, he tossed it, and she saw Satan catch it, snagging it easily from the air.

"No!" Faith screamed, struggling to tear herself free from his embrace, but he wouldn't let her.

"It's done," he murmured softly. "Don't forget about me, okay?" He bent his lips to her stricken face, and stole one last, bittersweet kiss.

"Oh, for fuck's sake." The Devil sighed. "Such devotion, such self-sacrifice."

Finn ignored him, for the only thing that mattered was the feel of Faith in his arms, the softness of her hair against his cheek. If he could die like this, holding her, then he would die a happy man.

"Very well," Satan said, almost wearily. "Luckily for you lovebirds, I occasionally find myself a sucker for a happy ending." A flash of lightning and a huge clap of thunder shook the room, and as it died, rumbling away into the distance, they both heard the Devil say, "I release you both from your bargains."

In disbelief, Finn searched the shadows, still holding Faith close, but the Devil was gone, vanished into thin air.

"I got what I wanted, and may you both have everything you wished for," came the familiar voice, still taunting, but with an undertone of finality.

"Go forth, keep your promises to each other, and live happily ever after . . . one big, happy family."

Laughter, cruel and mocking, died away into the distance.

"Of course, should you ever make the mistake of inviting me in for another visit, I can't promise to be so merciful next time."

Chapter Twenty-eight

"An employee of the Ritz-Carlton was found dead this morning, apparently by his own hand. Herve Morales, night shift manager, leapt to his death from the roof of the hotel, his body landing atop the parking garage. A suicide note at the scene has not yet been released to the press, but authorities revealed that Mr. Morales was under investigation for violating child pornography laws and unlawful use of company equipment. Management of the Ritz-Carlton had no comment, other than to say that they will be cooperating fully with authorities."

The television clicked off, filling the hotel room with silence. Without stirring from his chair,

Sammy said idly, over his shoulder, "How rude of you, Gabriel. I was watching that."

The Archangel Gabriel sighed, sinking down on the couch, which gave him a glorious view of the city of Atlanta. "Nothing is ever simple with you, is it, Samael?"

"I have no idea what you're talking about."

"Liar," Gabe said softly, without heat.

"What does it matter," Sammy said, just as softly, his eyes on the city, spread out before him like a banquet. "The Darkness must have its pound of flesh, after all. You should be grateful I let your little protégée off the hook. You can go back to the One and report that Faith McFarland will live a long and happy life, just as you desired."

"That's all well and good, but I was never appointed Faith McFarland's guardian angel," returned Gabriel, with a smile in his voice.

Samael the Fallen sat up straight, twisting in his chair to regard his old friend. "What?"

"I was appointed Nathan's," Gabe returned, eyes twinkling. "Faith was just a bonus."

Once again—for it was happening all too often lately— Sammy found himself speechless.

But only momentarily.

"You bastard," he growled, a dangerous glint in his eye.

"Oh, Sammy," the archangel answered. "You and me both. We have only one parent, after all. Thanks to you, Nate now has two." Gabe took a step back before adding, "And perhaps, one day, if you're lucky enough, your son, Cain, will, too."

And then he was gone before all hell could break loose, in a flash of light that could've been the sun, reflecting off the tall buildings outside the window.

Leaning back in his chair, the Devil began to chuckle, laughing at himself, and at all the world. The trickster had been tricked, and one must give credit where credit was due. His laughter died, though, after a moment. He sat there, staring at the view, lost in thought, for several more.

"Fuck it," he finally said, and snapped his fingers.

Gone was the presidential suite at the Ritz-Carlton Atlanta, and in its place was Ariadne's cavern, the black pool still and quiet beneath the tainted ground, the atmosphere cloaked in silence.

"Welcome back, Samael," said Ariadne, from her place beside the pool.

He said nothing, merely looking at her, knowing she knew all she needed to know without him saying a word.

"Past, present, and future," she said, "patterns

and circles, all repeating endlessly in one way or another." She reached out a hand to wave it over the pool before turning and gliding noiselessly into her cave, leaving him alone.

Always alone.

Then, because he couldn't help himself, Samael the Fallen knelt beside the black pool and looked into its mirrorlike surface, seeing not himself, but the future of the one he most longed to see.

There, in the dark depths, a scene emerged: a dark-haired young woman, pink streaks in her hair, a babe in her arms. She cooed down at the child, holding it close, moving the pink blanket away from its face as she gazed into it, obviously enraptured.

The two were joined by a third, a tall man with dark hair who leaned in, slipping his arm around the young woman's shoulders. Together they gazed at the new life they'd created, a touching tableau that pained the heart Samael thought he no longer had.

"And they all lived happily ever after," he murmured, reaching out a hand to swirl the black water and erase the scene from his sight.

"Enjoy your family, Nicki, my love, and don't forget the Devil who loved you."

He rose, ready to return to Sheol and face the eyes that constantly watched, judged, and demanded.

"There's no fool like an old fool, and I'm one of the oldest, after all."

Next month, don't miss these exciting new love stories only from Avon Books

Silk Is For Seduction by Loretta Chase
Climbing her way to the top of London's fashion empire, dressmaker Marcelline Noirot knows just the move that will get her there: designing a gown for the intended bride of the charming Duke of Clevedon. But when the two meet, a spark ignites and erupts into desire. Is passion worth the price of scandal?

Waking Up With the Duke by Lorraine Heath
When Lady Jayne's husband tells her that he's entrusted his friend, the Duke of Ainsley, to give her the child that he himself cannot, she's furious. When she at last relents, the duke's surprising tenderness melts her resistance, awakening a most impossible desire.

Loved By a Warrior by Donna Fletcher
Cursed to never love without bringing death, Tara is frightened by her intense feelings for the Scottish warrior who saved her life. Reeve MacAlpin resolves to make the beauty his. But will Tara turn her back on a passion so strong, or will she leave true love up to fate?

This Perfect Kiss by Melody Thomas
Christel stole a fiery, unforgettable kiss from Camden St. Giles at a masquerade ball. But now, nine years later and unmasked, they meet again. With previous misdeeds and long-guarded secrets filling the years in between, could their past destroy any hope for their future?

At Avon Books, we know your passion for romance—once you finish one of our novels, you find yourself wanting more.

May we tempt you with . . .

- **Excerpts** from our upcoming releases.
- Entertaining **extras**, including authors' personal photo albums and book lists.
- Behind-the-scenes **scoop** on your favorite characters and series.
- **Sweepstakes** for the chance to win free books, romantic getaways, and other fun prizes.
- Writing **tips** from our authors and editors.
- **Blog** with our authors and find out why they love to write romance.
- **Exclusive content** that's not contained within the pages of our novels.

Join us at
www.avonbooks.com

AVON

An Imprint of HarperCollins*Publishers*
www.avonromance.com